Love and

FAT-FREE
Cheese

Love and FAT-FREE Cheese

♡ CRISSY SHARP ♡

SWEETWATER
BOOKS

An imprint of Cedar Fort, Inc.
Springville, Utah

ISBN 13: 978-1-4621-1939-4

Published by Sweetwater Books, an imprint of Cedar Fort, Inc.,
2373 W. 700 S., Springville, UT 84663
Distributed by Cedar Fort, Inc., www.cedarfort.com

LIBRARY OF CONGRESS CATALOGING-IN-PUBLICATION DATA

Names: Sharp, Crissy, 1985- author.
Title: Love and fat-free cheese / Crissy Sharp.
Description: Springville, Utah : Sweetwater Books, An imprint of Cedar Fort, Inc., [2016]
Identifiers: LCCN 2016030498 | ISBN 9781462119394 (perfect bound : alk. paper)
Subjects: | LCGFT: Humorous fiction. | Romance fiction. | Thrillers (Fiction)
Classification: LCC PS3619.H356445 L68 2016 | DDC 813/.6--dc23
LC record available at https://lccn.loc.gov/2016030498

Cover design by Michelle Ledemza and Priscilla Chaves
Cover design © 2016 by Cedar Fort, Inc.
Edited and typeset by Deborah Spencer

Printed in the United States of America

10 9 8 7 6 5 4 3 2 1

Printed on acid-free paper

To my sweet sister and guardian angel Yvonne, who spent her time on earth lifting those around her. She always encouraged and believed in me.

♡ Chapter 1 ♡

Yoga is supposed to make me tranquil, peaceful, and sculpt my legs into those of a Greek goddess. However, as I strain every muscle in my body in an effort to do this Downward-Facing Dog pose, I am anything but calm or goddess-like. At least it's clearing my mind. The intense physical pain helps me forget how nervous I am to step foot inside The Bradley Corporation.

"Breathe. Remember to breathe," the instructor, sporting head-to-toe spandex, sings out as she demonstrates a One-Legged King Pigeon. *Where do the names of these poses come from?* I'm already gasping for breath, shaking profusely, and I have sweat pouring down my face. To top it off, I'm being referred to as a boat, camel, cow-face, plow, and now a one-legged king pigeon.

"Jules, you're not breathing," my brother, Everett, whispers.

"I can't breathe when I'm trying to touch my feet to my head," I say as spit shoots out of my mouth.

"Relax. The whole point of coming here was to help you calm your nerves before this afternoon, but you're more worked up than before."

I flop down on my mat, ignoring the angry look from the woman next to me. Her shirt bejeweled with the word "enlightened" is contradicted by her furrowed eyebrows. Closing my eyes, I picture myself inside The Bradley Corporation, meeting a man whom I know nothing about. I do have his name and office number written on a paper in my purse: Owen Denny, 9B. Everett scribbled it out for me this morning after he told me he'd arranged an interview for me with the vice president of the company where he works as a junior legal advisor.

"You're sure he wants to meet with me?" I ask Everett, doubt filling my mind.

"Yes, I'm sure."

"How well do you know this guy? I mean, could he actually have meant—"

"Jules, he wants to meet with you. I know him well and he said to send you over at two-o'clock for an interview."

"Know him well, how?" I prod. TBC employs thousands of people. It's hard for me to believe that my brother—the same brother I'd seen cry while watching *My Little Pony* not too many years ago—is chummy with someone in such an authoritative position. Although before today I also wouldn't have believed he did yoga. I'd watched him play years of football and basketball, but seeing him flawlessly transition from one yoga pose to the next was not something I had anticipated.

"Stop worrying," he answers.

The sing-song voice of the instructor sends all thoughts of Owen Denny and The Bradley Corporation flying out of my head. I start to open my eyes when she says, "Imagine your thighbones are rainbows, spiraling outwards." Maybe I don't want to open my eyes. Thankfully, she adds that we only have one final pose before the end of class. One more, I can do that. She calls it "The Crow Pose." With little effort, she proceeds to put her palms on the floor, her knees up by her shoulders, and balance on her hands. Is the human body supposed to do that? I look around and see everyone follow-ing suit. A few people are struggling a little bit and their arms are shaking, but they are still making that crow pose look pretty good. I decide it must not be as hard as it looks. It is. It is every bit as hard as it looks. I put my palms on the ground. I throw one leg up, but by the time I get the second leg up, the first one is back on the floor. I think I've just created my own yoga move I'll name "Bucking Bronco."

I roll my mat, grab my bag, and head for the door. Today was definitely the wrong day to try something new. Instead of the inner peace Everett promised, my insides want to be on my outside. I'm still just as nervous, but now I'm also wincing with every step from the pain shooting through my thighs, shoulders, and stomach.

Everett runs to catch up with me. "My lunch break is almost over. I have to get back to the office. Good luck. You got this."

After a quick shower and change of clothes, I stand next to the tallest building downtown. The dark glass radiates an ominous gloom and the theme song from *Jaws* plays in my head. As I walk through the large double doors and into the ornate lobby, I'm out of place. Everything about this building screams "fancy." I kick myself for opting to wear dress pants and flats instead of a pencil skirt and pumps. With each step I'm reminded of my mistake by the mirrors on each side of me. I straighten my posture, suck in my stomach, and enter the elevator. As the doors close, I'm staring at my reflection again. I quickly change my worried expression to a half-hearted grin. A couple of feet above my head are the words, "The Bradley Corporation—Keeping Your World Safe."

Ding. The doors open to reveal an even fancier lobby. Everything around me oozes with sparkle and shine. Oversized gold frames hang against the back wall. The floor to ceiling windows are covered with shiny purple curtains.

There are mirrors surrounded in purple and gold. It is the most overdone, gaudy room I have ever been in. As I walk toward the desk, I recite his name in my head one more time: Owen Denny.

The middle-aged woman behind the desk has a lime green shirt that matches the color of her long, acrylic nails, which are clicking against the keyboard as she types. Her hair, a shade somewhere between red and orange, is in tight, bouncy curls all over her head. A large crochet hook is tucked behind one ear and a pair of gold reading glasses sits on her nose. The nameplate on her desk says only "Celia," but the dot of the *i* is scratched into a small heart. Somehow this woman's quirky appearance calms my nerves. I smile. "Hi, I'm Juliet Easton. I'm here to see O—"

"Mr. Denny, yes." She replies with a Southern drawl that has me picturing her sitting on a front porch sipping iced tea. "I'll let ya know as soon as he's ready for ya, darlin'," the woman continues, the color in her cheeks resembling that of her hair.

"Oh, okay. Thanks." I turn around and scan the room for a place to sit. There are chairs against the opposite wall, which must be at least thirty yards away. My entire apartment could easily fit twice in this lobby. As I approach the chairs, I realize there is a girl, probably in her early twenties, standing a few feet away. She's pretty with straight, dark hair. Her long legs are emphasized by a pair of at least four-inch stilettos and a short, shiny dress. Diamonds are practically dripping off her. Although she looks better suited for a night club than this office building, she fits in with this room's decorations perfectly. Maybe that's why I hadn't noticed her until now; all the glitz and shine are like camouflage in here. I try to make eye contact to smile and say, "Hi," but the girl won't move her eyes. They're locked on the front desk in a glare.

"Are you here to see Mr. Denny as well?" I ask, for lack

of anything better to say. It comes out as a whisper, since this room seems to demand hushed tones.

Without so much as a nod of acknowledgement, she holds her icy stare. Then, as she intensifies the glare at the secretary, she spits out, "Celia, I am certain Owen was not intending for me to be left sitting in his waiting room when he said to hold all of his calls and visitors." The way she says "waiting room" makes it sound as if it is infested with disease.

"Again, Miss Lila, I'm very sorry I can't help ya. Ya don't need to pitch a hissie fit about it. I'm just doing as I've been told," the secretary replies matter-of-factly.

"And I'm just trying to see Owen before my flight leaves, but his obviously incompetent secretary is making that difficult. I think it's about time he tries out some new front desk help, don't you?" She snaps her head in my direction and aims her glower at me. "Um, yes, to answer your little question. I am here to see *Mr. Denny* as well." She rolls her eyes as she says, "Mr. Denny." "I don't, however, have an appointment." She shifts her stare back to the front desk. "I was not aware that *I* would need one."

Celia stares at her computer screen as if no one's speaking to her. I quickly grab the closest magazine, flip it open, and pretend to be engrossed in the article. My stomach flip-flops as I try to convince myself I belong here. I'm definitely out of my element. I have zero experience in the professional world, unless I count working as a kayaking instructor every summer while I earned my master's degree in Statistics from Penn State.

I need this job at The Bradley Corporation. It's never been my dream to work at a surveillance tech company since I hardly know what that means, but I've sent my resume out to forty-eight companies and haven't heard back from a single one. No one seems to want a statistician without any professional statistics experience. Meanwhile, I paid

May's rent with the last of my student loan money. My bank account has exactly twenty-two dollars remaining in it and I've existed solely on Malt-O-Meal and a four-pound bag of slightly freezer-burned hash browns that my roommate left when she moved out. My debit card *and* my self-esteem are relying on me nailing this interview. Plus, it would mean I could move back to Eden Falls, Pennsylvania. I only lived a couple of hours away while I attended Penn State, but I missed my hometown. Tucked in next to the Delaware River near the Pocono Mountains, it's idyllic. This time of year is especially picturesque with light pink and white blossoms everywhere and the air filled with the sweet scent of mountain-laurels.

My thoughts are interrupted by the purposely loud, irritated breathing of Lila. "Celia, unlock that door right now!"

"Oh, honey, just sit down. I'm sure he'll be done shortly," Celia responds, pulling some yarn out of her desk drawer. She takes the crochet hook from behind her ear and quickly slips it into a bright pink loop. She mutters to herself, but the words are clear. "She ain't got the good sense God gave a goose." Her fingers settle into a rhythmic pattern and her mouth is moving as she counts stitches.

I smile and steal a quick glance at my bedazzled neighbor as she settles back into her chair with a "humph." Her eyes lock on mine and I hope any trace of amusement has disappeared from my face. I move my eyes all around the room subtly. Why doesn't she go bang on the door herself and let Owen know she is out here waiting for him? I look back down at my magazine and notice for the first time what I've selected. There's a large picture of a sheep being milked, with the bold words, "Milking My Icelandic Sheep." Flipping it shut to check out exactly what magazine this is, I see more sheep and the magazine title *Sheep—The Wooly Truth*, complete with a cover story of "Cheese Maker Takes Ewe Turn."

Not generally among your typical selection of magazines in a front office.

Click, click. The doorknob turns and out walks a tall, dark-haired man, not too much older than I am. I don't pay any attention to how good-looking he is. I definitely don't focus on his green eyes or his lean frame. Nope, he is a normal looking man about to interview me. That's all. The shiny dress girl flashes a huge grin and walks quickly—especially considering her four-inch stilettos—across the room. She throws her arms around his neck and kisses him like she hasn't seen him in years. Heat rises in my face and I look back down to my magazine. I really wish I had grabbed something a little more interesting. Learning all about milking an Icelandic sheep isn't something I care to accomplish today.

I peek over my magazine in time to see the guy pull back and hear Lila say, "C'mon O, just skip this afternoon. Come with me. You can fly back tomorrow, or Friday . . . or sometime next week. I need you there. I'll miss you." She sticks her heavily-glossed lips out in a pout and then a big smile creeps across her face as she leans in to kiss him again. This is hardly the same girl I saw a couple of minutes ago. She's all smiles and ease now. "Oh, and your secretary," she starts as she smiles at Celia, "she wouldn't let me come in and see you. I've been waiting for at least ten minutes." Her face returns to the playful pout.

"That's because I was on a very important call and I have a really busy afternoon, Lila. I can't go with you this time. Tell everyone sorry for me."

She leans in and kisses him again. How can she kiss him so much and still have such perfectly glossed lips? If I did that, the poor guy's face would be covered in Pink Pizazz lip shine. Once more Owen pulls away, whispering, "I'll see you when you get back." He walks her across the room and out the door and with that, Celia and I are left alone. I begin to wonder how close this Owen guy and my brother really are. Lila is not the type of girl Everett would be able to spend much time around, and Owen must not be too great if he is with a girl like that. I'm shaky and nervous again. Has Everett made me sound way more qualified than I am? How am I going to get another job interview? No one wants me. The only thing I've had a chance to use my statistics degree for is to conclude that zero out of forty-eight call-backs is not a good percentage. I better start rationing my hash browns better. Luckily Owen walks back in before I can work myself up any further.

He walks straight over to me, sticks out his hand, and says, "Hey, Juliet, I'm Owen. Are you ready?"

Willing my heartbeat to slow to a normal rhythm, I say, "Uh, yeah. Sure." I grab my bag, stand up, and shake his hand, frustrated with myself for letting my first word to the man be "Uh." He motions for me to walk through the door he came through a few minutes ago. Behind the door is what looks like another waiting area, only this one is much simpler. There are two offices. He directs me toward the one on the right and grabs a chair from the waiting area. "I haven't done an interview in here for a while," he explains as he puts the chair across from his desk. This is the office of the vice president of TBC? It looks like a college dorm room. There are posters everywhere of hockey players and cars. Now the connection between him and Everett makes sense. Everett played hockey in college and loves anything and everything hockey.

"Hmm, little bit of a hockey fan, huh?"

"Yeah," he says with a grin I'm sure has melted many girls' hearts, "but I guess you probably know all about hockey fans."

"I don't know about liking the Badgers," I say with a smile, motioning to one of the posters. I glance back at him and can't help but stare at his eyes peering at me from under thick, dark lashes. When I realize I've been focused on his eyes for too long, I nervously look away.

He breaks the tension by laughing and then watches me for several seconds. I'm dying to know what he's thinking, but his expression gives nothing away.

"Well," he says as he sits down behind the desk, "your degree is in statistics, right?"

"Yes," I say as I reach for my resume, but instead see that I have the crazy sheep-milking magazine.

"So you find statistics interesting?"

"I love it. I love how nearly everything comes down to numbers. Like every time you do a search on Google, that data is collected. Complex algorithms then process the data to give you relevant search results." My jitters are gone now that I'm talking about what I'm good at. "I love deciding how reliable something is or finding underlying patterns. Trying to predict an outcome is a like a treasure hunt for me." I stop talking when I notice a grin tugging at the corners of his mouth. I evaluate what I just said. What was funny? Is he somehow testing me?

He takes advantage of my momentary lull and says, "You definitely do find it interesting."

Unsure of the best way to respond, I nod and say, "Yes." Then I quickly add, "Although I can see why you might not if you have interesting material like this to read all the time." I hold up the magazine.

He laughs out loud. "Somehow all of the terrible magazines that no one else in the company wants in their waiting rooms end up in mine."

I pull out my resume and hand it to him, trying to ignore my embarrassment over the lack of experience on it.

He spends the longest minute of my life reading over it before asking me a few questions about a capstone project I did in Market Research Analysis.

I answer his questions and he responds, "Okay. Well we need statisticians in our finance department and marketing department. It seems like you'd be a perfect fit with our marketing department." He smiles.

"Uh." I'm caught so off guard by a job offer that I have to think about how to respond. Just as words start to form into a sentence inside my head, I look up and see his smile again. All previous thoughts disappear as I stare at his straight, white teeth. I know I've taken too long when he starts to talk again.

"When are you available to start?"

I blink hard a couple of times, trying to focus on a response. "Um, I have to get my stuff moved back to Eden Falls, but that shouldn't take too long. I can start next week." I still half-expect this to be some sort of a joke.

"Great. As long as you try to hide your horrible taste in hockey teams, I think that will work out perfectly. Celia, at the desk you passed when you first came in, can direct you to HR, where you'll discuss salary and benefits, and figure out your exact start date."

"Wow, I'm not sure what to say. Thank you!" I force myself to stop gushing. What I really want to do is jump up and hug him. Instead, I extend my hand to shake his and add one more time, "Thank you."

As I walk to my car, I'm not sure what to make of my interview with Owen Denny. It can hardly be called an interview at all. I spent more time watching Lila kiss him than I did talking to him. Thinking of Lila with her skin-tight dress and fierce scowl brings a knot to my stomach. I try to push thoughts of her and Owen Denny out of my mind and focus on the fact that I just landed a great-paying job that will allow me to move back to Eden Falls. Maybe I should go buy something extravagant to celebrate. I've been dying for some brown sugar to go on my Malt-O-Meal.

♡ Chapter 2 ♡

I start at TBC a week from Monday, which gives me twelve days to get moved. When my best friend since sixth grade, Elaine, heard there was a possibility of me moving back to Eden Falls, she offered to let me move in with her.

I want to tell her the good news in person. I pull up the text she sent me with her new address to get directions and see what the commute from her house to TBC will be. Seven minutes. That's closer than my current apartment is to the campus at Penn. I gas it to see if I can beat the GPS and make it in six and then I punch the buttons on my Bluetooth to call Everett.

"How was the interview? Are you moving back?" he answers.

"I'm moving back!" I shriek. I try to bring my voice back down to a normal volume and add, "I'm going to work in the marketing department."

"Nice. I figured he'd find you something."

"Thanks, Ev," I reply.

"Hold on a sec, Jules," he says and I hear his muffled voice talking to someone else.

I follow the directions from my phone as it tells me to take a right. As soon as I recognize the road I'm on, the hair on the back of my neck stands up. I hadn't realized I'd have to go down this road, by that house, to get to Elaine's. I breathe heavy and sweat beads on my lip. Images I've tried to bury away for two years come rushing back into my mind. As I pass the house, I can still see in my mind the slumped form pushed against the garage door.

"Okay, I'm back. Sorry." Everett says.

I take a deep breath and look back at the garage one more time. No body. Just two oversized flower pots, one on each side.

"Jules? You there?"

I look straight ahead and focus on the road. "Yeah, I'm here," I say, willing the shakiness to stay out of my voice.

"Anyway, you were saying Owen found you a job in the marketing department."

"Oh, yeah." I bring my mind back to our earlier conversation and Owen. "So, there's nothing weird with Owen, right?" The words come out before I think them through.

"Weird? No, what makes you ask that?"

"I don't know. He hired me so quickly." I respond. "And, his girlfriend seems crazy."

"You were just nervous and we've all been overly cautious the last couple of years. Ever since Will left and you and Eva saw that, well, you know . . ."

Yeah I know, I thought. I know that I can't get the images of it out of my head. I know that it still gives me nightmares, but that has nothing to do with why I'm asking him about Owen. "That's not what I mean," I argue. "This has nothing to do with Will." I sigh in frustration. "I just mean—"

"Oh, and he doesn't have a girlfriend."

"What? Yes he does. Her name is Lila and she's—"

"Hey, sorry to interrupt you, but I have a call coming in that I have to take. I'm really happy for you. Stop by the office around five and I'll take you out to dinner to celebrate."

And with that, he is gone. Disappointed, I hang up. I want to hear what he has to say about Owen, my interview, and Lila. My brother is friends with the VP of the entire Bradley Corporation and I want to know more.

I take the next left, happily leaving the horrible road that has nothing but dark memories for me. After two more turns, I pull into the driveway of the little house Elaine rents. Her car is gone so I call her. No answer. I text her and still get no response.

I walk around the front of the cute, ranch-style home and picture living here. It's nice, but my emotions are still such a mess from the drive, I feel skittish. I want excitement and celebration right now. I just landed a great job and I won't let old memories ruin this day. I decide to head to my parents' house so I can tell them I'm moving back. They moved thirty miles outside of Eden Falls two years ago when it became too dangerous for them to stay in the house I'd grown up in.

I pull up to a four-way stop and a loud honk makes me jump. I check my rearview mirror and see Elaine waving wildly from the front seat of her car. I quickly park on the side of the road while Elaine runs to my window. "Hey," she says, jumping up and down. "I was driving toward the house when I saw you headed in the opposite direction. I had to go get Mom some Mountain Dew. She's been staying at the house a lot lately while I've been working. Apparently I'm not clean enough so she has a list of projects to help me with. Today she's cleaning baseboards." I smile. It always takes me a second to adjust to the mile-a-minute way Elaine talks. It's like she's just consumed twenty-seven cups of coffee and there's no stopping her. She continues, "If you decide to move back, I'll talk to her. I'll let her know that it's our house. I think it will all be fine. I mean, she's really starting—"

"Elaine," I cut her off. "I am moving back. I got the job at TBC." My excitement makes my voice squeak. "I start in twelve days so I'll have to move my stuff as soon as possible."

"Yes!" Elaine shrieks, but her face immediately falls. "Twelve days, huh? That means I need to talk to Mom, like, today."

I shrug. Elaine's mom has always disliked me, though I've never understood why. When I convinced Elaine to apply to Penn, the problem only got worse. When Elaine moved away from Eden Falls and lived with me while we attended school, Mrs. McElroy quit speaking to me entirely—a change I was not too sad about.

I know this is difficult for Elaine. She desperately seeks her mom's approval. Over the past two years while I stayed at Penn getting my Master's degree, Elaine moved back to Eden Falls and made amends with her mom, which was why I was surprised when she suggested I move in with her. I smile to ease the tension. Elaine smiles again and leans in through the window to give me a hug. "I can't wait to be roommates again. It will be just like college." she says.

♡ Chapter 3 ♡

J ules! We're ready to go! C'mon," Everett's voice booms from downstairs. I jump out of bed, unaware of what is going on. "Do we need to bust in there and get you?" Footsteps pound up the stairs of my parents' house.

"I'm coming, Ev. I just need two minutes." I remember Everett agreed to help me move today. I didn't know he meant we would start at 5:20, but I need his help whenever I can get it. I wasted a lot of time thinking I could move into Elaine's, but that fell through. So I spent the past week looking for a new place to live. Elaine waited until the day I was planning on moving to tell me it wasn't going to work. She told me "it was putting too much of a strain" on her relationship with her mom. She kept apologizing and saying how much she wanted to be roommates, but that we would have to wait a few months while her mom warmed up to the idea. Frustration starts to build up inside of me all over again. I know it probably has more to do with her mom not wanting to lose control of Elaine than actually about liking me, but it doesn't stop the ball forming in the pit of my stomach.

Luckily, when Everett heard the trouble I was having finding a place, he offered to let me stay in his apartment.

"Juliet!"

"Just one sec." I throw on some workout pants and a t-shirt and only spend about twenty seconds brushing my teeth. Glancing in the mirror, I see that my normally straight hair has a few giant kinks from sleeping on it. I start to brush it, but decide to save time and do my hair and makeup during the almost three-hour drive back to my apartment. I grab my stuff and walk out the guest bedroom door. "Let's go. I'm tired of waiting for you." I yell to Everett as I groggily slide down the stair banister and look to the top of the stairs to see where he's gone. I reach the bottom, turn around, and see Everett standing there.

Right beside him is Owen Denny.

"Oh sorry, Jules. Did we wake you up? And we were trying to be so quiet." Everett flashes me a sarcastic grin.

Owen, who looks a lot different from the last time I'd seen him, now that he is in shorts and a t-shirt instead of a suit, holds out a box of pastries. "You're going to need some sugar. Your brother is surprisingly peppy for this time of day."

I take a maple bar. "Thanks," I say, remembering my crazy hair and lack of makeup. I'm pretty sure I have the beginnings of a zit on my cheek too. I try to subtly smooth my hair down. "What are you doing up this early on a Saturday?"

"I talked him into helping us," Everett answers for Owen. "We do have to stop at some restaurant called Meridian's that's twenty minutes out of the way and treat him to lunch on the way back though."

"You guys will be thanking me for making you stop. It's amazing."

"That's really nice of you, but you don't have to do this," I say, feeling guilty that Everett has roped this poor guy into helping. He's already given me a job. "Everett and I can do it. I mean, it's going to be six hours in the car and lots of moving. It will be your entire Saturday."

"Speak for yourself, Jules," Everett chimes in. "I'm not very excited to carry your bed, sofa, and that giant desk of yours with only you to help me."

"I want to help," replies Owen. "I've been thinking of Meridian's all morning. I'm going to eat there today. Since it's already three-quarters of the way to your apartment, I might as well help out. Plus, this way I don't have to pay for it." Owen grins. My pulse quickens and I turn away before he notices me gawking at his perfect smile.

Everett's sneering at me. Did he notice me staring at Owen? He turns to head out the door and then stops, "Where's Eva?"

"Um, probably sleeping. At least she was sleeping before you came in," I respond, unsure why he's bringing up our older sister.

"Well, she should come too."

I give Everett a look to try to stop him, but he continues. "She'd probably love to get out of here for a change." I stand there, mouth ajar, unsure of how to respond. Everett knows just as well as I do why Eva is nervous to leave the house. She has spent the majority of the past two years basically in hiding. She only leaves the house to go to the elementary school where she works as a teacher, and even then, she is uneasy about it. Without knowing who can be trusted, she limits her interaction with people.

"Um, Owen's met Eva before," Everett says quickly, trying to explain to me that what he's said is fine, but I don't care if Owen has met her before. We can never be too careful.

"I'll go talk to her," I reply, hesitantly. At least now I will have a chance to brush my hair and throw on a little make-up. I jog up the stairs and open Eva's door. "Hey Eva, you awake?" I whisper.

"You guys are so loud. Of course I'm awake. Why is Ev here?"

"He's helping me move today, remember? Anyway, he thought it would be fun if you came. I tried to shut him up. He has Owen with him and everyth—"

"Owen's going to help you move?" She interrupts.

"Yeah, there's some restaurant he likes out there or something . . ." I trail off as I grab a hair band off of Eva's dresser and pull my hair back into a ponytail.

"Right, a restaurant that's worth six hours in the car."

"Huh?" I say, focused on the mascara I'm applying.

"Oh, nothing. You know, it would be kind of fun to go with you guys."

"Really?" I ask, suddenly hopeful. "Eva, come. We haven't done anything together in so long. We'll be careful. Please come." I look at her in the reflection of the mirror. She's rubbing her eyebrows, something she does whenever she's nervous.

"But . . . well, maybe. I don't know. You know if I go, someone will follow us."

"I know." I flop down on the bed and put my arms around Eva. No one should have to go through the drama she's been through and is still going through, especially not anyone as sweet and innocent as Eva. "But it *would* be fun and you should come. They'll follow us there, check out wherever we go, and follow us back. You should feel satisfaction that you're making them waste an entire day." I finish with a smile. I hope making light of the situation will convince Eva to come. The fact that she's even considering coming is atypical. It has to be unhealthy for her to be stuck in this house as often as she is.

"Really? You don't mind having someone tail us all day?" Her giant, brown eyes are wide, waiting for my honest answer.

"Of course not. I miss hanging out with you," I answer as nonchalantly as I can. It *is* a little unsettling to have people watch our every move when Eva's around, but I'd still rather have her with us.

Eva gets out of bed and heads to her closet. "This will give me chance to wear that blue Juicy Couture shirt I was telling you about." she says. I shake my head with a grin. Eva's obsession with clothes may have been dampened a bit since Will disappeared, but going out in public seems to bring back her fixation with fashion.

"Perfect," I agree, but in my head I'm busy calculating all the groceries I could have bought with the money that shirt cost. I swear she must spend half her salary on clothes. "I'll tell them you'll be down in a few minutes." I jump to my feet and shut Eva's door. When I get downstairs, the guys are playing pool. "She's coming," I say coolly, not wanting to alert Owen to anything out of the ordinary.

Everett shoots me a subtle grin that says, "I told you so." I think of going back upstairs to be with Eva while she gets ready. I know this is a huge deal for her and she hasn't been to my apartment since Will left, but I decide maybe it's best to give her some time on her own. I settle in on the sofa and let my eyes shut.

"Why don't you go check on her?" Everett suggests after only a couple of minutes. Maybe he's more nervous than he's letting on.

As I start up the stairs, Eva comes out of the bedroom. I am expecting a change of mind, but her perfectly curled hair and flawless make-up suggest otherwise. How does she do that in less than five minutes? I watch her bounce down the stairs in her black skinny jeans and heels and glance down at my own apparel. Suddenly my t-shirt from high-school basketball camp that says, "Seven days without shooting makes one weak" seems far too casual. Eva grins at me and mouths, "ready."

The four of us head out the door. The sun is starting to

peek over the mountains with a pink glow. The air smells like grass clippings mixed with lilacs. My stomach is dancing. I haven't spent a day with my brother and sister in way too long and being able to look at Owen Denny's perfect face the whole way to Penn State makes it even more sensational.

♡ Chapter 4 ♡

Two and a Half Years Ago

O uch!" I yelped, grabbing my right hand to check for puncture wounds. Eva laughed and set down her fork. There were little red marks where the tines of her fork poked me, but not the bloody mess I was sure I'd see.

"Sorry," Eva said in between giggles. "But I've been fighting off some sort of sickness all week. You really don't want to share food with me." I glanced again at her enchilada suizas and tried to decide whether or not it was worth it to steal a bite. "Why are you so hungry tonight?" Eva asked.

I shoveled another bite of my steak quesadilla into my mouth before answering. "Elaine's been obsessed with losing weight and I agreed to help her. She's been begging everyone in the apartment to do it with her and I felt bad." Eva raised an eyebrow in amusement. I stabbed a stray slice of green pepper and a chunk of steak with my fork and eyed it excitedly while I finished my explanation. "She's decided the best solution is the baby food diet."

Eva laughed and had to cover her mouth so her food wouldn't shoot everywhere. "How long have you been doing that?"

"Four very long days," I replied while rolling my eyes. "This is the first chance I've had to cheat." I winded some melted cheese around my fork and enjoyed the sensation of eating food that I could chew.

"That can't be healthy, Jules. You need more than baby food."

"I agree. We better stop at the Dairy Barn on the way home and get frozen custard with brownies mixed in." Eva smiled at my remark, but she was focused on something behind me.

I turned around as someone approached our table. My face was less than an inch away from a blue button-up shirt and striped tie. When I looked up, a man with sandy brown hair and a five o'clock shadow was offering an apologetic smile, but he turned his attention to Eva before speaking.

"Do you mind?" he asked, pointing to one of the empty chairs at our table.

I mind. I mind a lot, I thought. I was trying to enjoy a dinner with my sister who I only saw on the occasional weekend when she drove over from Williamsport. We were having a very important conversation about what I had eaten for the last few days. I was about to launch into the specific kinds of baby food I had tasted and how expensive baby food was. I was not ready to give up my time with her so some playboy could flirt with her for the remainder of dinner.

Sadly, Eva smiled and motioned for him to sit down. I tried to contain my sigh of disappointment. I should be used to this by now. I could hardly spend an hour with Eva without someone hitting on her. It was one of the many joys of having a perfectly beautiful sister. We actually had very similar features; dark brown eyes, medium skin, and perfect teeth. Of course, Eva was born with her perfect teeth. Mine took thousands of dollars of dental work, four years of braces, and head gear that made eighth grade sleepovers especially traumatizing. Eva's hair was dark brown and seemed to perfect all of her features. Her eyes looked darker and brighter. Her teeth looked whiter and her skin appeared olive. I, on the other hand, had blonde hair.

"How are the suizas here?" he asked, pointing at Eva's plate. "I almost ordered them."

It took a lot of self-restraint to keep myself from rolling my eyes. Talking about what food she ordered, how creative.

"They're delicious," Eva answered.

"I'm Will," the man said, holding out his hand to Eva.

She seemed to consider him for one moment before offering her hand and replying, "Eva."

He turned to me and offered his hand. I begrudgingly shook it and grunted, "Juliet."

"Well ladies, I came over here because I know I recognize you, but I can't remember how."

I dropped my head into my hands. Was there a handbook somewhere that listed all these pick-up lines? It's like there were no creative men left. "C'mon, you can do better than that," I said.

Eva looked at me pleadingly. I knew she was telling me to be nice. "Sorry," Eva answered, shaking her head at Will, "but I don't recognize you."

He stared at me. I shook my head. "Sorry, me neither." As his eyes locked on mine, I could see why Eva was being nice. He appeared to have walked straight out of a Calvin Klein ad.

His face broke into a smile. "You're right, Julie."

"It's Juliet," I corrected.

"That sounded like a cliché pick-up line, but I promise you I'm being genuine. I know I recognize the two of you."

"I don't know, Will. I'm not even from here. I'm just visiting my sister." Eva said.

Will asked where she was from and that started a whole conversation about her being in town to watch me play in a volleyball tournament. We talked about volleyball, Penn State, and the delicious food we were eating. I was actually enjoying the conversation and was a little sad when he said, "Well I've taken up too much of your time. Plus, I'm here with colleagues and they're going to wonder what's happened to me. It was great meeting the two of you."

After he left, I noticed the confused look on Eva's face and said, "That was weird. He didn't even try to get your number." She shrugged and changed the conversation back to Elaine and baby food.

We finished the meal, payed our bill, and headed for the door. Will appeared by my side once more. "I figured it out," he said, triumphantly. He motioned for the two men accompanying him to go ahead. "I know where I've seen you two." We stopped walking and waited for him to continue. "Every day for nearly two years I walked into an office at my job at P&L Pharmaceuticals, where I'd pass a picture my boss had of two of his daughters sitting on the bow of a boat. That picture is engrained in my mind."

"The picture of us at Lake Havasu that Dad had in his office," I said when I realized what he was talking about.

I glanced at Eva as a smile spread across her face. "You worked at P&L?"

"Still work at P&L," he replied. "But your dad took that picture with him when he retired." We were holding up a group of people who were trying to exit the restaurant so Will motioned for us to keep walking to the parking lot. "How is your dad liking retired life? Is he still in Eden Falls?"

"Yeah, I don't think he'll ever leave Eden Falls," Eva answered, walking toward her car. Will followed.

"Wow, I'm impressed." I said. "It wasn't just a terrible pick-up line. You actually did recognize us."

Will laughed. "I did. It was driving me crazy that I couldn't figure out how, but it also gave me an excuse to come talk to you." He opened my car door and I slipped past him into the passenger seat.

"Well if you get bored tomorrow, I'll be watching Jules play volleyball most of the day. You're welcome to come," Eva said, watching him as he moved to her side of the car.

"Okay," Will responded, flashing a pearly smile. I strained to listen to everything being said in case anything was interesting,

but all I heard was her telling him when and where to go. She got in and he shut the door for her.

"If you get really bored tomorrow," I imitated Eva's voice. "I mean like really, really bored, there's always a slightly less boring volleyball match you can come watch." I stopped using my Eva voice. "Thanks for selling my match as so exciting."

Eva laughed. She watched Will intently as he walked away. "You know I didn't mean it like that. I didn't want him to feel obligated to come."

"Well, I'm pretty sure he didn't agree out of obligation," I said with a grin. "He couldn't have stopped smiling if he'd tried."

Eva beamed as she started the car. "Let's just hope it's not because he's excited about watching a court full of girls in short, spandex shorts."

I laughed and we waved as we passed Will and his colleagues talking in the parking lot. "Now," she continued, "where's this place that has frozen custard with brownie chunks?"

♡ Chapter 5 ♡

We all talk for the first hour of the trip. Owen is funny and surprisingly easy to talk to, but pretty soon I feel my lack of sleep. When Owen and Everett become engrossed in a conversation about the NBA playoffs, I decide to use the opportunity to shut my eyes for a few minutes.

"Jules, Juliet, JU-LI-ET," Everett is yelling by the time I open my eyes. I sit up and see we are driving by the Penn State campus and that Eva has fallen asleep as well. "I don't remember how to get to your place from here."

"Oh, sorry, I didn't think I'd actually fall asleep," I say, rubbing under my eyes to make sure there aren't any remnants of mascara left there. "Take this road to the second light and turn left." I continue directing him to my apartment for the next few minutes.

"That car, two cars back," Owen starts, "it was right behind us after we left your house. Do you have more people coming to help?"

My heart sinks. I knew we'd be followed, but I still hate that it's happening and I hate that Owen is so observant. We will probably be followed the remainder of the day though so I figure he might as well know that much. "Yeah, Eva's pretty popular," I smile at him, trying to make it sound casual. "She dated a guy a while back who has gone missing and now people are always following her and asking questions about him." I glance over at Eva, hoping she's okay with that version of the story. Although she is trying to hide it, sadness envelops her face. Everett's looking back in the mirror to check on Eva as well.

Owen looks really confused, probably not sure whether it is some weird joke or if I am serious. "Really, people *follow* you?" he asks skeptically. Eva nods. "Who are they? Has this been going on long?" He sounds concerned.

"Yeah, a while," she replies quietly, leaning over so her hair is blocking her face.

Owen, obviously sensing she doesn't want to go into details, lets it drop. We sit in awkward silence for a few seconds. I try to think of something to say, but it's easier to let it be silent. We pull up to my apartment. Eva and I go in to start packing everything, while Everett and Owen leave to pick up a trailer. The last time I'd been here was before my interview with Owen so I hadn't known if I would be moving or not. Luckily I don't own a lot of stuff that needs to be packed.

For the last two years, I've shared this apartment with three other girls. Two of them received their master's degrees at the same time I did and already moved out. The other, Ally, still lives in the apartment and found one other girl to split rent over the summer. Eva and I get right to work in the kitchen boxing up pots, pans, and dishes. After two minutes, a short girl whose expression makes her look eerily similar to Wednesday Addams comes marching down the hall. She's wearing what appears to be sparkly pink lingerie and doesn't look like she can possibly be old enough to live away from her parents. She stares at us for several seconds, arms folded across her chest before flashing a fake grin. "I never knew tape could be so loud, so disturbing, you know, like when I'm trying to sleep," she says, her eyes never leaving mine.

"Oh, uh, yeah," I stammer, glancing at my watch. 9:17. "Sorry. We needed to get an early start so we can get everything packed, drive home, and unpack it at my new place."

"Maybe you should try it without the tape." She's given up on the fake smile and can barely keep the anger out of her voice.

I'm at a complete loss for words so I'm thrilled when Eva responds. "I have a better idea." She's digging through her purse and grabs a small, plastic container. "Ear plugs." She holds them out to the girl, who doesn't take them. "Don't worry. These ones have never been used."

"You just happen to have ear plugs in that giant bag of yours?" I ask.

"The fifth graders have band practice in my classroom after school. Yes, I always have ear plugs."

The tween-looking girl watches our interaction with confusion. Eva takes hold of her hand, sets the plastic container holding ear plugs in it, and turns back toward me with a shrug and wide eyes.

The girl's eyes narrow, but she wraps her hand around the plastic box and turns around. She's in the middle of an overly dramatic sigh when the front door swings open and Ally comes in.

"Juliet! Hey." She runs in and gives me a hug. After introducing Eva to Ally and Ally ogling Eva's shirt, she says "*So* you guys met Lucy. Lucy, this is Juliet and," she stops talking because Lucy is already back down the hall shutting her bedroom door.

I raise an eyebrow at Ally.

"Yeah, I know. I'm about ready to live in my car," replies Ally, looking weary. "Do you guys need help?"

The three of us continue packing for another hour before Owen and Everett show up again. The two guys haul the bigger furniture downstairs and load it while Ally stares at them out the window. "I bet they could use some water. I'm going to see. Do you think they need water?" She keeps watching them. Eva and I smile at each other. Our friends are always in love with Everett and apparently Owen is having the same effect.

As soon as Everett walks through the front door, Ally is by his side. "I was just saying that you guys would probably like some water. Do you think your friend would like some too? Oh, or I have some lemonade and I'm pretty sure there's still some ice in here," she rattles on.

Owen comes back in and while the five of us are talking, Lucy comes strutting down the hall. She is still wearing her pink lingerie, but she has teased her hair up and put on what looks like an inch of makeup.

She walks right in front of Owen, brushing against him and then pushes herself up next to Everett. "The girls didn't tell me we'd have more company. I would have fixed up if I'd have known. I just woke up so you boys are stuck looking at me all frumpy now." She flashes a pouty face that looks like something she's rehearsed in front of the mirror a thousand times. She moves back toward Owen, apparently not wanting either guy to feel left out. Placing her hand on his chest, she says, "Are you guys going to tell me your names?"

"Uh, yes?" Owen answers, but it comes out as a question. "I'm Owen and that's Everett," Owen says, looking unsure.

"Well, Owen and Everett, are you the boyfriends?" She asks. Owen looks at me with wide eyes as Lucy runs her hand through his hair. I shrug and smile.

Owen pushes her hand away gently and scoots over. "Yes. Yes, I am her boyfriend." He scoots closer to me. "But," he continues, with a playful expression, "Everett is their *brother* and is very single." Everett shoots Owen a glare.

"Okay, let's start loading all of these boxes," Everett says, changing the subject.

Lucy runs and throws herself across the top of several boxes, giggling. "You'll have to move me first."

"Yeah, Everett, move her," Owen cheers.

Everett grabs one of the other boxes and heads out the door. "I think I'll move these ones first."

"In that case, I'll come help you," Lucy says as she jumps up and runs across the room. She stops midway, looks over her shoulder, and says, "C'mon, Owen. You can't let us do all the work."

"I'm trying to give you two some alone time," he responds. Then loud enough for only me to hear, he asks, "Does she always go outside in lingerie?"

I smile. Honestly, I feel bad for Lucy. She's obviously starved for attention. "Well, she definitely has the legs for it," I say.

He laughs. "So do I, but I manage to put on pants before leaving the house," he says, motioning at his legs.

I shake my head and laugh. "Yes, Owen, very impressive."

We grab boxes and head outside. Everett comes back up the stairs, with Lucy on his heels talking all the way, "You must be hungry with all this hard work you've been doing. Are you hungry? There's this really delicious little French place just a few blocks from here." She skips as she tops the stairs and twists her hair around her finger. "Do you like French food? I just love it. People are always saying, 'Lucy, how are you so thin? You eat all the time, but you look amazing.' So I say, 'Well, it takes hard work. I work out like every single day.' And I do. I work out every day. Do you like working out? Oh, well obviously. Look at you. I never really was much for sports though, kinda boring. How about you?"

"Thank you, Lucy, but I'm actually not hungry yet. I just want to get my sister's stuff moved right now," Everett, who hadn't been allowed even a second to reply following any of her questions, now butts in.

Frustrated with his response, she transfers her focus to Owen. She grabs the other side of the box he's carrying. He gives me a look begging for help, but I just smile back.

I jog to the top of the stairs. I look back down to see Owen and Lucy set the box in the trailer. She jumps on his back. He tries to force her off, but she's not giving up without a fight. Ally is busy snapping pictures of the scene. I can envision one of those inspirational perseverance posters now. It could have Lucy holding onto Owen for dear life and the quote by Persius that says, "He conquers who endures."

About twenty minutes and numerous attempts of seduction later, Lucy has finally given up. All of the boxes are loaded. Eva and I run back upstairs one last time to say goodbye to Ally. When I come out, Lucy is sitting on the curb looking forlorn. Owen sits down beside her and the two seem to be deep in conversation for a minute before they hug and Owen gets into Everett's car. Everett pulls up to the curb to wait for Eva and me.

"Bye, Lucy," I say as I jump into the back. She nods, but doesn't say anything. "What did you say to her, Owen?" I ask, impressed at his kindness.

He doesn't answer. He's staring at something. I follow his gaze to the black car that followed us from Eden Falls. It comes screeching into the parking lot as we pull out. A man, unconcerned about whether or not he is seen by us, jumps out, nearly trips over Lucy and Ally, and runs up the stairs. "What about that? Is that normal too?" Owen asks, his brows furrowed in concern.

"Let's get going," is Eva's reply.

I point to Ally, who is now sitting on the curb next to Lucy, "What about them?" I ask.

"He'll go in, look around to figure out what we were doing, try to search everywhere for a guy I haven't even seen in years, and leave. There's nothing we can do at this point.

By the time Ally and Lucy get back to their apartment, he'll be gone. Trust me, they're quick," Eva answers, her eyelids heavy.

There is no longer any hint of laughing or humor in the car. In an instant, it has been replaced with seriousness and, at least for me, fear. The air is heavy. I can tell Owen wants to ask more, but thankfully he stays quiet. The four of us drive in silence for several minutes. I glance at Eva. Although her eyes are shut, I'm fairly certain she is awake and probably thinking about Will.

♡ Chapter 6 ♡

Two and a Half Years Ago

Eva's laughter rang through my apartment as she entered. Will followed her inside. I sat up to make room for both of them on the sofa. "You don't need to move, Julie," he said.

"It's Juliet," I corrected him with a grin. I knew he knew my name by now, but he insisted on calling me Julie.

"I actually have to head back to Eden Falls tonight so I need to get going, but I just wanted to peek my head in to tell you 'hi' and that you played great today."

"Oh, thanks. I'm glad you came. I've never had a fan cheer for me so loudly." He and Eva looked at each other and grinned. The two of them had stayed for all three matches of my tournament and had supported me very enthusiastically.

"All right, I'm going."

"Have a good drive," I replied.

As he headed out the door, Eva followed him back out. "I'll just be one sec," she whispered to me.

A couple minutes later, Elaine plopped down beside me. "Didn't I just hear Eva?"

"Yeah, she'll be—" I started but was cut off when Eva came back in and fell onto the sofa with a sigh. "That good, huh?" I asked.

"*Definitely that good. He's so funny. And sweet. He's so sweet. And did you guys look at him? Man, he's fun to look at. And the kissing. Oh, I loved the kissing.*"

"*You already kissed him?*"

Eva didn't even hear my reaction. "*He asked me out again for next weekend. He said he'll be back here on Friday morning and wants to take me out as soon as he's done with business that day. Can I stay here with you guys again on Friday night? He said he could drive to Williamsport and get me and we could get dinner there, but I like staying here on the weekends anyway. Plus, it will mean I'll have more time with him.*"

"*You can stay here whenever you'd like,*" *Elaine answered.* "*I bought something special to celebrate Juliet's win today, but now there's even more to celebrate with you meeting Will. Let me grab it.*" *Elaine returned holding three jars of baby food and three spoons.* "*It's Blueberry Buckle!*" *she exclaimed excitedly.*

Eva nudged my shoulder and grinned. "*Perfect. Thanks, Elaine.*"

I held up my jar and clanked it on Elaine's and Eva's. "*Yes, thanks, Elaine.*"

♡ Chapter 7 ♡

Two Years and One Month Ago

Y ou're getting married?" the woman with bleached blonde hair and long, fake eyelashes sputtered.

"Yes," Eva replied, eyes on her menu.

"To What's-His-Name that you had just started dating when you brought him to Bethany's wedding?"

"Will. Yes, I'm getting married to Will."

"Hmm, well congrats. Make sure to send me an invite. I must be off now. It was lovely seeing you." She made a kissing motion and sauntered away, her sheath dress accenting her swaying hips.

"Who was that?" I asked as soon as the woman was out of ear-shot.

"Tiff Bradshaw. I graduated with her," Eva answered, teeth clenched.

"What's the story with you two? Why is running into her so upsetting? The veins in your neck are bulging." I removed the wrapper from one end of my straw and blew out the other end so the rest of the wrapper hit Eva in the face. She removed it without smiling.

"There's no story. I'm just tired of everyone acting like I'm rushing into something. I know I want to marry Will, so why won't everyone just be happy for me?"

I was unsure how to respond. Will and Eva did get serious fast, but they were perfect for each other. For a while, I'd wanted to dislike Will because with him in the picture, I'd hardly gotten to see Eva, but there was nothing to dislike about him. When Eva first told me she was moving back to Eden Falls to be closer to him, I wasn't surprised. When they announced their engagement after only four months, I was expecting it. I'd seen the way Will lit up when he saw Eva; the way he watched her so intently. I'd noticed how comfortable they were around each other and how they went out of their way to make the other happy.

I placed my hand on Eva's. "What you and Will have is not something everybody gets to experience. It's impossible for some to believe that it could be genuine; that it's not just some fleeting romance."

"I guess so," Eva responded.

"Okay, look at this one," I said, trying to change the subject. I pointed to a picture of a bouquet in one of the dozens of magazines Eva and I had been scouring. Planning the wedding always put Eva in a good mood. She'd dragged me along on trip after trip to bridal boutiques. We'd spent hours looking at pictures of dresses, bouquets, cakes, and decorations. We'd painstakingly weighed out all the pros and cons between winter or spring, azure or cerulean, gardenias or anemones. I'd even learned who Jenny Packham and Vera Wang were as Eva tried on every gown she could get her hands on. "Do you like the calla lilies? I think I like them." I pushed the magazine toward Eva, whose expression hadn't changed.

I squeezed my lemon into my water and some juice squirted Eva's face. "Jules!" She yelled. "Watch what you're doing."

I fumbled for words. Eva was usually so laid back and happy. "Sorry," I said, pulling the magazine back to my side of the table. She still hadn't looked at it.

"I'm going to go," she said as she pushed her chair back. "I'm really not hungry anyway."

"I'm sorry. I didn't mean to get lemon on you."

Love and Fat-Free Cheese

She stared at me for several seconds. "It's not that," she said, shaking her head. She fumbled with the handle on her purse.

"What's going on, Eva?"

She hesitated, but sat back down. "I really don't know," she started. "Will is . . . different. He's so upset." Tears welled up in the corners of her eyes. "It's not that we're rushing into this. It's not. I know him, but something has him on edge."

"Is he upset with you?"

"No. I mean at least he says he's not. He claims it's stuff at work. Ever since he switched over from sales to product development, it's been bad." She spun her engagement ring around her finger as she talked. "I can't figure anything out though. He won't talk to me about it. And now . . ." She cried harder. "Now, he's telling me that I should stop planning the wedding for a while."

I held my napkin out to Eva since hers was saturated in tears and mascara. I scooted closer and put my arm around her. "I'm sorry. It will all work out. Just give it a little time." However, even as I was saying it, my head was spinning. Why would Will act that way? What was he hiding?

♡ Chapter 8 ♡

Everett's been asking Owen questions about Meridian's and how to get there. As we pull into the restaurant parking lot, it's nothing like I pictured. The way Owen talked, I figured it would be some over-the-top, expensive steakhouse or something, not the little hut with giant pillars shaped like hot dogs that stands in front of me.

Inside servers are dressed as a variety of foods; a couple of hamburgers, a corn dog, some chicken fingers, and, of course, hot dogs. I laugh out loud when I see my chair. It's a large cushiony hamburger. It looks like it is open so I am sitting on the patty and the cheese, and the top bun is the back. Owen tries to convince all of us to order the Chunky Chili Cheeser, saying it is his favorite food of all time, but my stomach hurts just hearing the name. I am even more confident in my decision not to order it when the food comes and I stare at Owen's and Everett's plates. The menu calls it a "mouth-watering delight that mocks the standard chili cheese dog." I can't even see the hot dog. I see crushed up Doritos, fried onions, cheese whiz, curly fries, ranch, and other toppings I can't identify. My Cheeky Cheeky Cheeseburger is looking more and more appetizing by comparison. I watch Eva as the guys convince her to taste the "Cheeser." She's laughing and looks like she's enjoying herself, something that's rare since Will disappeared. I decide I'm going to make sure she spends a lot more time out of the house now that I'm back in Eden Falls. It's time to put the past behind us.

After lunch, Owen offers to drive and within five minutes Everett's asleep. Eva has her earbuds in and looks like she is about to drift off as well. "So," Owen starts, "you ready to start working?"

Suddenly Owen seems a lot more intimidating. He is Mr. Denny, vice president of TBC and my superior. I try to rid myself of that feeling and talk to him as comfortably as I have all morning. "Yeah, I'm actually really excited. Especially now that I have a place to live, I'm ready for something to do."

"Something like finding underlying patterns and predicting outcomes?" he asks, smiling. I laugh, surprised that he remembers my answer from our interview. He continues, "The Bradley Corporation is a pretty great place to work. I think you'll really like it."

We talk about my job for a few minutes longer before I ask him about his history with TBC and how he got to be VP. "I've been really close with the Bradley family for years. They're my second family and they've been amazingly generous to me." He pauses for a few seconds, starts to say something, and then stops. After thinking for a little while longer, he adds, "The only problem is that because of all that generosity they seem to feel like I'm—" He stops talking as his phone rings. "Sorry, just one sec," and he answers his phone. He's talked for a couple of minutes when he looks over to me and mouths, "Sorry." I smile back and, feeling funny listening to him while he talks, pull out my earphones and plug them into my phone. Two songs later, Owen hangs up the phone. I take my earbuds out as he apologizes again and then asks, "Who were you listening to?"

"Paul Simon."

We talk about music, which somehow turns into a conversation about pizza toppings; I love veggie pizza and Owen will eat any kind of pizza but veggie. We talk about places we've visited; Owen having been everywhere while I've been nowhere. Pretty soon it's hockey games, kayaking, and funny things about Everett. That's when Everett wakes up and joins the conversation. With the three of us laughing and talking loudly, Eva wakes up as well. Everett and Eva start telling about the time I practically burned the house down with a lighter, hairspray, and a pair of socks.

We are only twenty minutes outside of Eden Falls now so I call my parents and Elaine, who said they'd help unload stuff. Mom and Dad are waiting at the apartment when we pull up. We unload a few things, but stop when a white car with Elaine in the passenger seat pulls in. A man who looks vaguely familiar is driving. After they get out, he approaches me and reaches in with outstretched arms, "Juliet Easton." I look at him with apprehension as he picks me up in a giant hug.

Elaine immediately says, "Remember Josh, you know, from high school?" And then in a whisper, "He was your chemistry lab partner." Now I can place him. I'm having flashbacks of a genuinely nice guy who never stopped talking. I clearly remember his monotone voice and the mind-numbingly boring topics he liked to talk about.

"Of course I remember Josh," I say, smiling at Elaine. Then, turning to Josh, I ask, "Are you still living in Eden Falls?" We make small talk about what a great place Eden Falls is with its thriving businesses mixed with small town charm. Elaine explains that she ran into him and told him where she was going and he said he wanted to come see me and help me move.

"Yeah," Josh starts. "I told her, 'I haven't seen Juliet since high school.' But now that I'm thinking about it, maybe I have. I think I saw you the next summer at Target. Do you remember that? You were pretty busy and couldn't talk too long, but I still saw you. So, you're moving back, huh? I don't live too far from here. It's a great part of town. You'll really like it. There's this little store that just went in about ten blocks back that way that sells these . . ." He continues talking and although I am really trying to stay focused and listen, my mind drifts. I watch my parents begin to unload the sofa and Everett explain to them that it is going to the storage unit around the corner. I see Mom laughing at something Owen says. I long to switch places with her right now. I look back to see Josh staring at me. "Do you?" he asks.

"Ah, do I?" I respond, puzzled, hoping he'll repeat whatever he asked me, without realizing I've been tuning him out completely.

"Like Thai food? It's the best Thai food I've ever had and it's right here in this neighborhood. You should try their Bean Noodle Salad. It has ground chicken . . . and pickled cabbage . . . and um, let me see, cilantro. It might not sound great because I'm not doing it justice, but it is great. What else is in it? I'm pretty sure there's some lime juice. There are leeks. Um, I think it may have those, um, ah, what are they called? Those yellowish, brown vegetables, oh it's right on the tip of my tongue. They're ah . . . um . . . ah—"

"Yes," I say when he finally slows down enough for me to answer. "I generally like Thai food. I'll have to try that out one of these days. Thanks for the tip, Josh. I better get over there and help before everybody else does all of the work."

Josh continues talking while we walk over to help unload. I quickly grab a box and take it up the stairs. Elaine comes up behind me, "Isn't he cute?"

"Josh?"

"Yeah, in high school he was so boring, but it seems like he's really changed. We're having so much fun."

"That's great, Elaine. I'm glad." Fun is probably the last word I would use to describe Josh. I would go with dull, stale, or mundane, and in the two minutes I'd just spent with him, he seemed exactly the same as he had in high school. However, if Elaine can find something fun about him, good for her.

Owen and Josh come through the door carrying my mattress. Josh is busy talking, ". . . is number thirty-four, but sometimes I even go up to forty. I guess my taste in mattress density changes some days. I will never use anything but a Sleep Number bed now. My back has never been in better shape and I know it's because—oh Juliet, I remembered. Scallions, they use scallions in the bean noodle salad— Anyway, oh, what was I saying, Owen?" Owen looks at me grinning, obviously very amused by Josh.

"Oh, scallions, yum," I reply.

"Yeah," Josh says, looking at Owen. "I was telling Juliet about the new Thai place on the corner. They have a great bean noodle salad with ground chicken, pickled cabbage, cilantro . . ." His voice gets quieter and quieter as I walk out to get another load.

It only takes twenty minutes to unload everything with all the help I have. I bring some of the drinks from Everett's fridge down to the parking lot and am thanking everybody when Elaine's mom pulls in.

"I ran into Josh while I was working so he drove me over here. I needed Mom to come get me and take me to my house." Elaine explains.

I thank Elaine for her help and give her a hug. Mrs. McElroy stares at me so I wave. She turns away, pretending not to have noticed me.

Chapter 9

Owen told me to meet him at his office at eight o'clock on Monday morning. He said he could show me around and introduce me to my department. The lobby outside of his office doesn't seem nearly as foreboding this time. It smells like coffee and new carpet. I clickety-clack in my heels up to the front desk. Celia's busy counting stitches as she crochets. I wait for her to look up. She gives me a warm smile and says, "Well, don't you look darlin'? You can just go on back, honey." I walk through the main door to the second waiting area and knock on his door. Nothing. It looks dark inside. Great, he must have forgotten. Now I have to show up in the marketing department all on my own, several minutes late. That's going to make a great first impression. A doorknob clicks and Owen walks out a different door.

"Hey," he says, noticing where I'm standing. "Oh, sorry, this is my real office over here." He points to where he's standing. "That one is just an extra room that I kind of made my unofficial office. I hate the decorations in this place. Sometimes it's nice to have a simple, un-purple room to do my work in. I can't focus surrounded by shiny stuff." He motions me into his real office. This one matches the gaudy decorations in the lobby; gold and purple everywhere. There are giant paintings on every wall. I watch him as he walks behind his desk and can't help but let out a laugh. There, right behind his desk, is a painting at least six feet tall of a naked man. I know laughing is juvenile and makes me look like I have the maturity of a ten-year-old, but it caught me off guard. "Sorry," I say quickly, shaking my head.

"Oh, so apparently you have very little appreciation for fine art," is his reply. I'm so relieved that his tone is light-hearted.

"It's, um, it's a very nice painting and I'm sure the artist is incredibly talented. I just wasn't prepared to . . ." I trail off, unsure how to finish.

"Now you understand why I turned that room into my second office. Sometimes I don't want to work with a naked dude staring me down," he laughs.

"You can't take him off of that wall?"

"He is bolted to that wall very well. I've suggested he be moved to a place where he might be better appreciated, but that idea was shot down so I just pretend this is a locker room and Eddie here is headed to the shower."

I laugh.

"Anyway, you ready to get started?"

"I'm ready," I reply. Owen grabs some paperwork he has lying on his desk and starts going over it with me. "Do you want me to go to Human Resources to do all of this?" I ask.

"No, I had them send it up here. I figure it will be easier for me to show you everything, instead of you having to go from floor to floor trying to figure it all out."

"Okay, thanks." I would rather go over it with him than with someone else.

We finish the papers and are ready to go to level five, where I will be working. I open the door to the main lobby and run straight into Lila. She stumbles backwards for a second before she catches herself and her eyes narrow in my direction, but a giant grin immediately covers her face as

Owen walks out. She grabs Owen's arm and pulls him in next to her. He looks uncomfortable. "I'm on my way out," Owen explains. "I'll give you a call when," he can't finish his sentence because Lila is kissing him. He pushes her back and walks to the main door.

"O, you've been so busy lately. I feel like I never get to see you."

"Why don't we have lunch today?" he suggests. "I'll meet you here at eleven." He glances at me and smiles apologetically before opening the door for us.

Lila looks me up and down in disgust as she walks through the door. "Okay," she responds to Owen, disappointed, "but at dinner last night I was talking about how you've hardly had a spare second for me lately and there was a lot of concern."

Owen stops walking and furrows his eyebrows. I'm missing something important, but can't pinpoint it. Why does Owen care about what Lila was talking about at dinner last night? And why won't his girlfriend leave him alone while he's working? "I'm sorry, Lila. I'll try to give you some more time. It's been kind of crazy lately. Meet me here at eleven and we can talk, okay?"

"Well actually, I texted Daddy when I was on my way down here and he said he'd love to take us out to breakfast." Then, as she nods to me, she continues, "So, tell your little assistant here what to do while you're gone because you and I are supposed to be in Daddy's office in about . . . ," she stops and looks at her phone, "seven minutes. See? We have no time. C'mon, Owen. Let's go fill that tummy up with some pancakes," she finishes while rubbing his stomach. Ugh, I think I might be sick.

Owen grimaces. "She's not my assistant. This is Juliet. Juliet, this is Lila."

Lila flashes a fake grin for half of a second before saying, "Juliet, we have to go. So maybe you could come back and sell us your Girl Scout cookies another day, 'kay?" She grabs Owen and starts pulling him toward the elevator. I'm left completely speechless. Who is this girl and why is Owen letting her walk all over him?

"Hold on a sec," Owen says to Lila. "Juliet, I'm really sorry. I'll call Collin, the marketing supervisor, and explain to him that I had to leave suddenly, but that you'll be down shortly." Then, shifting his attention to the front desk, "Celia, can you go ahead and take her over to HR and make sure they show her everything?"

Celia happily nods. "Of course, sugar."

"I'll find you later, Juliet. I'm sorry about this."

"Seriously, Owen, she'll be fine," Lila chimes in. "Daddy's waiting."

Lila and Owen leave. Celia tells me she'll need another minute before we can go to HR. I sit down, trying to shake my feelings of frustration. Maybe it's not frustration as much as it is disappointment. Owen is not the person I thought he was. Why am I letting myself get upset about a guy I barely even know? I tell myself it's because I was expecting to have him around today. I'm comfortable around him and having him with me would make my first day easier. But now after watching him with Lila, I can see I don't want to spend any more time with him than I have to. Lila is needy and immature, and he let her walk all over him. I want to take her fancy Jimmy Choo handbag and fill it with cat litter. Wait, scratch that thought. That would be a terrible thing to do to such a pretty bag and Eva would kill me if she ever found out I'd disgraced a designer bag that way. I want to take the Jimmy Choo for myself and save the cat litter for her ugly diamond-encrusted tank-top.

"Are you ready, honey?" Celia tears my thoughts away from my vengeful fantasy.

I stand up and give my best Girl-Scout-salesman-smile and quickly answer, "Yes." I need to get my mind back to what's important. I've been given a wonderful opportunity and I can't let it slip.

"Let's get you over to Human Resources. Most people start there anyway. Mr. Denny just really wanted to show ya 'round himself, but that Lila has to make sure she's always in control. She aggravates me somethin' terrible." Celia shakes her head. Her face looks like she's just sniffed a dirty diaper as she continues, "She's as awful as a sweet Georgia pine is tall . . . such a character, that one. Guess I shouldn't be ranting like this to you. Sorry, honey." She stops talking for a couple of seconds before she continues, "It's always the awful one's that have all the control. She has Daddy at her beck and call. Everybody around here is scared of her because of what she'll run off and tell him." I give Celia a confused expression. "Of Lila, honey, they're scared of Lila."

"Who's her dad?" I ask.

"Oh, you are new. That was Lila Bradley, honey. Didn't you wonder why Owen was always so nice to her?

So that's why he listens to Lila. He's dating Mr. Bradley's daughter so he can move up in the company. Now the whole VP thing makes perfect sense. I remember in the car ride back from Penn when he'd been talking about the Bradleys and he said something about being really close with the family. Yeah, at least he's really close to one person in the family.

That also explains why Everett acted surprised when I mentioned Owen's girlfriend. "He doesn't have a girlfriend. I've hung out with him nearly every weekend for the past year and, trust me, he doesn't have a girlfriend. He has several girls that wish they were his girlfriend though," Everett had said. I had naively assumed he wasn't dating Lila exclusively or something. I had dropped it because I didn't want Everett to suspect me of having feelings for Owen.

I feel stupid for not having realized this earlier. I had just watched Owen drop everything and go somewhere he clearly didn't want to go as soon as Lila mentioned "Daddy." He's dating Lila to gain favor with the family and then still going out with Everett and picking up girls when Lila isn't around.

"Don't get the wrong idea about Mr. Denny though. He's a big ol' sweetie," Celia gushes. "He's just doing what it takes to survive in this corporation. If the Bradleys had a son, I'd be trying the same thing." Celia laughs at herself and waits for my reaction. I give her a half-hearted grin. She pats my arm and says, "Here we are, honey. Just sit down right there and Laura will help ya with everything. You have a great first day."

"Thanks," I respond with as much enthusiasm as I can muster.

"Here, this'll help." She takes the crochet hook from behind her ear and pulls some yarn out of her jacket pocket. "When I get all frustrated, this just melts the mad away. You ever crochet before, sugar?" I shake my head. "Well, ain't nothin' to it, really." She takes my hands and tries to instruct me on how to begin. I have a five-inch chain by the time Laura is ready for me. Celia wraps her arms around me in a motherly hug. "You keep that hook and yarn. You may need it some more today."

"Thanks, Celia," I say and I'm surprised by how much I mean it.

The rest of the morning passes quickly. I like all of the people I meet in my department, but I feel completely incompetent. It seems like I'm asking a thousand questions and still don't understand much. After lunch, one of the girls, Kelcey or Keeley or Katie (I can't remember what she said her name was), starts showing me a computer program that I need to learn when Owen walks in.

"Hey, how's it going? I wanted to make sure you were figuring everything out," he says with his million-dollar grin.

"Yeah, it's good," I reply nonchalantly.

"Hi, Mr. Denny," the girl who's name starts with an K gushes. "She's doing great." She continues staring at him, eyes wide.

"Good," says Owen, sounding skeptical. I can feel his eyes burning the side of my face. "Is everything making sense, Juliet?"

I force a smile. "Yes."

"Okay," he says, still staring intently. I look at the computer, feeling uncomfortable with eye contact.

"She's just had so much to take in today," the girl says. "But she catches on so fast," she says over-enthusiastically.

"Yeah, okay, well I didn't mean to interrupt. I'll let you go so you—"

"Interrupt?" she gives a fake laugh. "Oh, Mr. Denny, you can interrupt us any time. We're never too busy for you."

"Thanks. I'll see you later," he says, turning to leave.

As he walks away, I can hear a chorus of "Hi, Mr. Denny" and "Good afternoon, Mr. Denny."

"Oh, I can't believe he knows your name and comes and checks on you," the girl says, putting her hands on her flushed cheeks. "I'm going to marry him. He may not know my name yet, but I'm going to marry him." She fans her face with her stack of papers. "After he takes over this company and ditches Lila, it will just be me and him. Kat Denny, doesn't that sound right?" She continues staring down the hall he walked down long after he's gone. "Oh, he's beautiful. There are not a lot of guys I would call beautiful, but him, he's beautiful. And did you smell him? Ah, he smelled so good."

So does everyone at The Bradley Corporation know why Owen is with Lila? It must be pretty common knowledge the way this girl is talking about it.

"Yeah, he smelled good," is all I can bring myself to reply.

♡ Chapter 10 ♡

My feet are throbbing. I've never worn high heels for more than a few hours before, but now I've had three-inch heels on for nearly ten. I pull into the parking lot of Everett's apartment. I guess now it is my apartment as well, but I still consider it Everett's. That's probably largely due to the fact that everything about his place says "a single guy lives here." There are no decorations to speak of, unless you count the sixty-inch television or all of the sports equipment. The fridge is always empty, except for some pizza or a couple of bottles of Yoo-hoo.

I took my shoes off when I first got into the car and the thought of putting them back on to walk up the stairs is painful. I grab my purse and my heels and walk barefoot through the parking lot. I'm heading up the stairs when I get a call from Everett.

"Hey, I'm coming in the door now. I'll see you in a sec," I say.

"No, that's why I called. I have a few things to finish up and I probably won't be done for a couple of hours. I won't be able to eat dinner 'til at least seven." Everett and I made a deal that I would figure out dinners. I am getting to live at his place practically rent-free for now so I agreed to take care of dinner every night.

"Okay. Let's plan on seven thirty."

"Sounds great. Thanks, Jules."

I had completely forgotten about dinner. I turn around and go back down the stairs so I can make a quick trip to the grocery store. I'm absorbed in thoughts of tacos and sweet rice as I jog through the parking lot toward my car. "Ouch! Ow, ow, ow!" There's a shooting pain in my foot. I see visions of the giant shard of glass that must be lodged in my heel. It has to be the size of a dinner plate. Or maybe I stepped on a small dog and its teeth are still digging into my flesh. I look down and see a tiny pebble.

"Are you all right?" asks a guy about my age with a concerned look on his face. I stare for a second, taking note that I can see his muscles through his dress shirt. I smile back, feeling ridiculous for yelling about stepping on a pebble.

"Yeah, I'm fine. Thanks." He still looks concerned so I add, "I should probably lie right now and tell you I twisted my ankle or something, but I actually just stepped on this." I hold up the tiny rock. "You probably can't even see it from there. It's a tiny pebble and I obviously have a very high tolerance of pain." He laughs and walks over to me to see what I'm holding.

"Well that one does have some pretty sharp edges. You sure you're going to make it?" He teases.

I grin. "Barely, but I'll try to hang in there."

"I've heard that ice cream really helps wounds like yours."

"I guess I better eat some right away. I'd rather not lose this foot."

"And I definitely don't want to feel responsible. Why don't we head to that creamery across the street?"

Wow, this guy doesn't waste any time. I should dress up more often. "Thanks, but I'm actually in a hurry right now. Maybe I can take a rain check on that."

"Sure. I'm Luke," he says, holding out his hand.

"I'm Juliet. Do you live in this building?" He nods and I continue, "I just moved in."

"I live in 207," he replies. "Let me know when you want that ice cream."

"I will, thanks." As I get into my car, I'm mad at myself. Why didn't I go with him? Dinner with Everett isn't so important that I can't go get ice cream for a few minutes. I declined before I even thought about it. I could get Everett a burger at some drive-thru and he wouldn't mind. As I picture Luke with his bright blue eyes and muscles, I'm ready to go knock on door 207 right now. I convince myself to wait. Instead, I buy groceries and make dinner for myself and Everett before we head to the gym.

The following evening my parents ask Everett and me to come out to the house for a family dinner. As much as I enjoy time spent with family, I'm anxious to see Luke again. I don't want him to think I'm not interested. I ask Everett to tell my family "sorry" for me, but that I can't make it tonight. He smiles and tells me I am becoming more and more fickle, like Elaine. Within two minutes, I'm in Everett's car and we are on our way to family dinner. He always knows how to get under my skin. Seeing Luke will just have to wait another night.

On Wednesday I'm getting ready to take my lunch break when Lila comes strutting into the marketing department. Figuring she's here to yell at somebody, boss them around, or just ruin their day in general, I ignore her and gather my phone, purse, and food. Collin, my supervisor, steps in front of me as I try to leave. He corrects his posture and stands up as tall as his five-foot-six frame allows, trying to match my height. "Hey, Juliet, I need you."

"Okay," I respond. I like Collin. I'd guess he's in his late-forties. The way he dresses and styles his hair suggest he's younger, but his leathery skin and graying sideburns give him away. I follow him into his office, where he turns toward me.

"Ms. Bradley," he says, motioning behind him where Lila stands looking like she is absolutely disgusted with having to be in this room, "wants you for a little while."

"Uh," I can't think of anything to say. Why does Lila want to talk to me?

I am desperately trying to think of any reason I can give for not being able to talk to her when she says impatiently, "Grab your stuff and let's go. You're going to come to lunch with me."

"Oh, thanks, but I actually brought a lunch with me today." As I say it, Collin shoots me a weird look and motions for me to go with Lila. People really are scared of this girl.

"That," Lila starts, pointing to the bagel in my hands, "is *not* a lunch. That is a load of carbs that will park itself right on your thighs. Let's go have a decent lunch." She starts walking away before she even finishes her sentence.

"Go," Collin urges, pushing his hair back with his hands. I really can't think of anything I'd rather do less right now. I think back to my last job when I was showing a girl how to roll her kayak and she puked all over the place. I thought cleaning up her mess was terrible, but I would rather be doing that right now than going to lunch with Lila.

"When Lila asks something," Collin whispers, sensing my reluctance, "it's not really an option. She'll find a way to make it happen. Just do it." I don't want to make a scene or irritate Collin, who is technically my boss. Plus, he's probably right. As long as I am working at TBC, I should probably get used to Lila's crazy antics. I slowly walk out the door that Lila walked through. She's waiting at the elevator, looking at her watch and sighing.

And the fun begins, I think as we step into the elevator. We're both silent as we ride down to the front lobby.

We walk outside and Lila points to a brand new Lotus. Once we're inside, she begins, "My fiancé asked me to help you out a little."

Fiancé? I was not expecting that. She's engaged to someone? Or does she mean Owen?

She continues, "He thinks you have potential, but you could use a lot of refining in some areas. You could do well in this company, and Owen's great about taking people in and kind of mentoring them so they have opportunities that they never would have had without him." As she drives, she taps her acrylic nails on the steering wheel. "He and I will be getting married soon. I love doing things that make him happy, so here I am; your personal fairy godmother."

I open my mouth to speak, but have nothing to say. It's one of those moments where I want something wonderful and mean to say, but can't think of anything. She caught me completely off-guard. My own personal fairy godmother? Seriously? I know I'll be up late tonight thinking of a thousand come-backs that I should have said in response to this.

"First things first," Lila continues as we pull in to the parking lot of Aisuru, one of the new restaurants in Eden Falls that I've never been to. "You're probably not used to eating at places like this so we're expanding your horizons today." We walk in and the maître d' immediately seats us. Once at our table, Lila sighs and says, "Being here just makes me think of O. He loves coming here with me. We feed each other the California rolls, but not in a weird, creepy way. It's more of a 'we're so in love way . . .'"

Lila continues talking and talking. If she isn't talking about how in love she and Owen are, she is talking about how amazing other people think she is. I pull my phone out of my purse to see how much time has passed and am quickly reprimanded. "Okay, stop. That is so rude. It's not that I care, but it's really important for you to learn. You should never take your phone out during a meal." Then when we order Lila quickly tells the server to ignore my order and bring us both unago sashimi and a field green salad. I try to hide my shock at the twenty-nine dollar price listed next to the sashimi. Especially since I'm planning on eating my bagel that will park itself right on my thighs as soon as we get back to the car anyway. "If you want to look like this," Lila goes on, pointing to herself, "you need to be a lot more conscious about what goes into your body. Those saddle bags will just keep getting bigger." After several more priceless pointers on food choices and reasons why Lila's body is perfect, the food comes.

After she rips me apart for choosing my fork instead of chopsticks, I say, "I have a lot of work to do this afternoon so I really need to get back."

"No, this is your work. This is the best way you could be spending your time for TBC. We still have to go shopping."

I know I cannot handle much more of this girl. "No, I need to get back."

"Where should we start?" Lila asks, ignoring me. "Some dresses or maybe shoes. Whoa, you seriously have the biggest feet I've ever seen on a girl. Maybe we can find some shoes that make them look significantly smaller. You should probably use subtle toenail polish instead of that bright color too. It draws more attention to them."

"I'll walk back," I say as I turn to leave.

Lila grabs my arm. "You really shouldn't walk that far in heels. It will make your calves bigger." I pull my arm away and Lila smiles smugly. "Okay, we'll hang out later. My fiancé will be so glad we're friends."

♡ Chapter 11 ♡

'm really not," I laugh into the phone. I'm on my way home from work and talking to Eva .

After each detail I relay about my lunch with Lila, Eva says, "You're making that up." I keep telling the story as Eva laughs. It's much funnier now that I'm not living it.

"Saddle bags?" Eva asks, incredulously. "There's nothing on you that even remotely resembles saddle bags!"

When I finish the whole story, Eva responds, "It sounds like she's threatened by you."

"Threatened? No, she's just a horrible person who wants to make everybody else feel awful," I reply.

"She must be convinced that you are trying to take Owen away. There's no way he actually asked her to 'help' you. She's trying to make you feel inferior. She wants you to feel like he's way out of your league or something; that the only reason he'd talk to you is out of charity. You're in better shape than anyone I know and she wishes her calves looked half as good as yours." Eva pauses and then adds, "I saw the way Owen looked at you. If Lila saw anything like that, I'm sure she's really nervous."

"Yeah, well if only Dad owned a multi-billion dollar corporation, I could get a high quality guy like Owen to go after me."

"Are they really engaged?"

"I guess. I mean he probably has to marry her if he really wants her money. Oh, Eva, I gotta go. I see Luke."

"Is that the ice cream guy?"

"Yeah, I'll talk to you later," I say in a rush. I want to catch Luke before he goes inside. It seems much less stalker-ish if I casually bump into him in the parking lot rather than show up at his doorstep. I step out of the car and yell across the parking lot, "Hey."

He walks toward me. "Hey, I'm glad to see you're wearing shoes this time."

"Yeah," I smile, unable to think of anything else to say. "I have comfy shoes this time." I desperately try to think of something more interesting to add. Nothing. I stare at him. "They're very . . . cushiony." Since I met Luke on Monday, I have been thinking about him and the next time we would talk. Now that it is actually happening, the best thing I can think to say is, "They're very cushiony."

Luckily he starts talking, "I saw you out here this morning around six-thirty, but by the time I came out, you were gone. Do you always leave so early?"

"I like to run before work," I answer, smiling. Then I remember the poppy seed bagel I had at lunch and wonder if I have several poppy seeds between my teeth. I attempt my best-looking close-mouthed smile.

"So your foot didn't need to be amputated after all, huh?"

I laugh. "I fought through the pain."

He unloads a couple of grocery bags while we make small talk. I appreciate having an excuse to stare at him. I bet he never leaves poppy seeds stuck in his teeth.

We walk toward the stairs and I decide now is my shot to take him up on ice cream. "Is the offer still good to go to the creamery? Will you be able to go tonight?"

"Of course," he answers eagerly. "Does seven work for you?"

"Seven's great."

"Okay, I'll see you later." He smiles.

I stare at him as he turns to walk away. "Oh, Luke, I live in 304."

"I know." He grins again.

I go upstairs to the apartment and start to make a quick dinner for Everett and me. My mind is only half-way focusing on what I'm doing. The other half is dreaming about how tonight will go. I jump back when I accidentally drip some oil down inside the burner and flames shoot up. "Ev! Ev, come help me!" I shout, filling a bowl with water to pour on it. Everett comes running into the kitchen, shoves me aside, grabs a towel, and throws it over the flames.

"Nice, Jules," he sighs. "The hairspray story was starting to get kind of old. Now we have a new one to tell. It would have been an even better story if you'd thrown that water on it. It would have splattered the oil everywhere and the entire kitchen would have been on fire." He gives me a consoling smile.

"Great," I say, sitting down at the table. "Why don't I order us a pizza so I have time to get ready for tonight? I'll make dinner tomorrow."

"So you just met some guy in the parking lot and you're going out with him?" Everett asks. "You can't trust some random guy, Jules."

I told him about Luke when we met on Monday and he'd been very skeptical. "It will be fine," I say, walking into my bedroom as Everett follows me. "I'm not even getting into a car with him. We're walking across the street, eating ice cream, and walking home. That's about the safest date I could possibly go on." I grab two shirts out of my closet. "Which one?" I ask, holding them up.

"Either," he answers. This was one of those times when I really miss living with girls, especially Eva. She wouldn't say "either." She'd tell me to put each one on and look at it from every angle to decide which one made me look my absolute best. Then, even when one of the shirts was chosen, she'd have me put the other one back on just to check one more time. "All right, I'll let you get ready. Just be careful. Guys are jerks."

"Great pep talk, Ev. Thanks." Everett leaves and I choose a different shirt entirely. At two minutes after seven Luke is at the front door. I hurry out before Everett can try to scare him off. He's wearing a light blue t-shirt that shows off tan, muscular arms. It takes everything in me to stop myself from reaching out and caressing his arm.

"So, where do you like to run?" Luke asks as we walk down the street.

"All around the little neighborhoods back here. I found a path yesterday that runs alongside the river and goes by a small waterfall. I had no idea this apartment was right next to so many great trails. I love it."

"Do you have roommates?" I tell him about living with Everett and how it's a temporary arrangement.

"You guys must get along well if you're able to live in the same apartment without strangling each other," he responds.

"Yeah, we do. We've always been pretty close."

"Are you close with all of your family?"

I nod. "How about you? Do you have family in Eden Falls?

"No, just me," he answers.

I wait for him to tell me more about his family, but he doesn't so I decide to change topics. "Have you been here before?" I ask, pointing to The Whole Scoop Ice Creamery.

He laughs. "Yeah, I've been here this *week*. And probably about every week since I moved here."

The teenage boy behind the counter takes our orders without looking up from the counter. His shaky hands cause him to drop a brownie on the floor. He quickly picks it up, wipes it off, and chops it up before placing it on the top of my ice cream. I smile out of the side of my mouth at Luke.

Luke stares at the kid in disbelief and starts to say something, but I elbow him and motion for him to not to. The boy, with his acne-covered skin and mop of dark blonde hair, is visibly nervous. He still hasn't looked up from the counter. He scoots our bowls toward a cheerful girl, who rings us up.

We find an empty booth and sit down. "Why didn't you say something? You can't eat that," Luke says.

I pick all the brownie chunks off and set them to the side. "Look at the poor kid. It must be his first day or something. He looks miserable. I don't care that much about the brownie anyway." I shrug. "It's just one more thing to have to dig through to get to what I really want; the peanut butter sauce."

The girl from the counter appears next to our booth. She sets a brownie wrapped in tissue paper on the table. "Here's a fresh one. Sorry about that." She looks toward the boy behind the counter. "He's had a pretty rough day." She turns and walks away as we thank her.

Luke grabs the brownie.

I raise an eyebrow.

"You said you didn't care about the brownie anyway," He says, holding it just out of my reach while laughing.

"No, I said I didn't care *much*."

"I'm pretty sure she brought it for me anyway. I have that effect on girls." He winks at me jokingly.

"Oh yeah? I guess next time I need to wear a shirt that makes my arms look all tan and muscular."

Luke laughs. "So you think I look muscular?" He sets the brownie back down. I rip off a chunk and eat it while he watches me. We continue talking while we eat. He keeps putting his hand on my leg, which makes me nervous. He's constantly touching my arm or tucking my hair behind my ear. It seems a bit much for someone who just met me, but I merely have to look at his face for one second before I'm reminded that there are plenty of other girls who would love to have him touching their arms.

At a quarter past eight, we head home. He'd mentioned earlier that he'd like to meet Everett. He figured he'd at least recognize him since they'd been neighbors for a couple of years. As he walks me to the door, I wonder if that means he wants to come in now. I think about inviting him in, but hesitate. I really want to change out of my jeans that feel like they are cutting into my hips, put on my pajama pants, and watch some of the shows I have on the DVR. I know it's ridiculous, but if he comes in right now, he might stay for hours and that just sounds exhausting. Instead, I thank him, he kisses me on the cheek, and I go inside alone.

An hour later I have opted to save the stuff on the DVR and instead watch an episode of *How It's Made* about bacon. I don't even really like this show, but once I start watching one, it's addicting. I have to finish the episode. I hear the doorknob and turn around to see Everett and Owen walk in.

"Nine-eighteen and you're home watching *How It's Made* . . . so the date must have been great, huh?" Everett comments.

"Actually, it did go well, but we were just going to get ice cream and I was exhausted so it was short."

"Date?" Owen joins the conversation. "Was it Collin? I could tell he had a thing for you," he says, referring to my boss in the marketing department.

"Collin?" I try to hide my shock, but must not do it well because Owen laughs.

"I take that as a 'no,'" Owen says, sitting down next to me.

"Yeah, I mean no. I mean, yes, you should take that as a 'no,'" I fumble. "He's my boss and he doesn't have a *thing* for me. He's just friendly."

Owen smiles. "Someone's getting awfully flustered with all this talk about Collin." He jokes. Then, lowering his voice to a whisper, he says, "It's that whole silver fox thing, right? Don't worry. I won't tell him." He smiles and nudges me with his elbow.

I sigh and shake my head while he watches me, his eyes dancing. I stare into the pools of green, but quickly remember my awkward lunch with Lila and look away.

"Which one is this?" he asks, switching the topic of conversation to what's on TV. "Hmm, bacon, I've never seen that one. Have you seen the one about hockey gloves? It's pretty crazy." I don't answer. He holds up a bag of peanut M&Ms. "Want some?"

I shake my head. "After watching this show, I'm not sure I'll be able to eat anything for a very long time. Besides that, your girlfriend told me I have saddle bags and large calves. I don't want to disappoint her by eating something like M&Ms."

"What? When did you talk to her? And, she's not my girlfriend."

"Oh, sorry, your *fiancé* was sweet enough to take me out to lunch today and give me all sorts of helpful hints."

"Ugh, she's definitely not my fiancé. I'm really sorry, Juliet. She gets really weird about any other girl she sees me with."

"Who are you guys talking about?" Everett sits down next to me as he interrupts.

"Lila," I say with a big, fake grin.

"She told you that you have saddle bags and large calves?" Owen asks, only now catching what I said earlier.

"Yes, and I need to eat fewer carbs and I don't know how to act in nice restaurants or order correctly, but that's why I'm so lucky to have her. She's my own personal fairy godmother. Those are her exact words, by the way. Oh, and I got to hear several wonderful details about how in love you guys are." I immediately wish I hadn't said the last part. As soon as I do, Owen has a pained expression on his face and an awkward silence fills the room.

"I'm sorry. Just try to ignore the stuff she says to you." Then, turning to Everett he asks, "Do you want the rest of the M&Ms? I need to take off and I'm done." He tosses the bag to Everett. "Don't believe everything Lila says, okay? See you guys later."

As soon as he's out the door Everett smiles, "That got nice and awkward, didn't it?"

"Yeah, sorry." I hand him the remote. "I'm tired. Let me know how the bacon turns out. Oh, and Ev, thanks for letting me live here. I'll try not to scare all of your friends away."

"So you had fun with that Luke guy?"

"Yeah, I did."

"Okay, good. Goodnight, Jules."

♡ Chapter 12 ♡

Two Years Ago

J ules is here!" my mom yelled as I walked into the kitchen of the house I grew up in. She wiped her hands on a towel and wrapped her arms around me. "How was the drive, honey?"

"Good," I said before popping a chunk of a roll into my mouth. "And all of your finals went well?"

"Mm-hmm," I tried to answer with my mouth full.

"It's about time you got here," Everett said, jogging up the stairs from the basement. "You ready to lose at foosball?"

I gave him a hug. "Good to see you too," I replied.

"It is good to see you, Jules. I'm glad you're here. And not just because I need a break from Eva's crying."

My heart sank. "Is she worse?" I asked. Eva had been in a lousy mood for weeks, but I kept hoping she and Will would work things out.

Mom nodded. Everett sighed and said, "Yeah, she's worse. Now that it's officially called off, she's like a—"

"They officially called off the wedding?" I asked, shocked that I hadn't heard anything about it already.

"Shhh," Everett said, glancing upstairs. "Like a week ago, Jules. She didn't tell you?"

My mom wrapped her arm around me. "She wanted to tell you, but she was afraid it would distract you during finals week. She didn't want you rushing back here when you needed to be there."

I grabbed the nearest chair and sat down. "I was sure they'd work it out," I said to no one in particular.

"It makes no sense. He's still at her place all of the time," Everett replied, as he stole the rest of my roll and took a bite. "But he says they can only be together when they're in private." He rolled his eyes. "That's convenient for him."

"Stop it, Everett," Mom scolded.

"He wouldn't cheat on Eva," I responded. "He can't even take an extra straw at Wendy's without feeling guilty. Why would he only want to see her in private?"

"They even spent the weekend together at the cabin, but still claim they're not together," Everett said.

"Eva took him to the cabin?" I asked. The word "cabin" sounded a little too nice for the place Everett was describing. "Shack" would be more appropriate. Our parents bought it when we were small as a place for fun family outings. It was right on the lake and sat on some of the most beautiful land I had ever seen, but Eva hadn't ever had a love for the place. She'd spent a large part of our time there complaining about how tiny and rundown it was.

"Well, why don't you go talk to her, Juliet?" Mom suggested. "Maybe you can cheer her up."

"Oh, and make sure you don't complain about dinner tonight," Everett said, heading back toward the basement. "Eva made it." He grimaced.

I looked at Mom for confirmation. She threw a potholder at Everett. "I've made lots of sides to go with it. You'll be fine," she whispered. There was a long-standing joke in our family about Eva's cooking. Eva had many talents, but cooking was definitely not one of them. "She was trying to stay busy this afternoon and told me she was going to make dinner for us." Mom sighed. "It's in the oven now."

"I'm sure it will be great," I said, bummed that after months of college food I was not going to get one of Mom's home-cooked meals. I walked up to Eva's room only to find it empty. "Eva?" I called out, but the upstairs was quiet. I headed back downstairs.

"Did she come down?" I asked my mom, who was chopping tomatoes for a salad. She looked up long enough to shake her head. I moved into the living room and spotted Will's white truck through the windows. I opened the front door quietly. I didn't want to interrupt anything, but I wanted to make sure Eva was out there. No one had seen her come down the stairs.

Will was standing next to the garage, holding Eva's face in his hands. His face was closing in on hers. I slowly inched my way back inside when Will yelled, "Hi, Julie."

"Hi. Sorry. I was just trying to find Eva. I'll be inside." I yelled back before I quickly shut the door and leaned on it. A smile spread across my face. They certainly hadn't looked broken up. They looked happy. And Will hadn't seemed angry. Everybody kept talking about how angry Will had been lately.

There was a light tap on the door I was leaning against. I opened it to Will and Eva. "I wasn't trying to scare you off. I really just wanted to say 'hi.'" Will grabbed me and gave me a hug. "How were finals?"

"Good. Why don't you come in?"

"No. I wasn't trying to interrupt family dinner. I just needed to talk to Eva for a minute, but I need to go now. Say 'hi' to everyone else for me." He turned to Eva and squeezed her hand. She pulled him back toward her and kissed him before he walked back to his truck.

She shut the door and grabbed me in a hug. "I'm so glad you're home."

She was hardly the weepy, depressed girl Mom and Everett had described. "Yeah, me too."

"I have to finish preparing dinner. Come with me so we can talk." I followed her into the kitchen, which was now empty.

"So . . . things with Will seem better, huh?" I asked, hoping she would elaborate.

"Yeah, I think maybe," she answered with a guarded smile, putting on an oven mitt. *"Okay, now tell me about your finals."*

I groaned. *"Eva. There's obviously more to tell about you and Will and you want to know details about my finals?"* She shrugged so I continued, *"Okay, let me tell you all about my Field Biology final. It was riveting. My favorite part was identifying the different rocks. Would you like me to describe all of the different kinds?"* She stared at me, but I could see a smile tugging at the corner of her mouth. *"Or maybe, you'd rather tell me what's going on with you and Will."* She didn't answer so I waited in silence.

She glanced into the living room. *"There's no one in there, Eva,"* I said. *"I think they're all in the basement."*

"Okay," she lowered her voice. *"Do you remember how I told you that Will had been stressed ever since he switched departments at P&L? Since he started working in product development?"* I nodded. *"Well they've been in the middle of a product release, some new type of IUD they call Tipro. It's supposed to bring in billions of dollars in revenue for the company."* Eva's serious tone told me I should be focusing intently on every word she was saying, but I was having a hard time not staring at the blobs of brown she'd just pulled out of the oven. Were we really going to be expected to eat those?

"Well, he just told me that there's something totally amiss with this IUD."

And with those things you made and called dinner.

"I guess several weeks ago while going over some of the sample groups, he noticed some inconsistencies. He looked into it more and more and found that some of the initial sample patients now have endometrial cancer. He mentioned it to other colleagues, but they assured him that it was way below the number that would actually qualify it as a side effect."

I took my eyes off of the baking sheet. "So it's giving people cancer, but consumers will have no idea?" I asked.

Eva pulled out the cinnamon and poured an excessive amount onto each off-putting mash of ingredients. "Exactly. Although it's only documented to have affected less than one percent of the sample patients, Will found that almost half who did testing over three years ago now have endometrial cancer. Half, Jules. Isn't that awful?"

I nodded.

"And somehow those facts seem to be omitted from all other test results." Eva grabbed the baking sheet to move it closer to her and burned her hand. She let out a cry before holding it under the faucet and running cold water on it. "He was trying to get some follow-up information from a patient and found out the patient had passed away. He kept digging and calling more people and found more who had either died or were sick. The more he finds out, the guiltier P&L looks. They're trying to cover it up and still take the product to market."

"I don't get it," I said, grabbing Eva an ice pack from the freezer. "He broke things off because he's upset at work? And why did he stop by tonight?"

"He stopped by to tell me he thinks he's figured out a way for us to be together. He didn't want to wait for me to finish dinner and drive back to my place before he talked to me."

"Why couldn't you be together before?"

"The more he's tried to figure out, the more walls he runs into. And then several weeks ago he started getting threats in his work email and some of them mentioned me specifically. He wanted people to believe that we weren't together anymore. He was trying to protect me."

"Hmmm," I responded, thinking about how much Will was blowing things out of proportion. A few angry emails didn't seem a big enough deal to break off an engagement with someone you loved.

"But now, there's someone helping him," she said. "A guy he works with has started helping him gather evidence. I think he said he works in the finance department or something, but Will said this should all be over soon and we will get married. I don't know. It all seems so scary. I don't like him being involved in this." She walked to the top of the basement stairs and yelled, "Dinner's ready!"

The rest of my family joined us in the kitchen, all of them eyeing the serving dish Eva set on the table with trepidation.

"What do you call those?" Mom asked, an overdone, fake smile covering her face.

"Golden Beef Nuggets," answered Eva, placing one on Everett's plate. Brown liquid oozed out.

"Mmm," Everett said. "Is that squash beneath the corn flakes?"

Eva nodded. We spent the next few minutes forcing down dinner. I knew Eva must have been in a pretty rough emotional state if my entire family was willing to choke down something called Golden Beef Nuggets in order to keep her happy. Everett even took seconds. It seemed he could only stomach one bite of the second one, but I was still impressed with the gesture.

Eva pushed hers around with a fork before saying, "Sorry, I just don't seem to have an appetite tonight. I'm really tired. I think I better head back to my place."

"I'll come with you," I said, pushing my chair back. Not only would I get more time with Eva, but I wouldn't have to finish this dinner.

"Okay, and you can just sleep at my place tonight," Eva answered, heading toward the front door. "Do you need help with your stuff?"

"It's all still in my car." I pushed back my chair and smiled at my family. "You guys enjoy," I whispered, nodding at their plates.

"We'll be sure to save you plenty, Jules," Everett said.

I shook my head before heading to the office to grab a couple of bridal magazines out of a drawer Eva and I had kept them in. I *needed to get Eva back in wedding planning mode so she would stop worrying so much about trivial things at Will's work.*

♡ Chapter 13 ♡

I rush to grab shorts and a t-shirt. The clock says 6:24 a.m. and I am supposed to be downstairs at 6:30. Last night Luke stopped by and asked if we could run together this morning. I put my hair in a ponytail, but then decide to change it to a braid. Should I wear makeup? I've never been confused over how to properly get ready to go running. I really wish he had asked me on a normal date. I wonder if this even qualifies for a date at all.

The week after Luke and I went out for ice cream, he brought over Chinese food for the two of us. A few days later, we met at Barnes and Noble on my lunch break to eat at the little café and look through books together. This week he keeps catching me in the parking lot and we end up eating dinner together or at one another's apartment talking. And now we're running together. I keep hoping he will actually ask me out on a normal date, but I've come to the conclusion that he either only wants to be friends or he's a really slow mover.

After applying a small amount of mascara, the clock catches my eye. 6:36 a.m. I shove my feet into my shoes and head out the door. He's waiting by the curb.

"Hey," he says with a grin.

"Hi," I answer, quickly bending over to tie my shoes. "Sorry I'm late." I try to think of a good excuse that sounds impressive. I definitely don't want to admit it's because I couldn't decide how much make-up I needed on our not-so-date-ish date. I was warming up with a quick one-hundred push-ups? I was juicing some kale and spinach for my breakfast? I decide to give him no reason at all. "Where do you want to go?"

"You're the expert here. Just lead the way." He holds his hands in front of him, motioning for me to take the lead.

I jog toward one of my favorite trails with Luke keeping pace. "So in all the time you've lived in your building, you've never run back here?"

"Nah, I'm more of a gym kind of guy."

"Hmm," I answer as we fall into an easy rhythm and wind our way through several large Maple trees.

"Speaking of the gym," he starts. "I think I saw your crazy enemy on a stair-stepper yesterday."

"Lila goes to your gym?" Several days ago Luke caught up to me in our parking lot and decided to come along while I went to pick up Mexican food for dinner. I saw Lila outside the pet store next door to the restaurant. I ducked back inside my car as quickly as possible and hit my head in the process. Luke was full of questions after that so I'd had to point out Lila and tell him about our friendship, or lack thereof.

"It was hard to be sure, but I think it was her. She was pounding up that stepper with serious determination. The machine was going about as fast as it could and I thought she might go flying off of it."

"I wish," I respond, gritting my teeth. I run faster as I think about Lila. Anger seems to be the best motivator. "She was in a mood yesterday. She decided it bothered her that I had a couple of sticky notes around the border of my computer screen. She ripped them up and threw them in the trash while spouting ways I should improve myself, focusing on cleanliness in the workplace. It took me half an hour to find the pieces and tape them back together and then they smelled like the leftover fish sticks that someone had thrown in that trashcan."

"Okay, let's not talk about her. She gets you too upset." Luke stops running and grabs my arm. He pulls me off of the path and in close to him. I try to enjoy the moment and nearness to him, but all I can think about is that I forgot to put on deodorant in my rush to get out the door. "We can do this instead," he says, his lips locking on mine. I lean into him, but pull back slightly when his sweat-covered arm slides along mine. My heart feels like it might pound right out of my chest, but I'm not sure if that's because I'm kissing Luke or because I was running so hard before he stopped me.

"Now let's go back to my apartment and I'll make us breakfast." he suggests.

I nod weakly before turning back in the direction we came from.

♡ Chapter 14 ♡

There is an obnoxious banging noise hurting my head. After several seconds, I realize it's someone knocking on the front door. I roll off of the couch and open the door to find Eva standing there. She gives me a once-over and raises an eyebrow. "You don't look ready for the gym."

"The gym? Oh. I forgot. Sorry. I fell asleep." I answer the best I can in my half-asleep state. I motion for her to come inside and we walk back to my room.

"Rough nap?" Eva asks.

I glance at the mirror. I'm flushed and the hair around my face is damp. "Yeah, kind of. I just had a crazy dream."

"Will?"

I nod. "I hardly ever had any dreams about him until lately. I'm not sure what it is, but now I'm constantly having nightmares. Maybe it's because you and I are spending more time together so I think about it more. I don't know." Eva has been coming into Eden Falls quite a bit and hanging out at Everett's place. She seems a lot more herself than she's been in a long time. I love it, but I wonder if it's bringing up bits of my past that make my subconscious go crazy.

"Hmm, could be. Or maybe it's the time of year combined with you being back here," she suggests.

I think about the possibility. It was summer when he was forced to disappear, when Eva and I found that horrifying dead body. "Well anyway, it doesn't matter," I say, changing out of the black pants I wore to work. "I just need to fill my water bottle and I'm ready to go."

As we drive I think about how much fun I've been having with Eva. It's nice that she's willing to go out in public once in a while now. She even got the chance to meet Lila last week when she met me at work. We were headed to the elevator on the ground floor when Lila was getting off. After being introduced, Lila said, "I could tell you were sisters because you both walk kind of hunched over."

Eva started laughing and said, "She's exactly like I pictured." Lila flashed her typical scowl and marched away.

Twenty minutes later when we were leaving, we ran into Owen, with Lila clinging to his arm. He gave us a quick nod, but didn't say a word. Lila grinned and said, "Hi, girls."

I complained about how pathetic he was. I was used to him ignoring me, but it really irritated me that he would ignore Eva. It didn't bother Eva though. She said, "He's doing it for you. If he stopped and talked to either of us, you know Lila would try to make your life here impossible. I mean, she saw you talk to him like two times over a month ago and she still has it out for you."

"Oh that's so sweet of him," I'd answered, rolling my eyes. "He doesn't want his I'm-only-dating-you-so-I-can-move-up-in-this-company-and-make-more-money-girlfriend to see him talking to any other females because she's so crazy she can't handle it. He is sweet." I feel mad at Owen and Lila as I think about the incident.

Eva interrupts my thoughts. "Are the guys already there?"

"Yeah, they said they'd meet us there and have the net set up." I have been tagging along with Everett whenever he and Owen go to the gym in the evenings. I work out with them, attempt some of the classes, and avoid yoga at all costs. I love it. Owen being there doesn't even ruin the experience. In fact, he's starting to be part of the reason I enjoy it so much. I don't like what he's doing to move up at TBC, but I have so much fun with him. I'm disgusted by him, but I want him there. Maybe it's because he's such good friends with Everett. It's like having another brother to hang out with. Lila's boyfriend is a total jerk, but my brother's friend is great.

A wave of excitement ripples over me as I think about the volleyball match we're about to play. Volleyball is a part of me. I love everything about it, especially when I win. Our numerous trips to the gym have shown Owen I'm a very competitive person so he always tries to get a reaction out of me by making jokes about how he can beat me. Eva and I decided that tonight she would drive out and we'd challenge Owen and Everett to a match.

I toss my extra pair of knee pads to Eva as we walk into the gym. Everett and Owen are standing by the net. "I figured you two were going to call any minute with some fake reason about why you couldn't make it," Owen calls out. "Most likely because Jules lit something else on fire. But I admire your courage. You know you're going to lose and you're facing the challenge head on."

I laugh. "We were just trying to give you guys plenty of extra time to warm up so you don't have an excuse when you lose by an embarrassingly large margin."

"Wow, look who's bringing her big statistics words into volleyball. We're very impressed," Owen says with a grin.

"And look who's bringing his terrible sense of style into volleyball," I respond, eyeing his shirt that says, "I Workout So I Can Climb the Staircases in Hogwarts." Several weeks ago I made fun of a workout shirt Owen was wearing and he's been digging up worse and worse t-shirts ever since. I have no idea how he can find so many terrible shirts. They've ranged from quotes like "Luke, I am Your Spotter" to "Real Men Love Cats."

"Oh, c'mon. I thought you'd like this one," he says.

"How competitive is this going to get?" Everett asks. "You guys actually brought knee pads? I thought this was just a nice, friendly match."

"Some of us just have really tough knees." Owen says. "But if you guys need knee pads, that's fine. Really, they're cute."

I finish lacing up my shoes and putting on my knee pads. "If you guys are done talking, we're here to play volleyball," I answer, biting back a smile. This is the side of Owen I enjoy. It's hard to remember how frustrated I am with him for using Lila when he understands my banter and dishes it back just as well.

After an hour, we've each won one game. Though I hate to admit it, the guys are really good at spiking the ball. Luckily Eva and I are also really good at digging it up. As we start the third game, I hit the ball right in front of Owen and it falls to the floor. "Now if you were wearing knee pads, you wouldn't have to worry about hurting those dainty little knees and you would have had that," I tease while giving Eva a high five. When it's match point, Eva gives me a beautiful set and I spike the ball directly in between Owen and Everett. They hang their heads before walking off the court.

"Now, I'm pretty sure the losers should have to buy the winners pie at Sadie's," Eva says, referencing our favorite bakery.

Everett looks to Owen and shrugs. "Yeah, let's rub a little salt on the wound," Owen says. "As if this loss wasn't painful enough," adds Everett.

"Great, I can't wait for my S'more Galore. I'm sure it will be even better when you guys are paying for it," I say, grabbing my stuff and heading for the door.

♡ Chapter 15 ♡

B y 7:50 a.m., I'm on my way to work. As I pass the stop-
light next to my apartment, a loud honk makes me nearly
jump out of my seat. I cringe. Josh, my high school chemistry
lab partner who helped me move last month, is waving wildly
from his white Yaris. I pass him on my way to work a couple
of times every week. I look down at my passenger seat where
my cell phone is ringing. Every time he sees me, he has to
call and chat.

"Hey, Josh," I answer, wondering what exciting topic he'll
want to discuss today. Two days ago it was the ratio of whey
powder he uses in his protein drink along with the inner
battle he's had trying to decide between whey and egg white
powder. Last week he told me all about his car's insurance
policy. Exciting stuff.

"We've got to stop meeting this way," he laughs. "Can
you believe how often we see each other on our way to work?"

"Crazy," I reply, thinking about how it isn't crazy at all
since we live less than one mile apart, both get to work at
eight o'clock, and work in the same general direction.

"I was just telling Elaine I see you more than she does. I
mean, I really do only see you. A couple of days ago Elaine
called me just to see if I'd run into you that day. Did she call

you? She really wanted to see if you were busy this weekend. We were thinking we could all get together—"

"Oh, nope," I cut him off mid-sentence. "I haven't talked to her in a few days."

"Well you should talk to her and figure out when—"

"That's a good idea, Josh. I'll call her now before I get to work. I'll talk to you later. Bye." I hang up with a sigh of relief. Sometimes Josh talks for the entire seven-minute commute and continues talking when I tell him that I'm at work and need to go. I try to call Elaine, but get her voicemail. I park the car, grab my bag, and get out. I wince as the door brushes against my hip and pain shoots through it. I have several bruises from falling on the gym floor to get volleyballs last night. It's worth it though, to have beaten Everett and Owen.

I get into the elevator. As the doors are closing Owen walks into the lobby. I feel a twinge of excitement and put my hands between the doors to stop them from shutting. He smiles and stands next to me, "Hey, Jules." I try not to notice that his arm is against mine. I try even harder not to notice how happy that makes me. *He's with Lila. All he cares about is moving up in the company.* I focus on the reasons I'm mad at him.

"Hey," I respond. *He wears stupid t-shirts . . . and looks so good in them. Okay, this is not working.* "I'm surprised you can smile at all after your devastating loss last night," I say.

He looks directly at me and smiles, "Oh, did I lose at something? That doesn't ring a bell." He continues looking at me, but his expression becomes serious. I'm not used to this. Owen and I are usually so sarcastic with one another. He continues, "Will you have any extra time today? I'd really like to talk to you. Can we get lunch together?"

"Um, yeah," I reply. His somber tone makes me tense. I was expecting him to tease me right back. "I can take my lunch any time today. When were you thinking?"

The elevator doors open to reveal my floor. "I have a meeting across town at ten-thirty. Do you want to meet at Franco's at noon?" he asks.

I'm astonished that Owen is talking to me at work. Inside the elevator is one thing, but now everyone in the marketing department can see that we are talking. Anyone very close to us can hear we are making lunch plans, which means Lila will probably find out. "Yeah, that sounds great. I love that place, but I haven't been there in years." I realize I'm whispering, half-expecting Owen to either shush me or completely ignore me.

"Great. I'll see you at noon."

"Okay, see you later," I say, giving a slight wave as I turn to go to my desk. I can't help but look back to see if he's still there. He is. I wave. *Did I just wave at him twice?* And my hand is still in the air. I smile awkwardly and half-walk, half-run to my desk. I'm pretty sure everyone is staring at me. My cheeks burn as I sit down and pretend to be fascinated by my computer screen. Hopefully no one notices the power is off.

My coworker, Kat, is immediately at my side. "So, Mr. Denny, huh?" she prods.

"Yes, that was Mr. Denny," I try to mask my flustered feelings by sounding matter-of-fact.

"Remember he's my future husband," she laughs, poking me with her elbow. "You and Lila can have him now, but he'll be mine in the end."

"I don't have him now. I'm dating somebody else."

"Well so is Mr. Denny," she replies, giggling.

I give her an exaggerated eye roll, but then smile.

"So who is this other guy you're dating?" Kat inquires.

"His name is Luke," I say as I type numbers into a spreadsheet. I'll have to go back and delete all these numbers later since I'm only typing them to look busy. I don't feel like talking about my dating life. It's hard for me to explain when I'm still trying to figure it out myself. I want to be alone so I can think about possible reasons for Owen being so serious and wanting to talk.

She continues prodding about Luke. Then she'll throw in a question or two about Owen. Finally, when she notices she's not getting anywhere with her questions, she leaves me alone. I pick up on a project I started last week, but I can't help but check the clock every few minutes. *What does he want to talk about?* Finally, after what feels like at least twelve hours, the clock says eleven-forty. I log off my computer and head out the door.

I pull into Franco's a little before noon and see Owen's car in the lot. As soon as I get out, he walks toward me. "You know," he starts, "I was just thinking maybe we should get some Thai food instead. I heard from a pretty reliable source that the place near your apartment makes a killer bean noodle salad with ground chicken, pickled cabbage, and scallions."

I laugh, surprised that he even remembers what Josh said about the Thai place. "You forgot about cilantro and lime juice," I respond. "But as great as all that sounds, I was pretty set on Franco's today."

"Okay," he says, opening the door for me. The smell of fresh bread and oregano fills the air. I can't see anything for a few seconds as my eyes adjust from the bright sun to the dimly lit room. I'm busy focusing on not running into a table as we follow the hostess. Owen puts his hand on my back and an electric current runs from by back to my toes. After we're seated, Owen grabs the candle that's sitting in the middle of the table and slowly moves it away from me. I look at him inquisitively. He sets it as far from me as it can possibly be while still being on the table.

"What are you doing?"

"Oh, the candle? I've heard about your experiences with fire," he says, smiling innocently. "I figure it's best for everyone in the place if we keep any flames as far from you as possible. You may not have any hairspray or oil with you right now, but I don't want to underestimate your ability to create a fire catastrophe."

Laughing, I say, "Oh wonderful, thanks."

We order our food and continue laughing and talking. As much as I'm enjoying myself, I'm dying to know why he asked me here and when he's going to tell me. I let the conversation stall several times, hoping it will bring up his real reason for this lunch, but it doesn't. I take a bite of my delicious lasagna and see someone approaching our table out of the corner of my eye. Assuming it's the server, I continue talking.

"Well, Owen, what a surprise," a low voice booms. Owen's standing before the man even finishes his sentence. He laughs uncomfortably as he shakes hands with the man. "So who is this young lady?" the man asks, patting my shoulder with his enormous hand. I find his size intimidating. He must be at least six-foot-four, with broad shoulders, and a bulky neck. His dark hair is graying. The large bags under his eyes make me want to get my de-puffing concealer out of my bag and test it out on him. His red face looks droopy thanks to his large jowls. He's wearing two rings with diamonds in them, along with an expensive-looking watch.

"This is my friend's younger sister," Owen replies quickly. "Do you remember Everett Easton? This is his sister." Then looking in my direction, but avoiding eye contact, he points to the man and says, "And this is Mr. Bradley."

I hold out my hand to the hefty man before his name sinks in. Once I realize who he is, I have a hard time even letting my hand touch his. However, he's friendly and con-versational. Maybe it's just Lila who's horrible and he's a good guy. I can picture her screaming in a fitful rage and her poor dad giving into her outlandish demands. Now I feel nothing but sympathy for the man. The person I don't understand is

Owen. I'd really let my guard down during lunch. I'd even found myself wondering if we were on a date and hoping we were, but now I want to be anywhere but here with him. He was the perfect guy until he saw the man who has all the power to either promote him and pay him more or fire him. This further proves my point that he's entirely driven by money and power. I don't want to play second to Lila. I'm amazed by how quickly Owen felt the need to explain I was only his "friend's younger sister." He hadn't even called me a friend. He didn't want Mr. Bradley to think I was any closer than the younger sister of a friend.

"Everett's a great guy," Mr. Bradley says, watching me.

"He is, but he was a little too busy to come with us today," Owen adds, looking like a seven-year-old boy who got caught stealing and is trying to dig himself out of trouble.

I can't look at him. He invited me to go to lunch. Everett was never part of it.

"Well you two enjoy your lunch and, Owen, I'll see you this afternoon." Then looking at me, but still speaking to Owen, he continues, "Oh and Lila said you two had a great time this past weekend." He smiles at me as he continues, "And I can't help but notice all of the rings she's been checking out lately."

I break eye contact with Mr. Bradley. I take back any nice thoughts I had about him. He and his daughter are equally awful. They probably sit around the dinner table plotting whose life they'll try to ruin next.

Owen smiles politely at Mr. Bradley and says matter-of-factly, "It was a fun place and the boat was great. Thanks for letting us use it."

"Sure, anything for you and Lila. Well, Everett Easton's little sister, it was nice to meet you." He pulls at his tie, which looks like a mere thread against his massive neck. "I went ahead and covered you kids' lunch today. I hope you enjoyed it." He pats me on the head the same way I used to pat my childhood dog, a Golden Retriever named Tallulah.

Owen looks even more uncomfortable. "You shouldn't have paid for us." Mr. Bradley stares at him so Owen continues, "Thank you."

"Yes, thank you," I add.

Mr. Bradley smiles. He walks across the restaurant to a table where two men in suits are seated.

"I'm sorry about that," Owen says, sitting back down in his chair. "I'm really sorry." Then more to himself than to me, he adds, "And I can't believe he paid for our lunch. He does anything he can to make me feel indebted to him."

"Hmmm," is all I can say. I take another bite of lasagna. I might as well be chewing on my napkin. I push my food away. "I actually need to get back to work. I don't want to have to stay late today."

"C'mon. Please stay for a few more minutes. We haven't had dessert yet. You haven't had chocolate lava cake until you've had Franco's chocolate lava cake."

"I've actually had their chocolate lava cake before, but thanks, and thank you for having me meet you for lunch." I stand up. "I really do need to get back. You stay and enjoy the cake."

Owen stands up, a look of desperation covering his face. "Juliet, I'm really sorry if that made you feel awkward. Actually, I'm sure it made you feel awkward. It made me feel awkward." He follows me as I make my way to the parking lot.

"It's fine," I respond. I start to get into my car, but he grabs the door.

"I'm sorry. I have to act like that to him. I'll see you later, right?"

"Yeah, see ya," I say as I pull the door shut. I can see him waving as I drive out of the parking lot so I give a quick wave back. Why am I mad at him over this? It was stupid on my part to start having feelings for him. I'd seen him kissing Lila the very first time I'd met him. I knew he was with Lila and more than that, I knew he was with Lila to gain position in her family's company. I care for Luke and not at all about Owen. He can date whomever he wants. I'm sure we'll still see each other and we'll hang out, but I won't get mad at the mere mention of Lila. He said I was his "friend's younger sister." So, he will simply be my brother's best friend and nothing more.

♡ Chapter 16 ♡

I've only curled three-quarters of my hair when the doorbell rings. Everett is at the gym so I set the curling iron down and head to the door. A quick glance at the clock shows it's only 6:48 p.m. Why is Luke early? I tuck the uncurled part of my hair behind my ear and open the door to find Owen standing there. Surprised and a bit frustrated by the sight of him, I remind myself I'm not mad. He's just Everett's friend. "Hey," I say. "Everett already left. He thought you were meeting him there."

"No, I mean, yeah, I know. I was at the gym," he says, his eyes boring holes in my face. He fidgets with his keys for a second before looking back at me, his lips turning up and his dimples appearing. "I'm actually here because I need to talk to you."

"Okay," I reply skeptically. "Um, why don't you come in?"

"Thanks," he says, stepping inside the apartment.

I grab a glass and pour myself some water. This is harder than I thought. I want to act coolly toward him, but it's hard when he's staring at me like this. "Would you like some?" I ask, pointing to the pitcher.

"No thanks," he answers and then continues, "I wanted to talk to you at lunch today, but that ended terribly. I'm really sorry."

"Don't worry about it. It was fine," I say reassuringly, still trying to convince myself that it was no big deal. "It was a little weird for me meeting Lila's dad. I don't really love her, you know? But you can spend your time with whomever you like."

"That's kind of what I want to talk to you about." He looks directly at me and there's a long pause. His intense eyes are locked on mine. I try to ignore how attractive he is, how his thick, dark eyelashes and tan skin make his green eyes stand out. I attempt to match his stare, but my quickening heartbeat causes me to look away. He grabs my hand. I tell myself to pull it away, but apparently the message is getting lost somewhere between my brain and my hand. "Jules, I want to spend my time with you. The hours go way too quickly whenever I'm with you and when we're not together, I'm thinking up some excuse to see you again. This is the first time in my life that I've made it to the gym every day. And as much as I like Everett, I don't normally spend all of my free time at his apartment."

I pull my hand free. "Um, I don't, I can't . . ." My words come out like a tangled mass of yarn. Owen steps closer and a wave of dizziness sweeps over me. I have to lean against the table.

"I know this probably seems sudden and I'm sorry if I'm catching you completely off guard, but it's killing me to keep it to myself."

I pause thinking of exactly how to respond, but it's hard to think clearly when he's standing so close. I can feel the heat of his body. Pushing thoughts of his green eyes and how good he smells out of my mind, I force myself to think of how he acted at lunch today. "This is a lot to process. I haven't thought about the option of you and me because you're with Lila," I lie.

"No, I'm not with Lila," he says, shaking his head. "I'm not."

"I know, not technically maybe, but you act like you are. I don't like what you're doing there and I don't want to be a part of it. Besides it's more than that."

"Like what? What is it?"

"We're just a little different."

"We challenge each other, yeah, make each other better, but that's a good thing, Jules." I can sense the desperation in his voice as he moves closer. I consider leaning into him and admitting that I think about him constantly; that my heart rate doubles when he enters the room. Suddenly all of my reasons for pushing him away seem meaningless. I take a deep breath, trying to clear my head.

"You treat me so badly whenever there's a Bradley around. You're so fixated on moving up in the company or making money or whatever it is that you want. When I'm with a guy, I like to be the only girl he dates. I'm not okay with the little charade you have going on with Lila."

"It's not like that," Owen says quietly.

"It was like that at lunch today. I mean, it's fine, but it's only fine if I think of you as my brother's friend. If I let myself have real feelings for you and something like that happens, it won't be fine."

"Jules, I want to explain everything, but I can't. I need—" He's interrupted by the doorbell.

I freeze. I don't want the moment to end. I want him to stay next to me and give me more reasons why we should be together, but the doorbell rings again. "I'm sorry, Owen," I say, turning away from him. As I open the door, Luke is standing there with a smile, but as soon as he sees Owen, his smile drops. They stare at each other for several seconds.

"Okay, I'll see you later," Owen grunts, pushing his way past Luke. Luke stands in the doorway with a triumphant smile.

"Hold on," I yell after Owen. Then, turning to Luke, I say, "I'll be back in one sec, okay?" I sprint down the stairs and catch Owen on the bottom landing. I grab his arm. "Owen, wait."

He turns around, the pained look on his face filling me with guilt. "Please, please tell me you're not dating that guy," he pleads.

"Owen, it wouldn't work."

"I'm not even talking about that anymore, Juliet, but trust me when I tell you that you shouldn't be spending time with him."

I open my mouth to respond, but Luke comes jogging down the stairs. "You ready, babe?" he asks.

"Uh, yeah," I say, watching Owen walk back to his car. I try to smile at Luke. "So how do you know Owen?"

"Is he Owen?" Luke asks, nodding towards Owen's car. I nod and he continues, "I don't know him, but he does look a little familiar. Does he live in Eden Falls?"

"Yeah," I say, confused. "Anyway, let me grab my purse." I remember my hair is only partway curled. "Oh, I never finished my hair. Can you wait in the apartment for a couple of minutes while I pull it back?"

"Don't worry about it. I'm used to how you look when you go running or after a whole day at work. You look great now. Let's just go."

I stare at him, dumbfounded. Did I hear him right? Is he actually telling me if he compares how I look after work with what I look like now, then I look good? What kind of a guy says something like that? "Well thanks for putting up with the way I look when I run, but right now I'd like to go pull my hair back. Plus I need to shut off my curling iron."

He looks taken aback. Apparently he hadn't realized how insulting he was. "Oh yeah, of course. Juliet, I didn't mean it like that. You are gorgeous. I just mean that if you look that good without makeup on or doing your hair, you don't need to worry now." He grabs my arms and pulls me toward him. I shove my arms back down by my sides and he continues, "Babe, you are perfect. I wouldn't change a single thing about how you look." *All right, maybe he didn't mean it quite how it came out.* I feel silly for my little outburst. Of course he wasn't insulting me. Maybe the constant insults from Lila are starting to wear on me.

I put my arms around him and look up into his face, "Thanks, I'll only be one minute. Why don't you head down to the car and I'll meet you there."

Less than ten minutes later, we are inside the restaurant of Luke's choice, Aorist. There are several restaurants that popped up right outside Eden Falls in the few years I was away and Aorist is one of them. According to Luke, it is, by far, the best Greek cuisine around. I'm not a good judge of that. I'm not entirely sure what constitutes Greek food. My roommate, Ally, used to smear Nutella over pitas and serve them as dinner. Maybe that counts as Greek. Thinking of Ally makes me think of Lucy, which in turn makes me think of Owen. I think of Owen when I see the candle on our table. I think of Owen when I see the dark-haired server, who actually looks nothing like Owen, except for the dark hair. I even think of him when I read the specials and see "oven-baked lamb," which reminds me of the sheep magazine in his office. Everything I see seems to make me think of him and thinking of him brings an overwhelming sense of sadness. Why do I feel so bad? He's the one who's shallow enough to be dating someone as awful as Lila just for the money. Yet, I'm the one feeling horrible. I can't forget the pained look he had when I explained why it wouldn't work or the expression he wore when he saw Luke. I convince myself I must feel terrible because I hate hurting a friend so badly. Still, here I am with a great guy and my mind is consumed by Owen.

"Are you getting a salad?" Luke asks.

"I'm not sure what I'm getting yet. I'm still reading through everything." *What did he mean by that? Should I be getting a salad?* Now I'm second-guessing my original thought of ordering Moussaka, the Greek lasagna with cream sauce. What is wrong with me tonight? First I was upset about the makeup comment and now I'm making a big deal of him asking what I'm getting. I don't know what is making me so self-conscious, but I don't want to let it get to me.

When the server returns, I confidently order the Moussaka. "Okay, Ma'am, and for you, Sir?" the server asks.

"I'll get the stuffed peppers with the fat-free feta cheese and can you do her Moussaka without the sauce?"

It takes a second for me realize what he just said. "No, I want the sauce. That's the part I'm most excited about," I say looking from Luke to the server.

"Oh, okay, maybe on the side then?" Luke suggests to the server.

"Bring it exactly as it is on the menu, please," I say. The server looks as if he can't walk away quickly enough. He half runs away from our table. I glance at Luke with my eyebrows raised. "What was that about?"

"I don't like to eat things as fattening as cream sauce," he replies.

"Oh, well I adore things as fattening as cream sauce," I respond.

Luke laughs, "Okay, good, I'm glad you ordered it just as you want it. Sorry," he says, smiling and shaking his head. "I guess I assumed we'd kind of share everything like we did the other night. I wasn't thinking about how terrible that would come across."

I smile back, realizing he looks much less attractive than usual. My thoughts return to Owen.

♡ Chapter 17 ♡

Two Years Ago

Y ou have to keep your torso facing forward," I yelled. My voice cracked as it echoed off the tile walls surrounding the pool where I taught people how to kayak. I wiped a trail of sweat off of my cheek with the shoulder of my shirt. It was already damp thanks to the humidity in this room.

A quick glance at the clock showed I still had another five minutes with Joel. I walked closer to the edge of the pool so I wouldn't have to yell so loudly. "Power comes from untwisting your torso," I reminded him for the sixth time. He straightened his torso, but kept his eyes on me while flashing another smile. He'd spent at least half of the session watching me with a goofy grin on his face. I gave him a forced smile in return, but quickly looked away and focused my eyes on the other side of the pool.

My phone lit up on the bleachers next to where I was standing. I tried to ignore it and focus on Joel, but found myself leaning closer to check the screen. It was Will. Why would he be calling me? My curiosity won. "Go up and back again practicing everything we've talked about. I'll just be one second," I shouted before grabbing my phone.

"Hey, Will," I answered.

"Have you heard from Eva today?" He asked. I could tell he was upset by his shortness of breath.

"No, why?" I asked, giving a quick thumbs up in the direction of the pool.

There was no response from Will other than a few swear words muttered to himself.

"Will, what's going on?"

"I don't know. It's probably nothing, but I can't get ahold of her and things at my work are pretty crazy. I need to make sure she's okay."

"What do you mean crazy? Why wouldn't she be okay?"

"It's nothing. She's probably sleeping in today or something, but I need to go so I'll talk with you later."

He was trying to downplay whatever was going on, but the fear in his voice gave him away. Plus, Eva never slept past eight so there was no way she was sleeping in. I glanced back towards the pool and Joel's leering smile.

"Good job," I hollered. My hands tapped my thighs as I wished the next four minutes away. I needed to finish up and get back to Eden Falls. The instant the session was over, I yelled "Okay, Joel. That was great. I'll see you next week."

"Uh, okay," Joel responded, rowing towards the edge.

After grabbing a few clothes at my apartment, I was in my car and on my way to Eden Falls. I had allowed myself to get more and more worked up since talking to Will. Sweat trickled down my forehead and my heart was racing as I thought through all of the reasons Will could have been nervous for Eva. I called Mom, Dad, and Everett, who all told me they hadn't heard from Eva. With each phone call, I had a harder time sounding calm and casual. I needed to quit letting my mind wander. I found some hard gummy worms in the console of my car and shoved one in my mouth. Before I knew it, the bag was empty, I was nervously chewing on a gooey mass of sugar, and I was no more relaxed than when I'd started. I called Eva for the seventh time since leaving my apartment.

"Hey! Good timing," Eva answered. "I was just trying to decide between two shirts. They're both really cute and fit well so I'm going to send you pictures of both and you help me decide, kay? Call me when you get them."

I stared at my phone. She hung up. She was shopping that whole time? I was relieved, but wanted to bang my head against the steering wheel at the same time. I called her again.

"Which one? The teal one, right?"

"Why haven't you been answering your phone?" I shouted.

"Wow, you're cranky today. Did you call me earlier?"

"Yes. Yes, I called you earlier. And Will has been trying. He's really worried about you."

"Oh, sorry. There are awesome sidewalk sales this morning and my phone was in my purse. It must be turned down low. I never heard it until now. I better call him right back. Sorry, Jules. I'll call you after I talk to him."

I pulled into a gas station. There was no reason I needed to go home now that I knew Eva was fine, but I was over half way there and I had cleared my schedule for the next two days so I was going to go see my family anyway. The mass of gummy worms I had eaten had me feeling a little nauseous so I grabbed a sandwich and got back in my car. I was pulling back onto the road when Eva called me back.

"Is everything okay now?" I asked.

"No, he's really worked up," she answered. "Remember how I told you about that guy who works in the finance department at P&L, Matt? The one who was helping Will?"

"Yeah," I replied.

"He didn't come back from lunch today and he left a really weird voicemail for Will. It's mostly him breathing heavy and whispering undecipherable words, but then he yells and it cuts off. Something big is going on here, Jules. Will's kind of freaking out. He doesn't want me at his place or to meet me at mine so we're meeting at Mom and Dad's."

"I'm only about a hundred miles away from there so I'll meet you too. It's going to be fine, Eva. I think things have just gotten blown out of proportion."

"You're on your way here?"

"Yeah, I was worried about you when Will couldn't find you and now—"

"Oh, I'm so glad you're going to be here," Eva cut me off. "You can help calm Will down."

"I'll try," I said, wondering how much help I would actually be.

"Thank you, Jules. I'll see you soon."

An hour and a half later, I walked through my parents' front door. Eva was sobbing and Will was pacing back and forth. Eva jumped up and hugged me. After I hugged her, I pulled back, but she didn't let go. I glanced at Will. His shoulders were slumped and his eyes were wide as he watched Eva.

"Eva, what is it? What happened?" I asked.

"He's leaving," she answered. "Please, Jules. Tell him this is ridiculous. Tell him how things are blown out of proportion."

I cringed as she quoted what I had said earlier. I had been trying to comfort her, not make Will feel bad.

"I wouldn't be leaving unless I thought it was necessary," Will said as he approached us and grabbed Eva's hand.

"Why do you need to leave?" I asked.

Will hands me a sheet of paper. "This was on my desk this morning." I skim over the first couple of paragraphs. It's a conversation between Will and Eva, but I don't understand why it's typed out. It's nothing important, just Eva telling about her day at work. I look at him waiting for an explanation.

"That was a phone conversation Eva and I had last night. Somebody was listening to every word and now they're trying to warn me to back off."

"Hmm," is all I can answer, trying to process what he's telling me.

"Then Matt left work this morning, telling everyone he was just taking an early lunch. He was actually going to meet with one of the patients who'd used Tipro and now has cancer. He told me he'd be back right after the appointment and we'd add any evidence he collected to the report we were working on." Will leaned against the wall and rubbed his eyes with the palms of his hands. "He didn't come back. He left me a voicemail that I couldn't understand more than two words of and when I called him back, it didn't ring through. I went to his house and his wife told me he was at work." Will paused as Eva pulled him over to the sofa and sat down next to him. He continued, "I started getting nervous so I figured I'd go home until I could figure out my next move. As I got to my street, there were two cars I didn't recognize parked at my house. There was a man going through the gate on the side of my yard and two more by my front door. Something shiny caught my eye and I realized the guy by the gate was holding a gun." He shook his head.

"Did you call 9-1-1?" I asked. My heart was racing.

"I didn't even think about it. I was still just trying to make sense of everything. That's when I started trying to get ahold of Eva and couldn't find her."

Eva looked up at Will and mouthed, "sorry."

"When I couldn't find Eva, I drove to the police station. I told them what was going on with Matt. They said they'd try to get something off of the voicemail he sent, but they couldn't do much more until he'd been missing for twenty-four hours. As for my claims about endometrial cancer, they need a lot more evidence. They did agree to send a couple officers out to my house and make sure no one was trespassing."

I sighed. "This is crazy. You definitely didn't blow anything out of proportion." Eva shot me a glare.

"So now I need to get out of Eden Falls, way out of Eden Falls," Will replied. "Hopefully I've distanced myself from Eva enough in public that no one will bother you guys. I just don't know how far P&L will go to cover this up." He stared at Eva for several seconds. "What if they still come after you for information? Eva, you need to leave too."

Eva perked up instantly. "Yes." She hugged Will. "That's perfect. I'll go with you."

"No, you can't go with me. It's too dangerous for you to be with me right now, but you need to get out of here. Please."

Eva set her jaw. "Will, stop it. I want to be with you. Let me decide what is and isn't too dangerous."

"I'll spend the next few weeks getting evidence and then we can be together wherever we want. You just need to go somewhere else until then."

"If I can't be with you, I need to stay here." Eva answered. "At least then no one will suspect me of having any connection to you. If I disappear too, they'll know I'm involved. I'll act like nothing is going on, like I don't even know you're gone."

"All right," Will agreed, shaking his head. "I hate this though. I hate you being here." Eva grabbed Will and they hugged. I walked away until I could no longer hear their whispers. I sat in the kitchen to give them some time alone.

Several minutes later, a red-eyed Will came through the kitchen door. "Julie, can you come outside for a second?" I followed him out the back door. "I don't want to tell Eva this because she's already mad enough about me leaving, but I can't take my phone. I can't email her. I can't send her letters. It's all too risky. It can be traced," he said as he ran his hands through his hair. "I know she'll think I'm being paranoid, but I set up a safety deposit box at Falls National Trust." He looked around as if he thought we were being watched. I got goosebumps on my arm thinking of the possibility. "I talked to a buddy of mine and he'll check the box every week and mail any messages to me. I'll send him any messages I have for her and he'll leave them in the box."

"Okay," I replied, rubbing my arms. The eighty-degree air was suddenly chilly.

"Will you make sure she's not the one checking the box?" he asked, handing me a key. "If she's doing anything on a regular basis, I'm afraid she'll have people checking out what it is and

why. I know she thinks this is insane, but I'm really worried that there will be people following her."

I tried to agree, but nothing came out. I stared at him wide-eyed. "Following Eva?"

"I don't know. Probably not, but just in case."

I nodded. It all sounded a bit over the top, but I wasn't about to tell Will that.

He hugged me. "Thanks, Julie."

"It's Juliet," I said with a smile, even though I had grown attached to his nickname.

He squeezed me. "This will all be over before we know it. I'll be back and Eva and I will be married and this will all be funny."

I nodded again, even though I was afraid he was wrong. He headed to his truck. "Will, come here," I hollered. I walked to the garage and he followed. "There's a chance someone will recognize your truck, right?"

"Yeah, I'll try to get something else as soon as I can, but I don't know what else to do."

"I do." I pulled back a tarp revealing my dad's vintage motor-cycle, a Moto Guzzi V7 Special from the 1970s.

"Where did that come from?"

"It was Dad's in high school," I replied.

"I honestly can't even picture your dad on that."

"That's why you're going to take it. I don't think he's ridden it in at least twenty years. Everett takes it out every once in a while just to make sure it works, but he has his own bike. He won't miss it."

Will pulled the tarp the rest of the way off and sat down. "Well if you're offering, I'll definitely take you up on it," he said, grabbing the helmet I offered. "I'll have to put it in my truck until I get away from this house though. I can't leave the truck here. I don't need anything else implicating you guys."

I opened up the main garage door and helped him move the bike to his truck. "Be safe, Will. I had kind of gotten used to the *idea of you as a brother-in-law and I don't want you messing that up now. Plus, Eva's not going to relax until you're back."*

Will grinned and hugged me again. "Take care of her. I'll see you soon."

I watched Will drive away and wondered how soon it would actually be.

♡ Chapter 18 ♡

Late Saturday afternoon, I drive out to my parents' house for a girls' night with Eva and my mom. As I pull into the driveway, I let out a sigh. Right in front of the house is Grandma's maroon Cadillac. My grandma is not your typical loving grandma. She's more of a makes-you-want-to-shove-marbles-in-your-ears-so-you-don't-have-to-listen-to-all-of-the-snide-remarks-she's-making kind of grandma. Last time I saw her I was given an hour-long lecture about how inappropriate it was for me to wear a skirt without wearing pantyhose. "If you want all of your coworkers to think you're a floozy, then you're on the right track," she'd said. "It's a wonder to me all of these women are complaining about sexual harassment when they dress like they do. Of course you're going to have men wanting intercourse when they're looking at your bare legs. That's not the way to get a husband, Juliet." I cringe as I think about the conversation.

Maybe it's Grandpa, I think hopefully. My grandpa is the sweetest, funniest man I know and he should be sainted for spending the last fifty plus years with my grandma.

I haven't even opened the front door before I hear Grandma. "Oh, Eva, quit moping around. Use your smile to change the world. Don't let the world change your smile."

I laugh to myself as she quotes what she must have recently read in Reader's Digest and say, "Hey," as I walk through the door.

"Jules!" Eva shouts and grabs me in a bear hug, obviously appreciative of the distraction from the current conversation.

"Hello, Juliet," Grandma says, looking me up and down. "Are you going to bed?"

"No, Grandma, I'm not," I respond, bracing myself for the snarky comment that will undoubtedly follow.

"You could have fooled me. You are wearing pajamas, you know."

"These aren't my pajamas," I reply with a forced grin. I'm wearing sweat pants and a faded t-shirt from a 5k I did several years ago.

"Aren't your pajamas? Sweat pants are part of your normal wardrobe? And that shirt leaves hardly anything to the imagination. There's nothing wrong with a nice turtle neck every once in a while."

"Good to see you, Grandma," I say as I wrap an arm around her boney shoulders, then walk towards the back where Eva disappeared.

Grandma follows. "Is it too much to ask for a little respect? I know a lot, Juliet. You're always going to be single if you dress so casually."

I see Mom, Dad, and Eva in the backyard and long to be with them. I inch my way toward the door as Grandma talks. When I finally open the door, they're all laughing. "Oh, Juliet, I can't believe you come to this house dressed so casually," Mom says, grinning. Eva has obviously already shared the most recent lecture with them.

"I know. How am I ever going to get a husband?" I say grumpily, but stop talking when the door opens and Grandma joins us on the deck.

"Hey, Grandma," Eva begins, "I was just telling Juliet she should do her hair differently. What do you think?"

"All right, I know when I'm being made fun of," Grandma responds, folding her arms and standing rigidly against the deck railing. "By the time I was Juliet's age, I was married and had three children. I know times may have changed, but is there anything wrong with me wanting you girls to settle down and find a man?" I tune her out. I detest these rants, especially when they're about finding husbands. Grandma never specifically mentions Eva or Will, but leaving Eva out of the lecture makes things just as awkward. I listen again when I hear my name. "Juliet had that wonderful young man and let him go. What was his name? It was Zachary, right?"

"Zach," I correct her.

"Yes, I thought so. Zachary was a fine boy. Have you seen him lately? Are you sure things are completely over between you two?"

"Yes, they're over and have been over for more than a year, Grandma," I reply. Zach and I dated in college and it had been a bit of a disaster from the beginning. We met at the fitness center at Penn when I was in the middle of a grueling volleyball practice. I'd eaten lunch right before practice, not expecting the coach to make us run sprints to start things off. Within ten minutes, I was hurting. My coach was yelling that I wasn't pushing it hard, there was a shooting pain in my side, and my head was spinning. I ran out of the gym, barely making it to the nearest garbage can before remnants of my chicken salad sandwich came right back up. Hoping no one had seen me, I turned to go back to practice, but ran straight into someone and fell backwards. I opened my eyes as some guy helped me stand up. "Sorry," I'd mumbled, my head still spinning.

"Why don't we go sit down over here for a second?" the guy said as I took a couple of wobbly steps. He put an arm around me, trying to hold me steady. All I could think about was how sweaty I was and how his arm was probably getting wet.

"I'm fine, really. I need to get back to practice," I said, trying to free myself from his hold.

"Okay, can I get you some water or something first?"

"Thank you, but I have water in the gym."

"Um," he said, looking at me uncomfortably. I was horri-fied to see that he was good-looking. He continued, "There's a restroom over there. You may want to go wash up." He dotted at his own chin as he said it. When I got to the restroom, I discovered a piece of chicken stuck to my chin. There was more chicken-like substance running down my shirt. My face was a dark shade of purple, my hair was drenched with sweat, and I had sweat marks on my collar and under my arms. Then to top it all off, I had a big sweat ring under my chest. I wanted to hide in the bathroom until the guy was gone and hope we never crossed paths again, but I knew my coach would already be mad about the practice time I'd missed. I washed my shirt and face, walked out of the bathroom, and waved to the guy who'd helped me.

"Feel better?" he yelled.

"I'm great. Thanks for the help." I forced a smile, even though I wanted to bury my head in my hands. I told myself that with a campus the size of Penn State, I'd never see him again.

I was proved wrong less than a month later. My friend Chelsey and I were getting slices of pizza on campus when I saw him. He was sitting at the table with several of Chelsey's friends. I quickly sat down and tried to remain inconspicu-ous. I knew he wasn't looking at me and hoped he wouldn't recognize me now that I wasn't purple, sweaty, and covered in chicken. At one point, I heard him ask the girl next to him what my name was. After lunch, he approached me. He made some joke about how I cleaned up nicely and introduced himself as Zach. We talked for nearly half an hour before I had to get to class. We met for lunch the following day. We went to a basketball game that weekend and within a month we were dating each other exclusively.

I spent a lot of Saturdays traveling around, watching Zach compete in triathlons. I had fun with him and even enjoyed watching him compete for a while, but it seemed to consume his life. He woke up early to swim and his afternoons were spent bike riding (very serious bike riding). I went with him once on a bike ride, expecting it to be a fun way for the two of us to spend time together and decided I would never go again. He pushed himself as hard as he could and tried to find the most challenging hills in the area. Having me with him was no excuse to slow down.

Zach graduated that spring and decided to move to Colorado, where there were better places to train and the high altitude would present him with more of a challenge. He asked me to come with him, saying I could transfer to a school out there, but I said no. I used volleyball as an excuse, but knew the real reason was that I wasn't in love with Zach. He meant a lot to me, but his need for constant competition was nauseating.

After he moved, I found myself relieved to have my Saturdays back. I was pretty certain he wasn't too crushed either, since the newsfeed of my Facebook showed him and some cute brunette competing in triathlons together.

"He's still in Colorado," I say to Grandma, hoping that will end all talk of Zach.

"I'm sure he comes back here to visit every once in a while," Grandma argues.

I know her advice is filled with love, but I can't take any more of it. "Okay," I say, cheerfully changing the subject. "Who wants to go wakeboarding?"

"I definitely don't think that is a sport for ladies so that's my cue to leave," Grandma says.

We quickly tell her good-bye. Once she's gone, we all agree it sounds way too exhausting to hook up the boat and actually go wakeboarding. Instead we watch a Hallmark movie on TV and eat cereal for dinner.

The movie ends and no one moves as the next one starts.

During a commercial break, Mom says, "I want to hear more about this Luke guy."

"Eh, I'm not so sure about him lately," I say. Eva and Mom sit quietly waiting for me to elaborate. "He seems so wrapped up in himself sometimes. And, he's one of the only guys I've ever met who makes me feel self-conscious. Maybe that's not even his fault, but I find myself getting offended at everything he says."

"I don't like him," Mom replies.

I laugh, "That probably wasn't the most selling description of him. He's actually a great guy."

"If he's making you feel bad about yourself, I don't like him. You've always been so confident and a good guy should make you feel even better about yourself. You'll like you better when you're with him," Mom says. Eva nods.

"So . . ." Eva starts. "Maybe you're not in to Luke because you are in to . . ." she drifts off, waiting for me to finish her sentence. I say nothing so Eva continues, "Maybe you're falling for Owen."

"I love that boy," Mom says.

"Mom, you only see one side of him; Everett's fun friend. There's another side . . . and it's not nearly as attractive," I explain.

"I know, I know, but I can't help but love him. And picturing him telling you how much he wants to be with you makes me weak at the knees," replies Mom. I shake my head in disgust, mainly at the term "weak at the knees." I'm wishing I hadn't been so open about the details of my conversation with Owen last night.

"So you think it's totally fine that he ignores me at work, and—"

"He ignores you for your own benefit though," Eva interrupts. "I know it still sucks, but he's not doing it to be mean. If he didn't, Lila would torment you even more."

"Yeah, maybe," I agree, surprised that Mom and Eva are defending Owen so much. "But she wouldn't be mad at me if he weren't leading her on to get ahead in her family's company."

"He probably donates all of his money to the children's hospital or something," Eva adds. I grin and shake my head.

"Okay, so he has one minor flaw," Mom says.

"Are you two being serious? That's one pretty major flaw. It tells me a lot about him," I respond, but as I say it, I feel that ache I've been feeling ever since my conversation with Owen. I want to see him.

Sensing my seriousness about the topic, Mom says, "I know, honey. It is a big deal. I guess it's hard for me to believe because I've only ever seen the wonderful, funny, charming side of him. You know him better than we do, so if your gut feeling is that he's a jerk, he's probably a jerk."

"Thank you," I say, hoping we can stop talking about this. I nod toward the TV, where our movie has resumed. I don't think he is a jerk. I don't even like hearing him called a jerk, but I don't understand it. He's so two-faced. When I was little, one of my closest friends was Ollie Williams. By the time we were in fourth grade, it wasn't cool to be friends with the opposite sex so Ollie started telling everyone he couldn't stand me. He'd ignore me at school, but as soon as school was over, he'd be waiting by my front door seeing if I wanted to play basketball or come to his house for dinner. I'd get excited thinking we were friends again, only to have him kick rocks at me at school the next day. I stopped hanging out with Ollie. Then, in the seventh grade when it was cool to be close with the opposite sex, Ollie started writing me love letters and trying to kiss me, but I was still mad. And I was still mad at him when he moved away our freshman year. I don't get along well with two-faced people.

The movie ends and I'm still thinking about Owen. I look over at Eva and Mom. Eva looks enveloped in sadness as she stares blankly at the rolling credits. Sometimes girly movies seem to have no effect on Eva and other times, they send her swirling into an I-miss-Will-so-much state for several days. Mom is glancing over in Eva's direction with a look of concern. I jump up and shut the movie off. I start talking about Grandma, which is completely out of the blue, but the quickest way to lighten the mood. Within minutes we are all retelling stories and laughing. At one a.m., Mom goes to bed. Eva and I keep talking, but at some point I fall asleep because before I know it I wake up to the smell of cinnamon; Mom's breakfast cake. The rest of my family is already in the kitchen eating. I love being here. This is so much better than the boring bowl of oatmeal I have for breakfast nearly every day. When breakfast is over, I lie down on one of the lounge chairs on the patio and quickly find myself replaying my conversation with Owen.

♡ Chapter 19 ♡

Two Years Ago

After Will left, Eva spent a good part of the afternoon just sitting on the couch staring into nothing. I suggested we go for a run and she unenthusiastically agreed. Once we started our run, her aggression over the day's events turned into adrenaline. I pushed as hard as I could to keep up with her, but after three miles, I couldn't match her pace. I slowed to a jog as she sprinted up the final hill. It took her a while to notice I wasn't still by her side, but after a quarter of a mile, she turned back searching for me. She stopped and waited as I caught up.

When I reached her, she was bent over with her hands on her knees. Sweat dripped off of her face and onto the asphalt. Her breathing was loud and her face was crimson. I stood by her, waiting. As her breathing evened out, she stayed silent. I set my hand on her back. When she finally stood upright, there were tears in her eyes.

"I need to go to Will's place," she said.

"What? Why?"

"He had my good phone charger over there and a bunch of my DVDs."

"Eva, we can't just show up at Will's place now. Did you hear the part where there were men with guns at his place?"

"*That was hours ago. The police said they were going over there to make sure no one was trespassing.*" When I continued looking at her skeptically, she added, "*I'll just run in and out.*"

"*For a phone charger and dvds? I'll buy you new ones instead.*"

"*I like mine.*"

I stared at her, waiting for her to tell me what was really going on. There was no way she wanted to go over there for easily replaceable items.

She walked away back toward the house. "*Eva, wait.*" I jogged after her.

"*You don't have to go with me, Jules. I just wanted you to know where I was going.*"

"*And I just want to know the real reason.*"

She sighed and turned toward me. "*That is the real reason. And . . . if I happen to see anything else, anything that would help explain all of this, that would be okay. I can't believe that he's really in so much danger that he needs to leave. So Matt didn't show up after lunch. There are hundreds of possible explanations.*"

"*It sounded scary to me,*" I said.

"*Yeah, I noticed. You didn't help talk him out of leaving at all. You sided with him.*"

"*Eva,*" I started, but her wide eyes about to spill more tears stopped me. "*Okay, let's go to Will's,*" I agree. "*But, we're just running in and out, right?*"

"*That's all I want,*" Eva said, grabbing my arm and pulling me toward the driveway.

I got in the passenger side of her car and she sped toward Will's house. "*Why don't you at least park a few houses down?*" I suggested, nervous I'd let her talk me into doing this.

She rolled her eyes, but agreed.

The sun was still visible over the top of the Poconos Mountains. If I hadn't been so fidgety, I would have enjoyed the beautiful orange and pink sunset, but as it was, it all just seemed ill-omened. I took a deep breath and hurried toward

Will's. He'd mentioned a man by the gate earlier so I stared at the gate intently. Everything looked as it should. A loud gasp pulled my attention back to Eva. The blood drained from her face and her body shook. I followed her eyes to the garage door and a slumped figure. As I looked closer, dried blood was visible around a circular wound on his forehead and trailed off down his face and shirt.

I turned around and grabbed Eva to turn her away, but had to move away from her when I realized I was about to throw up. I tried to make it to the street, but couldn't. I got sick right in the middle of the driveway. Eva was still staring at the body. "Uh, Sir?" she said shakily.

I pulled on her arm. "Eva, he's not alive. We need to get out of here." My own body was shaking too much to be strong enough to pull her away.

"We can't just leave him there," she said through tears.

"Yes, we can. We'll call the police, but we can't stay here right now."

She relented and moved toward the car. I took her keys and helped her into the passenger side. I wasn't entirely sure I could drive either, but I figured I had a better chance than Eva, who still hadn't looked away from the body and was paler than the white brick of Will's house. I only needed to drive to a different neighborhood, just a block or two.

I shut her door and leaned on the car as I moved toward my side. I got in, turned on the engine, and drove forward.

"That must have been Matt," Eva said flatly.

I swallowed and nodded. "But why was he there?" I asked.

Eva was silent as I rounded the corner. "I bet it was meant as a warning for Will. Why else would the killers leave the body right there? And there was no blood on the concrete or the garage door. That body must have been moved."

I was surprised at the details Eva had noticed. I hadn't noticed any of that.

"I think they put the body in front of Will's house to tell him to back off."

That made some sense, but in the middle of the day? The sun was still out. I stopped the car on a side road. I had no idea how long I'd actually driven, but it had to be close to a mile from Will's. I parked and dialed 9-1-1. "Yes, hello, I just found a dead body."

♡ Chapter 20 ♡

I stumble to my desk on Monday morning. Everett and I were in a heated game of Tri-opoly until well past three o'clock this morning. We both kept saying we needed to quit and go to bed, but neither of us was willing to concede. Since I eventually fell asleep at the kitchen table, I guess I forfeited. I stare blankly at my computer screen. It's like I'm staring at one of those 3D image books where your eyes are practically crossed before you can see the image. Except, no image is materializing, unless you count my own reflection. I know what I need to work on, but I can't seem to get myself to do it. I decide, instead, to show Owen's secretary my progress on the scarf I'm crocheting. It's pretty lopsided with tight stitches on one side and big, loose ones on the other. Crocheting has been great for helping me clear my mind in the middle of the night when I can't sleep, but it's definitely not a hidden talent of mine. Still, I know Celia will still act like it's beautiful. She always does. My first project was nothing but a few rows of yarn and she oohed and aahed about the skill I had.

Carrying my work of art, I walk into the lobby where Celia's desk sits. Celia's nowhere to be seen, but Owen's sitting in her chair, propped up on his elbows staring at the computer. "Hey," he says as he sits up with a smile.

I haven't seen him since Friday night and all I can think about is him telling me he had feelings for me while I pretended I had none for him. Trying to act casual and ignore the awkwardness between us, I respond, "Hey," but it sounds more like a question than a greeting. "I, I thought Celia would be up here," I stammer. *Great job not sounding nervous, Juliet.*

"She had to run home. Her son's school called and said he was sick."

"Oh, okay."

"Do you need her for something?"

"No, not really. I was going to show her my latest project." I have to force a smile as I hold up the mass of yarn that I call a scarf.

"Ah, she taught you her method of getting rid of stress," he says. "I think Celia alone keeps that craft store in Town Square in business with all the skeins of yarn she purchases."

I relax and remind myself I'm just having an easy conversation with Everett's friend. "I'm just impressed that *you* know what a skein is."

"Oh, you're not the only one to glean some of Celia's crochet knowledge," he says while raising an eyebrow.

"You?"

"She was adamant that I learn. Told me it would save me from a heart attack. She used to always worry about my lack of down-time. I remember her constantly saying things like, 'Honey, you're busy as a one-legged cat it a sandbox.'" He does a spot on imitation of her accent. "The first year Celia was my secretary, my mom got several crocheted pot holders for Christmas from me."

I laugh, trying to picture Owen holding a crochet hook and yarn. He holds out his hand toward my scarf and says, "Let me see."

I raise my eyebrows at him.

"C'mon, Jules," he urges with a smile.

Still reluctant, I hand it over. He untangles the scarf and holds it up. A large grin spreads across his face. "I like the style with one side smaller than the other," he teases.

I snatch the scarf back. "And that's why I will never show you anything I make ever again."

Laughing he says, "I'm just kidding. It's good."

I roll my eyes.

"I'm serious. You must have had a lot of stress lately because it looks like you've gotten plenty of practice on that thing. It really does look good." He pauses. "Well, not if you compare it with one of my potholders, but it wouldn't be fair to you to put your work up against mine."

"Oh yeah? Kind of like it wouldn't be fair for you to have to play volleyball against me?"

Owen smiles, but is distracted by something on the computer screen. He stares at it for several seconds, types using the ten-key pad, and stares again. "Sorry," he says, turning his attention back to me.

"What are you doing?"

He turns the monitor slightly so I can get a better look. "I'm on Ebay. Celia was in a bidding war on a duck call before she had to leave and didn't want to step away from her computer until she won it. I told her I would watch and bid for her."

"A duck call? Really?"

"Yeah, she's very serious about these, has quite a collection."

"I had no idea," I laugh.

"You'll have to ask her about it. She'll talk your ear off for hours." He checks the screen again. "Here," he says, standing up. "Sit down and help me. I'll grab another chair."

I sit down and check the time left on the auction; three minutes. I'm sure no one in the marketing department will miss me if I'm only gone for another three minutes. Owen sets a chair down next to mine and scoots toward me as he checks the monitor. *Why does he always have to smell so good?* I want to lean in closer, but at the same time I'm frustrated with myself for thinking about it. "So, how long have you known Celia?" I ask, trying to change my thoughts.

"Um, she's worked here for almost three years."

"Were you the one that hired her?"

"Yeah. I was interviewing people to be my secretary and most the candidates drove me nuts. They were such suck-ups. Celia came in here telling me something about how it was hotter than a goat's butt in a pepper patch. Then she asked if she could help me tie my tie properly because I 'looked undone.' I knew immediately she was the one. She's been watching out for me and fixing my tie ever since."

I laugh, picturing Owen interviewing Celia. "I want to learn all of her sayings. They're so eccentric and wonderful. It makes me want to move to the South."

"She definitely has some good ones," Owen agrees. He puts in a final bid with seconds to go and we're silent as we wait for the outcome.

"Woohoo," I let out a small cheer when I see he won the duck call. Owen grins at me, but then stares long enough that I feel awkward again and my thoughts are back on Friday night. "Okay, well I better get back to my desk," I say. "I'd like to think I'm so important they're missing me down there."

"I'm sure they are," he says in a monotone voice. "Thanks for helping."

"Sure, I know you couldn't have done that without me," I say, trying to lighten the mood as I stand up.

His mouth turns into a grin, but his face still doesn't look happy. "See you, Jules."

I go back to marketing and sit at my desk. Something feels different. I look around the room slowly. Everything seems as it should; Kat sitting at the desk next to mine chatting away on the phone, a couple of interns with eyes half shut doing data entry, Collin's office door slightly ajar so I can see him clicking away on his keyboard. I try to shake the feeling that someone's watching me. My awkwardness with Owen must still have me on edge. I glance down to the pile of papers that I always keep right next to my stapler and it has been moved a touch to the left. I adjust it so it's in its proper spot and notice my bottom desk drawer is open a couple of inches. I slide it open and view the contents of the drawer; a box of envelopes, some unused folders and my lunch. However, sitting on top of my Greek yogurt is a red and black flash drive. I stick it into the USB port on my computer, but hesitate and take it back out. I have no idea where this thing came from. What if it has some horrible virus or a really, loud, embarrassing video that starts playing as soon as it's opened? I roll it between my hands as I contemplate my next move.

"Hey," Kat says, causing me to jump. "You okay?"

"Yeah, I'm fine. I was just daydreaming and you scared me," I explain.

"I'm going to grab some coffee. You want to walk over there with me?"

"Thanks, but I've got too much to do," I reply. "Eat a doughnut for me though." She starts to walk away, but I call after her, "Oh Kat, was anybody at my desk while I was gone?"

"No, I don't think so," she answers. "Why?"

"A few of my papers were kind of messed up, but it's not a big deal."

"Sorry. I didn't see anybody. See you later."

I know someone was here. I sat my lunch in that drawer twenty minutes ago and there wasn't a flash drive on it. I decide to check with Collin.

"Hey, Juliet, what can I do for you?" Collin asks when I walk through his door.

"Did you see someone at my desk while I was gone?"

"Yeah, one of the interns from finance said he had a couple of reports you requested. He wanted to know which desk was yours."

"Oh." I definitely didn't request any reports from finance, but I'm not going to tell Collin that until I find out what's on this drive.

"Why? Is there a problem?"

"No, no problem. There were some papers scattered around and I was curious what had happened, but it's fine. I'll go check out those reports and see what . . ." I trail off as I leave his office.

By the time I get home and pull out my laptop, I have imagined hundreds of possible scenarios involving this flash drive. In many of them, I end up with millions of dollars, but in several others I end up dead. Images of Matt's crumpled body next to Will's garage door flash through my mind over and over. Suddenly it seems like it's two years ago and Eva and I are driving back to Will's to meet the police and watching them determine the body is in fact Matt.

I try to push the memory from my mind and wait impatiently as the computer powers on and gets to the home screen. With shaky hands, I insert the drive and open the file. There are several folders and they're all full of coded gibberish. After years of doing the cryptiquotes in the newspaper with my mom, this shouldn't be too difficult to decipher. I work on it for forty-five minutes before realizing I'm wrong. Very wrong. This is nothing like a cryptiquote. I give up and try to make dinner.

I can't focus on cooking. Everett's going to have to endure some toasted waffles because my mind is too busy to concentrate on anything else. Curiosity is pulsing through my veins. What is on this thing? Why was it left in my drawer? Why would someone give it to me without a way of cracking the code?

Everett spends nearly an hour trying to help me, but doesn't do any better with it than I did. Unless "Goobits like us shnals" means something I don't understand because that's the closest he gets to a sentence that looks remotely like English. At least I don't feel like as much of an idiot now. I had initially thought this might have something to do with Will or Matt, but now I wonder if it was left for me by mistake. Were they trying to leave it for somebody else? I think about the flash drive well into the night, but can't decide what to make of it.

♡ Chapter 21 ♡

On Wednesday afternoon, Collin asks me if I will come to his office when I have a second. Expecting Lila to be waiting with some outrageous request, as has been the case several times before, I take my time finishing a spreadsheet before I slowly walk to his office. I knock on his door, hoping I've taken long enough for Lila to have given up on me and left. As the door opens and I see Collin is the only one in the office, I breathe an audible sigh of relief and grin at Collin. "Sorry it took a little while. I had to finish up some stuff," I explain, looking around one more time to make sure Lila isn't behind the door or something.

"Don't worry. She's not here," he says.

"What? Who?" I ask, pretending I don't understand what he means. I'm not sure why I'm pretending. It's obvious to everyone that Lila and I don't get along.

"What? Who?" Collin mimics in a high-pitched voice intended to sound like mine. I laugh and he continues, "This isn't one of Lila's weird, random tasks. I actually have something to talk to you about."

"Oh, okay," I say as I sit in the chair he's motioning to. His office smells like Tommy Hilfiger cologne. Everett used to wear it in high school so I know the scent well. Collin starts by explaining that the work I've been doing has been outstanding. He goes on complimenting me and telling me what an asset I've been to the company. I'm not sure if I should sit back and feel proud of myself or brace myself for what's coming next. Couldn't he hurry up and get to the point? Have I upset Lila enough that she's actually seeing to it that I lose my job?

". . . and all of those reports have really helped us understand our target audience better. Thanks to you, our marketing strategy has never been better." He's saying a lot of really nice things. I wish I could focus on what he's saying instead of waiting for the words "let you go." He continues, "What that means is you will have a group of three to four interns working for you as well as one or two salaried employees. I'll narrow it down to a few potential candidates and then we'll leave it to you to decide exactly who you want. We really love what you've done and can't wait to see what you'll do when you're heading up an entire team. You'll get the office across from Fitz's and your salary will increase by about, um, I just saw it on here. Yeah, there it is, uh, forty-two. What do you think? Do you want to try it?"

I feel like a bobble head as I nod eagerly, but can't make my mouth move. I finally squeak out a "yes." I take a deep breath and continue, "That sounds amazing. Thank you! And, um, what do you mean by forty-two?" I don't want to sound ungrateful, but I don't understand what he means. "You said my salary would increase by forty-two. Is that some term I don't understand or am I really getting an increase of forty-two dollars?"

He laughs. "No. It will increase by forty-two thousand dollars."

I stare in disbelief. When I finally find my voice, I ask, "Are you sure?"

"That's what it says right here and it's signed by Mr. Bradley himself."

I can't stop the giant grin that's spreading across my face. It turns into a laugh. I know this isn't professional, but I'm way too excited to try to contain it. "I was excited about the forty-two-dollar raise, but this is beyond amazing. Thanks, Collin."

He tells me we'll go over the details tomorrow and start interviewing Monday. It's difficult to look composed as I leave his office. I really want to take a flying leap out his door and dance around the room. I call Eva to tell her about the promotion and we make plans to celebrate. She's already deciding how we'll update my wardrobe with some of the extra money. A few minutes later Luke texts to see if I want to get together after work. I tell him my news, that Eva's meeting me at work, and that Everett, Eva, and I are going out to celebrate. At five o'clock on the dot, I log off my computer and head out. As I step off the elevator into the main lobby, there is Luke holding a bouquet of roses. My feelings for him are so hot-and-cold. One day everything he does seems to irritate me and the next day he seems perfect.

"Since you're busy tonight I wanted to see you for a couple of minutes and bring you these. Congrats on the job," he says, handing me the roses with one hand and grabbing me around the waist with the other.

"Thank you. They're beautif—" is all I can say before he pulls me into a kiss.

After a few seconds, I pull away. I feel funny making out with him in the middle of the main lobby of my workplace. I look up at Luke, a smug look covering his face. His eyes are focused on something behind me. I turn around and feel as if I've been kicked in the stomach. There is Owen, his brows creased and his eyes looking darker than ever. He immediately turns around and gets back in the elevator.

"Let's go," I say, pulling on Luke. The sinking feeling in my stomach grows worse with each step. Of course the one time Luke shows up at my work, Owen sees me kissing him.

"Go where?"

"Let's go outside," I suggest. He follows me into the parking lot. "Thanks for the roses, Luke. It's sweet of you to bring me these." We walk to my car and wait less than a minute when Eva calls and I tell her where I'm parked. I kiss Luke and say, "I'll call you tomorrow."

"Are you trying to get rid of me?"

I laugh and kiss him again. "No, but she's here and she doesn't know how to get to Everett's office building so she's going to follow me."

"You mean I'm still not going to actually meet your sister?"

"You can wave at her," I suggest, smiling.

"Okay, I'll see you later," he says, kissing me good-bye as Eva pulls up. He walks back to Eva's car. I can see him shake her hand through the window. The two of them talk for several minutes before I start inching forward. Eva waves good-bye to Luke and follows me. We drive two parking lots over, where Everett's office is, but he calls and says it will be a few minutes before he can leave so I park the car and jump in the passenger side of Eva's.

"So what was that about?" I ask.

"He said he's heard lots about me and wanted to put a face with the name," Eva says. She tips her head to the side at me with a grin. "You're right about him being fun to look at."

"I know," I agree with a smile. "Plus he does stuff like show up with roses and he makes it pretty tough to resist him. I ended up kissing him in the main lobby, where Owen saw, looked at me with daggers, and walked away."

Eva covers her mouth with her hand. "No," she says, sadly.

"Yeah," I reply, waving at Everett as he walks toward the car.

"Hey," Everett says as he gets in the backseat. "I'll ride with you guys. Can you bring me back to my car after dinner?"

"Yeah, I'm already bringing Juliet back to get hers," replies Eva.

"Congrats, Juliet!" Everett says, grabbing my shoulder. Then with a smile, he adds, "You can start paying rent now."

♡ Chapter 22 ♡

"Why didn't you show me this sooner?" Eva looks almost purple as she fumes. Little beads of sweat are accumulating on her forehead. I can tell she's trying to stay calm, but not succeeding. "You've had it since Monday?"

"Eva, I couldn't call you up and tell you about it. You told me not to say anything about Will on the phone and I was afraid talking about an encrypted flash drive might spark suspicion. I knew I'd see you sometime this week and I could show you then. It's been killing me too." Everett, Eva, and I had finished dinner and were heading home when I told her about my odd discovery on Monday morning.

"Will's definitely behind this. Who else would leave you something like that?" Eva asks. "Can I spend the night at you guys' apartment so I can look at it tonight? Maybe I can figure it out." Everett shoots me a glance that says, "Yeah right," and I smile, but tell her she can give it a shot.

My clock shows it's 2:32 when Eva bursts into my bedroom and flips on the light. "I've got it, Jules!"

"What?" I mumble, my mouth full of cotton.

"The Rosetta Stone," she yells.

"What about Rosetta Stone?" I look longingly at my light switch, wishing it were in the off position.

"Do you know what it is?"

"Of course. I was there when you learned French, remember?" I mutter. "Is that French? It sure didn't look like it to me."

"No, not the Rosetta Stone course," Eva shakes her head in frustration. "The actual Rosetta Stone, like the rock, the *stone*."

"Okay," I yawn. "I didn't know there was an actual stone."

"There is," Eva replies, looking at me like I'm a four-year-old. "It's from like 200 B.C. The text on it appears three times, each one in a different language."

"Okay," I nod, trying to follow what this has to do with the flash drive.

"Anyway, when the stone was discovered in the early 1800s, they couldn't read one of the languages. They didn't know what it was. So, by comparing it to the first text, one guy knew where the proper Greek names should be and was able to create a twenty-nine-letter alphabet that he identified from those proper Greek names."

"I really am trying to understand all of this, Eva, but I have no idea . . ." I trail off.

"Okay, you don't have to understand that. Will had a weird fascination with certain historic pieces and one of them was the Rosetta Stone. It made me realize there are a few words underlined in those files and they're underlined because they're proper nouns; proper nouns like Will, Matt, and P&L Pharmaceuticals. Using those we can decipher the rest."

"Did you try it? Does it work?" I jump up, sleep suddenly unappealing to me.

"No, I mean, yes, kind of. I just went through and picked out all of the underlined words and figured them out. I have most of the alphabet figured out from those. I'm going to get Everett," she hollers running down the hall.

Within the hour, Everett's found a program that's made for cracking cryptiquotes and pasted all of a three-page document into it along with the answers Eva has come up with. However, when it decodes the text, it still makes no sense. I sigh. If this is from Will, why is he making it so difficult for us to figure out?

"Yes!" Eva shrieks. "That's it." I stare at the monitor again, trying to understand what she's excited about. I sound it out *Progredi no litante . . .*

"That's what, Eva?"

"It's Latin."

"Oh, good, Latin," I sigh.

"It's easy, Juliet. There are a million programs out there that can translate from Latin to English." Sensing my lack of enthusiasm for the task, Eva continues, "Why don't you guys go back to bed and I'll find a way to get this translated? I'm not tired anyway." Everett puts his hand on Eva's shoulder before silently heading back to his room.

"Okay, let me know if you need anything," I yawn, hoping she can figure it out on her own while I sleep. I *am* curious to find out what those files are, but not curious enough to spend hours in the middle of the night translating Latin.

Once I wake up for the day, I head out to check on Eva. She's sitting at the kitchen table, bright eyed, smiling at me. "Good morning?" I ask, lamenting that I have giant circles under my eyes while Eva looks like a person straight out of a Folgers commercial.

"Good morning," she sings. "I got everything translated."

"And?"

"He needs your help."

"*My* help? How can *I* help him?"

"He needs a pharmaceutical statistician."

"I'm not a pharma—"

"You're the closest he's got. I mentioned your new job in a

letter I wrote months ago and now he needs your help. You'll have to read the files, but apparently P&L is phasing out all of the old Tipro and replacing it with a new one."

"That's good, right?"

"Well it's good that they're getting rid of it so it can't hurt people anymore. However, if they succeed, it will be much harder to prove the problems the initial Tipro caused and no one will be held responsible. He needs you to run some statistical analysis to compare the competence intervals of cancer statistics from two—"

"Competence intervals?" I smile. "Are you sure it wasn't confidence intervals?"

"Oh, probably. See, you need to read it. I don't know what I'm talking about. He spent like three paragraphs explaining that he thinks they kept their percentages the same by expanding competence, er, I mean confidence intervals."

"Okay, I'll read it after work today."

"Thanks, Jules. I'll understand if you don't want to get involved. If P&L ever found out you were helping Will, they'd be after you like they are him. He must really need you if he's risking that."

"They won't find out, Eva. And maybe this is exactly what he needs to speed things up and be able to come back."

♡ Chapter 23 ♡

'm going to grab another drink," Luke says, jumping up from the circular sofa we are sitting on. Elaine, Josh, Luke and I are at The Orchid Lounge. Elaine has been suggesting we get together for a while so I asked Luke if he'd go out with a couple of my friends. He said that sounded great and suggested we go to one of his favorite clubs. Clubs aren't exactly my scene, but I figured it could be fun anyway. I was wrong.

Elaine is busy watching Josh's every move and acting like everything he says is either genius or the funniest thing she's ever heard. And nothing Josh says seems even remotely humorous. Maybe it is really funny and I am missing all the punch lines when my mind blocks out what he's saying as a form of self-defense. Then there's Luke. He's apparently not impressed with my friends, but honestly who can blame him? Elaine is not acting like the friend I know. I am frustrated that Luke makes sure we all know how bored he is. Every few minutes he lets out a long sigh. Then he looks at me and rolls his eyes while Josh talks, which is ninety percent of the time.

"Juliet, how do you like your apartment?" Josh asks as Luke walks away.

"I really like it. I'm falling in love with the north part of Eden Falls. The town square has so many cool places. I'd never spent much time up there 'til now, but I went—"

"Yes! There is so much to do there," Josh cuts me off. "There's also a lot of cool history about the north side of town. Have you ever noticed the apartment building that's a couple blocks south of you called La Chute?" I shake my head slightly. By this point, I know it doesn't matter whether I answer or not. He's going to go on and on, no matter what my reaction is.

I glance around me to see if anything interesting is going on. I love watching random people interact with each other. At the bar, there is a woman laughing with a short, balding man. Every couple of seconds she glances to her side where her friend is sitting and rolls her eyes. Then she turns back to the man, makes a comment, touches his arm, and laughs. A few feet away is a woman with long, dark hair. She can't be more than five feet tall, but her heels probably add six inches. She has a large bust that she is very proud of. It's practically popping out of her teeny-tiny purple dress and she looks down at it every ten seconds or so, probably to make sure it hasn't slipped out. She is busy talking to two guys, who look at her chest even more often than she does.

"He he he he he," Elaine's high-pitched giggle rings in my ears. I have known Elaine since the eighth grade and have never seen her try so hard to impress a guy. "Oh stop, Josh, that's too funny!" Elaine squeaks. Part of why Elaine and I have been such great friends is that neither one of us is obsessively guy crazy or ditzy. In the eighth grade, that was a pretty rare thing. Now, Elaine is acting exactly like all of those eighth-graders who'd driven us nuts. It seems even worse on a twenty-five-year-old.

"It's so annoying when people call them croissants," Josh remarks, saying "croissant" exactly as I've always heard it pronounced. "That's not even close to the correct pronun-ciation. Have you heard the story about how croissants were invented? It's absolutely false, but it's a fun story anyway," Josh says enthusiastically.

"You can't be serious," I hear Luke say behind me. He's starting to sit down when Josh begins his croissant story. "Croissants? I can't take this," he adds and walks away again, head shaking.

I look at Josh so I can apologize for Luke, but he doesn't seem even slightly bothered. He simply picks up his croissant story right where it was interrupted. I mouth "sorry" to Elaine and get up to find Luke. I'm actually thankful for the excuse to get away from Josh's story. As soon as I stand up I see Luke about twenty feet away, talking to a group of people. He's laughing with a couple of the guys. My head spins. All this flashing messes with my head more than I thought. As I walk toward him, swaying slightly, I see one of the women reach out and grab his arm. He smiles and talks to the woman. "Hey," I say as I approach him.

"Oh, hey," Luke answers, barely looking up. "These are a few of my friends and this is Juliet," he grunts, irritation in his voice. I give a small wave and two of the guys imme-diately start talking to me. Luke keeps whispering to the woman next to him. I talk to the guys for a few minutes when one of them, Marcus, gets close. He's a muscular guy, about the same height as I am. He puts his arm around me and his face gets closer and closer to mine as we speak. I look at Luke, but he's still engrossed in a conversation, which is apparently hilarious judging by the way he and the woman are grinning. I glance back at the sofa where Elaine and Josh are sitting, when I feel Marcus' breath in my ear. I can't understand half of what he says, but I clearly hear him when he asks "Why don't we go outside?" His breath reeks of his last drink.

I laugh nervously while trying to think of how to respond, but words won't form in my foggy mind. "Thanks, but I want to stay in here. I should probably get back to my friends," I say, motioning to the other side of the room. The lights are flashing faster.

"I'm sure they can manage without you for now." He gently pushes me toward the back door. I feel the same nauseating sensation I feel every time I walk by an Abercrombie store. He must have dumped at least half a bottle of one of their colognes on himself. Smells this strong always make me feel sick.

I try to distance myself from him as I say, "No, I really need to get back. It was nice to meet you, Marcus."

He's not getting the message. He puts his arm around me and pulls me in until I'm tight against him. "You're making a scene," he says into my ear. I push away, but that only makes him pull harder. His arms have a layer of sweat that dampens my arms. Again, he's whispering things I can't understand. I hear him say something about the parking lot and not letting people see. If he didn't have my hands pinned down by my side, I would slap that superior look right off of his face. I stare at the sofa, wishing I was sitting on it listening to Josh talk about croissants. Elaine is too busy hanging on Josh's every word to look up for one second and see my desperate looks. Another wave of dizziness passes over me. With every flash of light, I feel pain in my head. Has the music been this loud and obnoxious the entire night? Marcus detours from the path to the bar and begins pushing me toward the door. I'm trying as hard as I can to get away, but my attempts are futile. I don't seem to be slowing Marcus in the slightest. As we get closer to the door, fear paralyzes me. I try to flail my arms around to attract attention, but they don't move. Marcus has me completely restrained. I scream for Luke.

"Juliet! Juliet!" I hear a voice behind me. Marcus immediately loosens his hold. I turn around and see a pale-faced Josh. "We've been looking all over for you. Elaine needs you."

I quickly move away from Marcus while he's distracted. Josh takes off in front of me in a sprint. I walk to the sofa, but it's empty. Josh is by my side again steering me toward the door. "Just keep moving," he says.

Elaine is waiting outside the door with wide eyes. She grabs me in a tight hug. "Are you okay? That was so scary. Josh saw you over there with that guy. He was ready to fight him if he needed to." Elaine gazes at Josh in admiration.

"Thanks, Josh," I say, waiting for the nausea to pass. I think of Josh, walking toward gargantuan Marcus. He was so scared that there was no color left in his face and he took off running as soon as he'd distracted Marcus. I'm so appreciative of what he did, I feel bad for my previous negative feelings for him.

"Oh sure, it wasn't a big deal," Josh shrugs. "It actually reminded me of this documentary I saw where this girl w—"

As Josh continues, I whisper to Elaine, "I really need to get out of here. Is it okay if I ride with you guys?"

"Of course. I won't let you go back in there!" Elaine gasped. "Who is that guy? Do you know him? I was truly scared for you. You should go to the police."

I look back to see if Luke has noticed that I'm gone or if he's still talking to the same woman. He's moved across the room, but not because he's looking for me. He's busy talking to Miss Teeny-Tiny in the purple dress. He has his hand on the small of her back and is walking to a table with her. I turn away and follow Josh and Elaine out the door.

As we reach the parking lot, I feel everything coming up. I stand by a neon sign that says, "The Orchid Lounge," and throw up. This hardly seems fair. I only had soft drinks, and

I am the one puking. It was induced by everything tonight: cologne, loud music, flashing lights, Marcus, Miss Teeny-Tiny Dress, and Luke.

♡ Chapter 24 ♡

Thump Thump Thump. I sit up on the couch. I convinced Elaine I wanted to go home. I had to tell her repeatedly that I wanted to be by myself and that I would be fine. I laid down in front of the TV to wait for Everett to get home, but apparently I fell asleep. *Thump Thump Thump.* The pounding is louder now. It shoots pain into my head with each knock. It sounds like someone is about to knock the door down. I grab my cell to check the time, 1:13 a.m. "Juliet! Juliet, are you in there? I need to talk to you." It's Luke. Almost immediately my cell phone starts ringing. I check the name. Luke.

I answer the phone. "Luke, go home. I don't want to see you right now." Then I hang up.

Thump Thump Thump. "C'mon, Juliet. Let me in." My phone dings with a text saying, "Please let me in, Babe. I'm sorry. I really need to talk to you," followed by several hearts.

"I'll talk to you tomorrow," I text back.

"Please give me one min to explain," is his reply.

Desperate for him to go away, I get up and open the door about two inches. "What?" I growl.

"You scared me. I looked everywhere for you."

"I was scared too . . . when your creepy friend Marcus tried to force me out the door with him."

"Marcus? Oh, he's harmless. He'd just had too much to drink," Luke says, flippantly.

"Okay, great, well I'm glad we talked," I say sarcastically as I shut the door, but Luke wedges his foot in to stop it.

"I'm sorry I didn't stay with you all night. Your friends were hard to be around, you know?"

"You didn't have to stay right with me all night, Luke. It would have been nice though, if you hadn't stayed right with every other female in the place."

"Wow, I had no idea you were the jealous type. I've got to tell you this is not your most attractive side. We never said we were dating exclusively, Juliet," he proclaims.

"Are you serious?" I fume. "You and I were on a date. So, yeah, on the nights that we're on dates, I kind of expect to be the only woman you're with."

"Do you want to date exclusively?" he asks.

"AH," I growl. "No. I. Do. Not. Please leave." I can't believe this guy. He obviously doesn't care for me or he wouldn't have treated me the way he did tonight.

"I'm not leaving. Let's talk this out," he insists.

"Okay," I hiss, grabbing my purse from beside the couch. "I'm leaving." I jog down the stairs. Luke follows, trying to convince me to stop and talk to him. I jump in my car, lock the doors, and take off. Anger is consuming my entire body. Celia would be telling me that right now is a great time to start crocheting. I shudder to think what might have happened to me if Josh hadn't stepped in tonight. And Luke doesn't seem to care at all. He said he just didn't like being around my friends, but I'd left my friends to go talk to him and he'd been too busy talking with another woman to care.

I have no clue where I'm driving. I'm mindlessly following the bright white lines in the middle of the road. I see my reflection in the mirror and wince. Mascara is smudged in big spots beneath my eyes. My hair is in a messy bun on top of my head, but chunks are falling out all over.

I drive in circles for thirty minutes, before calling Everett to see if he's home yet. I figure he can make sure Luke is nowhere in sight. He answers, but all I can hear is yelling. I recognize Owen's voice and I'm pretty sure I can hear Luke as well.

"I'll call you back in five, Jules," Everett shouts and hangs up. I gas it and make it back to the apartment parking lot in less than three minutes. There's no sign of Luke. I run up to my apartment. Owen's sitting at the kitchen table with an ice bag on his face and I can see blood.

I gasp, "What happened?" as my weak stomach does a somersault.

"Luke happened," Everett responds, digging through the freezer. He finds a bag of peas and tosses them to Owen, who immediately uses them to replace the bag of ice. "Owen looks great compared to him," Everett assures.

"Compared to Luke? What happened? You two really got in a fight? I mean, why were you fighting?" I realize I might know exactly why they were fighting. Luke was mad at me. Owen was probably still angry about seeing me kiss Luke. Once they saw each other, they took their anger out on one another. It seems so stupid and juvenile. "Owen, what happened? Why did you guys fight?" Owen looks up at me and then looks away, shaking his head. I'm so frustrated that he won't explain what happened. "Owen, I can't believe you'd fight with him. This is ridiculous!" I turn to face Everett to see if he'll give me some details. Everett watches Owen, waiting for him to explain. I throw my arms up in frustration and walk toward the hall. Owen stands up and grabs my arm. I turn around so I'm facing him.

"Don't assume you understand everything here. I can assure you that this had nothing to do with you," he sighs, before turning to Everett and saying, "Thanks for the ice, man. I'm going to head home."

I stand motionless, dumbfounded, watching him leave. I can't tell if he's angry with me or if he's trying to comfort me by saying it had nothing to do with me. Either way, I feel awful. I yelled at him for getting in a fight and he was right; I didn't understand what happened. It makes me feel sick to watch two people beat on each other, but I shouldn't have been so self-centered as to assume the fight had anything to do with me. On top of that, I've had such a long, horrible night. But I know the long night isn't Owen's fault and I wish I hadn't yelled at him. My head is pounding. I want to get in my bed and have this terrible day be over.

"You don't look so good," Everett winces, sympathetically.

"Yeah," I try to laugh, but it sounds more like a cry. "I don't feel so good."

Everett wraps his arms around me. "Look, Jules, I don't want to get involved in something between you and Owen, but I guess I'm kind of already in it. It's a little weird for me to have a friend who obviously has feelings for my little sister. Anyway, I feel like you often get the wrong impression of him." Everett pauses and pulls out a carton of ice cream and two spoons. He hands me a spoon and takes the lid off of the carton of Cookie Dough Explosion. "Like tonight, it was actually pretty impressive."

"Impressive?" I shake my head in disgust.

"I'm not talking about the way he fought, Jules," Everett says, sounding annoyed that I interrupted. "I know you like Luke and you think he's a great guy and all that, but I have never been happier to see somebody get beat up. Owen and I pulled into the parking lot and Luke was beating up some guy. I'd never seen the guy before, but he was small. I'm talking like maybe five-foot-five and probably not an ounce over one-thirty. Luke was wailing on him. The guy wasn't even fighting back. Owen jumped out of the car and yelled at Luke to stop, but that got him going more. So Owen grabbed Luke off of the guy. Of course that made Luke start swinging at Owen. Owen told him to back off, that he wasn't going to fight him, but Luke kept swinging and hit Owen a couple of times. So, Owen hit him back twice, hard. You know, from the few stories I'd heard about Owen's childhood, I knew he could probably hold his own in a fight, but that's the biggest understatement. It wasn't even ten seconds before Luke was on the ground. And even then, when we were helping the other guy get up, Luke was still yelling at Owen to come back and fight. But Owen didn't do it just to fight Luke, like you seem to think. It wasn't over you. He did it to get Luke off of that other guy."

We sit in silence as I try to make sense of everything he's related. I've definitely seen a new side to Luke tonight, but still, it's hard to think him capable of being quite so malicious. "Why were they fighting? Not Owen and Luke, but Luke and that other guy, why were *they* fighting?" I ask Everett.

"They weren't fighting. Luke was punching and the other guy was in a ball on the ground trying to protect himself," Everett explains. "As soon as Owen stepped in, the guy took off running."

"Okay," I reply, desperately searching for some possible explanation for Luke's behavior. However, I'm not sure why I'm trying to find a reason to defend him. I can't stand him right now. I guess I would like to think I have better taste in men than to be completely blind-sided by such a creep. "But do you know why Luke was so mad at the guy? I mean the other guy must have done something to make Luke so mad."

"I have no idea. I just wanted you to know it wasn't Owen's fault."

I feel sick all over again, but it's not from the ice cream I've been shoveling into my mouth. The thought of Luke beating some guy senseless makes me both nauseated and angry, and I feel awful for yelling at Owen. I grab my phone, scroll down the contacts list, and push "send."

"What are you doing? Don't you think you've had enough drama for the night?" Everett asks. "Why don't you go to bed and deal with Luke in the morn—" Everett is interrupted by a cell phone ringing. We look at the floor, where Owen's jacket lies.

"I wasn't calling Luke. I wanted to apologize to Owen," I explain, pointing to the pocket of Owen's jacket.

"Oh, yeah. When he ran after Luke he threw his jacket at me, and I guess we both forgot about it. I think you need to get some sleep though. You can talk to Owen later."

"Yeah, I guess so, g'night, Ev," I yawn and turn toward my bedroom.

"Have you made any progress on the project Will gave you?" he calls after me as he puts the ice cream away.

"Yeah, but it's going to take a while. There's a lot of information there." The pulsing pain in my head sharpens as I think about all of the work I should be doing. Will sent me nearly ten pages just outlining the stuff he needed help with. The actual files containing the information were hundreds of pages.

"I'm sure he didn't intend for you to do it all within a week. He's spent two years gathering that information. Take your time, Jules." He pulls me into a hug. "Anyway, you've had a rough enough night without stressing over that. I'll see you tomorrow."

"Okay," I reply before dragging myself down the hall. I'm exhausted, but instead of falling asleep, I lay there thinking of the way Owen looked at me when he said, "I can assure you that this had nothing to do with you." He seemed so hard. I wonder if all feelings he had for me are gone.

♡ Chapter 25 ♡

gaze at the clock for what seems the thousandth time this morning; 11:04 a.m. I'm trying to focus on the project Collin gave me, but time is dragging. Yesterday Everett and I tried to take Owen's jacket and phone back to him, but when we got to his place, he wasn't there. I'm dying to talk to him and apologize for getting mad at him for fighting Luke. I hate to consider what a brat he must think I am. First, he knows I've been dating Luke who's turning out to be a complete jerk. I really wish I hadn't kissed Luke at TBC. Owen probably thinks I set that up on purpose where he could see. And second, after the fight, I treated Owen like he was so stupid for fighting; like the fight had been over me. I'm embarrassed as I think about it.

When Sunday passed without me getting the chance to see Owen, I decided I'd go to his office during lunch today and talk to him. I know he may not want me there if any of the Bradleys are around, but it's killing me to not be able to talk to him. Although it's still early for lunch, I gather my stuff and head out the door. I move quickly, watching all around for Lila. It's ridiculous trying to be so stealthy, but I don't want Owen to have another reason to be irritated with me right now. I take the stairs so I can peek through the window into the lobby without being seen. It looks empty. I approach Celia's desk. Celia looks up and, seeing it's me, flashes a huge grin. "Hey there, honey, haven't see you in a while. How are things in marketing? Isn't Collin just a doll?" She stands up and grabs me in a hug.

I smile back. "Yeah, he is."

Celia eyes me suspiciously. "What's wrong, sugar?"

"Nothing. I think I'm tired or something," I say shrugging, but her second hug and motherly concern have me ready to sit down and pour my heart out to her. However, the last thing I need right now is to get worked up and emotional in the lobby of Owen's office. "Is your son feeling better?" I change the subject.

"Oh, yes, he is. He's better than ol' Blue layin' on the porch chewin' on a big ol' catfish head."

My mood is instantly better. I laugh as I repeat what she said. I tell her about stopping by her desk last week to show her my scarf and seeing the duck call she won on Ebay and then I listen for several minutes as she describes her new treasure to me.

When she's finished, I ask, "Is Owen, or, ah, I mean Mr. Denny in his office?"

"Oh, honey, it doesn't bother me if you call him Owen. In fact, I'm sure he'd prefer it for you to call him Owen. Yes, he is in his office, but he's with someone right now."

"Dangit," I mutter under my breath. Then looking back to Celia, I whisper, "It's not Lila, is it?"

Celia lets out a burst of laughter. Her large frame shakes. I give a smile as I wait for her to explain what is so funny. "No, no it's not Lila, sweetie." She takes a couple of deep breaths in between chuckles. "She really gets my goose, though, thinking she's so high and mighty. You should have seen your face as you said her name. You looked like you were ready to cream her corn." Celia stares at my smile and continues, "But no, it's not her. It's a client Mr. Denny's always been very close to. I have no idea how long they'll be. Why don't ya let me give him a message, honey?"

I try to mask my disappointment. "No, I don't have a message, but could you tell him that I stopped by?"

"Of course. Is that all?" Celia gives me a skeptical look.

"That's all. I'll catch up with him later." As I say it, I hear loud laughter from behind the door. The knob turns and out walks Owen. My breath catches in my throat and butterflies are swarming through my stomach. He looks amazing with his black suit and air of confidence. There's a man standing next to Owen, but I don't notice any details about him. I'm too busy staring at Owen. Owen meets my eyes and stares at me intently for several seconds. I wish I could figure out what he's thinking. I wince at the purplish knob on his forehead and his face spreads into a grin. Suddenly I feel nervous. Owen's never made me this nervous before. I'm speechless, staring at his dimpled smile.

"Hey, Jules," he says, and along come more butterflies. He turns to Celia, "Celia, can you get me the earnings report from June? Michael thinks I'm padding the numbers." The man next to Owen lets out a booming laugh. Owen moves closer to me and whispers, "This could be a while. I'll let you know when I'm done." Goosebumps cover me head-to-toe as he talks. He squeezes my arm before moving away. I give him a slight nod, but still can't get any words out. My arm feels all tingly where he touched it. I want to grab him and pull him close to me again, but instead, I turn to leave. "Oh, and Jules, here you go," he says, throwing me a magazine. "I thought you might want the current issue." I look down to see this quarter's issue of *Sheep—The Wooly Truth* in my hands. Owen turns to the man who's apparently Michael and says, "You have to watch out for her. She stole a magazine right out of my waiting room. Now all the sheep fanatics have no good reading material in here." He smiles at me while Michael, obviously a little confused, gives a lighthearted chuckle. I smile, hoping some of what I want to say to him is conveyed through the expression and he and Michael disappear behind the door.

"Oh, honey, you two are absolutely adorable," Celia coos. "Don't you let that Lila get in your way. He's never that happy to see her."

I smile and shake my head, "I'll see you later, Celia."

"Ba-bye, hun."

I practically skip down the stairs. *Owen's not mad at me. Owen's not mad at me,* I chant in my head. I think about his smile and replay everything he said. Then looking down at the magazine in my hands, I laugh. I walk into the cafeteria to eat last night's leftovers; cheesy chicken and asparagus. However, once there, I can't make myself sit down. I'm way too excited to sit. I decide to walk to the bank. It's been over two weeks since I've been there to check for a letter from Will and this new project has me thinking more and more about him and when he will come back. The sky looks masked in gray, but dreary sky and sticky air can't ruin this mood.

I walk along the sidewalk, noting the pretty scenery. There's a small fountain with several ducks swimming along. I swear they're smiling at me. I think through exactly what I want to say to Owen. I had just been going to apologize, but part of me wants to say more. He'd told me I didn't understand what was going on with Lila. Maybe I've misjudged him, but as I try to justify the way he's acted with Lila, I can't. I'm angry with myself for having these feelings for a man who is so obviously taken.

A fat raindrop hits my arm. I look up and see heavy, dark gray clouds rolling in. I jog the last hundred yards to the bank and quickly duck inside. I open the safety deposit box where a thick manila envelope is waiting. It's so large I have to use both hands to pry it out of the box. Once I get it out, there's still another paper in the box. It's the typical, small, easy to conceal in my purse letter from Will. So what is the giant envelope? It has Eva's name on it, but that's all. I try to jam it down into my purse, but it's way too big. I make a mental note that I have a new reason to buy another handbag.

Will and Eva have never exchanged anything more than a letter so this hefty envelope has my curiosity piqued. There is no way to hide it. Should I leave it here and come back later with a bigger bag? No, that seems like more effort than it's worth. I'll put it in my car as soon as I get back to TBC. I grab the envelope and stick the two-page letter over the top where Will wrote "Eva" in big letters. If anyone is following me, which I seriously doubt, they won't be close enough to read the small handwriting on the letter. I step back into the bank's lobby. A glance out the large windows shows a black sky. Rain is coming down in bucket-loads. I step outside and begin jogging the six blocks back to TBC.

I've gone almost four blocks when the sky is lit up by lightning. The rain picks up even more and is coming down in sheets. Everything is dark and blurry. I'm so glad that I didn't wear the white silk shirt I'd initially had on this morning. I'm completely soaked from head to toe. "Jules!" I hear someone yelling behind me. I turn around and hear Owen's laugh. "I've been trying to find you." I stop running, but he grabs my arm and pulls, saying, "That's okay, keep going. Let's get to that awning."

We run another block before stopping in front of Lisa's Dry Cleaners with its blue and white striped awning. It helps, but the rain is still coming in on the sides. "Michael had to leave a few minutes after you did, so I figured I'd find you eating lunch somewhere. That kid from accounting with the crazy hair told me he'd seen you take off this way. I had just turned back when it started pouring," he yells. Even with him yelling, the pounding of the rain and the wind whipping in my ears make it difficult to hear. He continues with a grin, "You enjoy taking leisurely walks in the middle of torrential downpours?"

I smile. "I had some errands to run so I thought I'd get them done now."

He nods as lightning blasts through the sky again. "We should get going. Standing under an awning during a lightning storm probably isn't the best idea."

"Okay," I agree. As we start running again, I yell, "Did Everett give you your phone? We went to your place yesterday, but you weren't there."

"Yeah, thanks. He brought it up this morning."

"Look, Owen," I start, but have to pause as the thunder cracks loudly. I continue to yell, "I'm really, really sorry about the other night. I was having a terrible evening and I, I mean, I know that's no excuse for yelling at you, but," I stop. I had thought out a good apology, but now I'm jumbling it all up. "What I mean is it was really good of you to step in and help that other guy. I'm sorry I jumped to conclusions."

Owen stops running. TBC is less than a block away, but I stop next to Owen. "Don't worry about it," he replies, his eyes piercing mine. "Do you still have some time before you have to be back? Why don't we get something to eat?" He leans in and starts to say something else, but stops when he notices the envelope and papers. I'm hugging them in an attempt to keep them dry. He grabs them from my hands and tucks them inside his suit jacket while saying, "Your papers are getting soaked. You should have had me put them in here earli—"

"No! Um, thank you, but no," I burst out, grabbing them out of his jacket quickly.

The shock is evident on his face.

I try to explain. "I really don't mind them getting wet. I'm going to hold them." I shove them against my stomach and look up at Owen's face. It's a mixture of confusion and sadness. Suddenly things feel very awkward and tense between us.

"Okay." He starts walking and I follow. We pass the fountain and I notice how ugly it is. And those ducks, those stupid, smug-looking ducks.

"Owen, I meant no about you holding my papers. I want to get something to e . . ."

He cuts me off, "I should probably get back to work."

"Owen, stop." I grab his arm. We've reached the lobby of TBC. Owen quickly looks around and I realize he's probably worried about being seen by a Bradley. I let go of his arm.

"I'll see you later," he sighs, holding eye contact with me for several seconds before turning and walking away. I lift up the envelope and papers in my hands and hit them against my head. I want to scream, but instead let out a much quieter, "AAAAhhhhhhh." Once in the elevator, I smack the button for the parking garage. As I take Eva's stuff to my car, I get angrier and angrier. Stupid Will. Why didn't he stick to the normal letter? If he hadn't sent a giant envelope, everything would have gone differently with Owen. I unlock the car and throw the envelope and letter under my seat. I take a deep breath, trying to calm down so I can return to my desk. I think about telling Collin that I don't feel well and driving Eva's stuff out to her now so I can talk to her. However, Collin's arranged interviews this afternoon for me to decide who I want on my statistics team. This would be the wrong afternoon to play hooky.

I ring some water out of my hair as I step into the elevator, but quickly stop when I see the puddle I'm creating on the floor. My clothes are weighed down by all the water they're retaining. I grab my compact mirror out of my purse to see what my makeup, or lack thereof, looks like now. As I open it, the elevator doors open again and several people from the lobby enter. I feel someone staring at me and look up to see Lila standing next to me.

"Rough day?" Lila smirks.

"Nope, just a new style I'm trying out," I mumble.

Lila grabs a strand of my dripping hair. "Your hair gets really brassy when it's wet. It's way over-processed. Oh, and it smells awful," she says in disgust as she throws the piece of hair as if it's a venomous snake.

Two women in front of me turn around. One eyes me up and down curtly and the other flashes a sympathetic look. "So what happened?" Lila asks.

I stare at Lila, who's grinning smugly. "I went swimming during lunch . . . in my clothes," I answer.

"Oh, I don't mean how you got wet. I mean you look like you're about to cry." The elevator doors open on my floor and I get out, but Lila follows. So does the lady who looked me up and down curtly. She continues her look of disgust as she pushes past me.

"That's because I have mascara running down my face," I reply to Lila, hoping she'll let it drop.

"You should use waterproof mascara if you plan on playing in the rain. But no, that's not it. You look pretty upset. It think it's more about your little boyfriend, Luke. Isn't that his name? You got in a fight with him and now you're torn up over it."

"What?" How does Lila even know that Luke exists and more specifically, that we had a fight?

"Yeah. I met him earlier when he came by looking for you. He told me about how mad you are at him, that you won't return his calls or texts. He said you're doing everything you can to ignore him. Lucky for you, I am the one he ran into. I went ahead and had Collin let him into your office. You can't ignore your problems forever, Juliet."

"My office? Lila, Luke and I are none of your business."

Lila laughs and coyly says, "Oh, so you don't want to see him? If only I'd known. You know, I never would have put you and him together. He's pretty hot. If I weren't taken, I would have grabbed him for myself." She pauses to look me up and down once more before continuing. "Maybe not, he must be a little desperate."

With a sigh, I walk away. I want to get as far from Lila as possible. However, I want to see Luke even less so I duck into the restroom. Once inside, I stare at my reflection. What little makeup remains is now smudged beneath my eyes. My hair has separated into large chunks that are matted down. I'm shaking. I'm not sure if it's because my wet clothes are making me cold or because I'm so angry, but my whole body is quivering. I take a couple deep breaths to calm down and use a hairband from my purse to pull my hair up on top of my head. I wash my face and scrounge through my purse for any makeup, but can only find lip gloss. Ever since Luke's comment about how I look in the mornings when we go running, I've been more self-conscious without makeup. "At least my face is tan right now," I think as I muster the courage to leave the bathroom.

Before I open the door to my office, Collin stops me. "Hey, Juliet, it looks like you had an eventful lunch break. Crazy rain, huh?"

"Yeah, crazy," I agree.

Collin looks uncomfortable as he fidgets with his pen. "Look, there's some guy in your office. Lila said you'd been looking for him. I wasn't sure what to do. I know Lila's not generally looking out for your best interest, but she was so adamant that I couldn't argue. I think his name is Luke. Do you know a Luke?"

"Yeah, it's okay, Collin. Thanks."

Relief floods over his face. "Okay, but as soon as you're

done, your first interview is here so you should probably get him out as quickly as possible."

"I will. Trust me. No one wants him out of here quicker than I do."

I take a deep breath and open the door. "Hey, babe," Luke says, as if nothing is wrong, "Some beautiful flowers for my beautiful girl."

"Luke, why are you here?"

"I needed to see you. I miss you." He holds out the bouquet of flowers to me; lilies. I decide lilies are one of my least favorite flowers. If you get too close to them, you're covered in nasty orange stuff that stains your clothes, I don't like the smell, and right now they look especially ugly.

"Luke, let's not make this a big deal," I say as I flip through papers on my desk. I do need to look at the resumes Collin gave me, but I'm mostly trying to look busy and uninterested. "We have nothing in common." Luke stands up and walks over to me. He grabs me around the waist and pulls me close to him. Noticing how wet I am, he grimaces and loosens his hold. I push away. I find everything about him repulsive, even the big, hideous muscles that are forcing me in close to him.

"Juliet, I don't care what we do or don't have in common. All I know is that I've hated being away from you these last few days." I continue pushing against him and turn away from his kiss.

"Luke, I really need to get back to work. I have to interview a bunch of people this afternoon and I'm already running late."

"You're pretty cute when you're mad. Kick me out again."

Luke, I need you to leave," I plead.

"Okay, I'll leave, but will you please at least talk to me later?"

"There's no point, Luke."

"Please, Juliet. Please." His haughty attitude is gone and he looks desperate. Part of me feels sorry for him.

"Please leave."

"C'mon, just agree to talk to me."

"Okay, we'll talk later, but I need you to go right now."

"Great, how about tonight? Can I take you to dinner?"

"I'm busy tonight," I reply casually. He gives me a skeptical look. "I'm serious. I'm going out to my parents' house."

"All right, what about tomorrow night? Where do you want to eat?"

"I don't have a lot of time tomorrow night either. Let's not go out to eat. You can come over and we can talk at my apartment." I figure he probably knows that I'm not busy tomorrow night, but I don't want to sit through an entire evening with him. Hopefully this way, we can talk for five minutes and be done.

"Okay, what time should I come over?"

"I don't know. I'll text you," I answer, trying to push him out of the office.

"I've seen how great you are at texting these past few days. I'll never hear from you. Why don't we plan on seven?"

"Sure, come over at seven, but I have to leave at seven thirty."

"C'mon, Juliet. You're not giving me much to work with here."

"Luke, you can either come over at seven or not. It doesn't matter to me, but that's all the time I have tomorrow night. Now I'm bringing someone in here to interview so please leave."

He looks disappointed as he sets the flowers on my desk and walks out. "I'll see you tomorrow at seven, babe."

I let out a sigh of relief and look down at the resume I'm holding to see who I'll be interviewing first, Mary Sorensen. I had seen the pile of resumes and applications Collin had received in response to these new statistics positions. There were easily over a hundred. However, many of them were immediately thrown out. One woman's resume showed that she had a "bachelorette degree in statistics." There was a cover letter that read, "Enclosed is my resume for you to overlook." There were multiple typos such as "detail-oreinted," "thype 70 wpm," "deals well with any problems the might arouse," and "B.A in slatics." Collin threw one after the other in the trash. "Slatics?" he'd asked incredulously. "That's not even close to 'statistics.' If they can't even spell that correctly, how are they going to come up with entire reports that are error-free?" I'd left his office laughing, glad I wasn't the one sorting through them all. In the end, he'd narrowed it down to five people, all of whom would have interviews with me today. I'd read over all five resumes, but skimmed Mary's again to remind myself of the details.

I walk into the front of the marketing department where two women are sitting and say, "Mary?" Both women look at me. One of them is the rude-looking woman from the elevator. The woman continues to wear her look of disgust. "Are either of you Mary Sorensen?" I ask.

"I am Mary Sor-EN-sen," the woman from the elevator says, putting emphasis on the second syllable of her last name, obviously angry that I had not.

"Are you ready for your interview?" I ask, fairly certain this interview is not necessary. I do not want to work with this woman every single day.

Without answering, Mary stands up and walks toward the hallway of offices. I'm guessing she is in her mid-fifties. She's wearing a white suit with a blue, sparkly scarf and her dark hair falls right below her ears, which display large diamond studs. Her skin, spotty and wrinkled, is more orange than tan. She looks like she rolled in a giant tub of Doritos before coming here. Once in the hallway, she stops and turns around, waiting for me. "Has your boss seen how you look today?" she asks.

Unsure of what to make of this question, I answer, "Yes."

"Well, I think you should know that it's very unprofessional to be at a place of work, such as this, sopping wet. It reflects poorly on the establishment as a whole. You should always look your best when you're representing a company. You should wear makeup and your hair should never look so unkempt. A classy woman never leaves the house without her hair fixed and a nice pair of earrings," she says, giving my naked ears a look of disgust. I'm too taken aback to respond, which Mary takes to mean she should continue. "Also, I heard you speaking so rudely to that young woman in the elevator. Sarcasm doesn't suit you."

I feel like I'm listening to my grandma. "Okay, well I think we're done for today. Thanks for coming in. We'll let you know if you get the position."

She looks confused, but the confusion quickly turns to anger. "Oh, I don't think so. I'm here for an interview. I'll wait here until someone is ready to interview me." I realize this woman doesn't know I'm the one who is supposed to interview her. She must think I'm a secretary or assistant or something.

I laugh and say, "Okay, I'll show you to your seat."

Mary, unsure why I'm laughing, but looking triumphant anyway, follows me to my office and sits down in the chair I point to. I walk behind the desk and sit down. She looks at me with a sneer. "Well?" Mary asks.

"Well . . . ," I reply. I take out the resume and look at it. "It says here that you work well with others. Please tell me more about that."

Mary's expression changes to one of horror. "You're interviewing me? Why are you interviewing me?"

"Because . . . I am the Stat—"

"Statistics Director," she finishes the sentence and immediately flashes an ear to ear smile. "Wow, you are so young. You must be incredibly intelligent to have a position like this at such a young age." Her tone has completely changed. "You'll have to excuse the way I acted. I want what's best for TBC and for my boss so I wanted to help you do your job better, but what do I know? You obviously do your job spectacularly." She lets out an uncomfortable laugh and grins at me. I smile back, but say nothing. I can't help but smile. It's fun watching her try so hard to schmooze her way out of the hole she's dug.

"Ms. Sor-En-sen," I say, overemphasizing the "En" this time. "I appreciate you wanting what's best for TBC. However," I pause, enjoying Mary's disappointed expression. "There are many days I come to work without earrings. Sometimes I only brush my hair and stick it in a ponytail. And once in a while, I don't wear makeup at all. I can only imagine the discomfort and anxiety you'll feel being forced to look at me on those days. So thank you for taking the time to come in today, but we're going to go with one of our other applicants."

Mary's face is a shade somewhere between red and purple. "That's fine," she spits as she scoots her chair out and stands up. "You're going to learn that it's more important to ignore personal biases and go with the person who's most competent. I was the head of statistical analysis for six years at Boston Green. You're not going to find anyone more competent than that at this pay level."

I flash my largest grin and open the door. "It's been a pleasure."

"You are a power-hungry girl who will not make it far, and I plan to talk to your superiors about the lack of professionalism demonstrated during this interview, if you can even call it that!" she fumes. As she speaks, there are spit strings between her lips. Grossed out, I look away.

"Good-bye, Ms. Sorenson," I say while closing my door. Mary continues hollering as she walks down the hallway, but I don't even try to make out what she's saying. I pull out the next resume and prepare for my interview with William Malone.

♡ Chapter 26 ♡

At 4:15 p.m., I head out the door. To say this day has dragged by is an understatement. The morning had inched along slowly as I'd anticipated talking to Owen. However, that was nothing compared to the afternoon. Following my interview with Mary, I met William Malone, who confided in me that he didn't technically have the degree that his resume said he did. He was smart enough, but his advisor had suggested the wrong classes. He insisted I call him "Pack Attack," because that's what everyone called him and then unbuttoned his shirt partway and showed me his "eight-pack" telling me that I could "touch them if I'd like." Then every few minutes, he'd yell "pack attack" and act like he was going to rip his shirt open again. He explained that it was a good way to lighten the mood in the interview. Maybe on another day I would have found it humorous, but today it made me want to stab his abs with my pen. The next two people were very knowledgeable in statistics and would probably do the job very well, but back to back, they were the two most boring interviews I could imagine. I was having a hard time staying focused anyway. I was freezing cold from getting so wet, dreading the fact that I'd have to see Luke tomorrow night, and worrying about how things had gone with Owen earlier. When it was finally time for my last interview, I was burnt out. Collin came in and told me that we'd have to reschedule because of some crisis with the man's daughter. I was thrilled, not thrilled there was a crisis, but happy that it was getting me out of another interview right then. After Collin stared at me for several seconds, he'd told me to go ahead and go home. I must have looked as bad as I felt. Without any hesitation, I grabbed my stuff, thanked Collin, and headed for the elevator.

As I walk down the hall, I can hear an obviously irate woman yelling. I quickly identify the voice as Mary Sorensen's. *This woman does not give up.* Without hesitation, I turn around and head for the stairs, but don't seem to be getting any farther from the voice. "The amount of disrespect I was shown was unfathomable. I will not tolerate this and TBC should not tolerate this. Is that how you want to be represented?" Someone responded, but I couldn't hear what was said. Her rant continued, "I've been trying to talk to someone in charge all afternoon. I keep getting passed around from office to office, with empty promises that Ms. Easton will be talked to. I certainly hope you're the one who's actually going to take action against her." The mention of my name makes me pick up my pace to try to get to the stairs before being spotted. I'm not in the mood to try to deal with her. "There, that's her." I keep walking, my back to Mary and whomever she's talking to, and act as if I've heard nothing. "This is the perfect example. Here it is, barely past four o'clock and she's leaving for the day. I think TBC expects a little more ambition out of their employees, don't you, Mr. Denny?"

Mr. Denny? My stomach is in my throat and my cheeks are on fire. How in the world has he been roped into dealing with this? I turn around. There stands Mary with her boney, wrinkled finger pointed at me, a look on her face like she's eaten a lemon. Next to her is Owen. I offer a weak smile, but Owen stares at me, his expression making me wonder if he's been awake for a week straight. He turns to Mary and motions for her to walk back from where they'd come. "Ms. Sorensen, I'm sorry that your experience with TBC was not a positive one. However, Miss Easton is a fantastic employee. She is incredibly hard-working, and the time of day that she leaves is no indication of her level of ambition."

Before he finishes his sentence, Mary is marching toward me. She pokes the front of my shoulder and puts her nose less than an inch away from mine. "You may use short skirts and cat walks to get the males in this office on your side, but I can see right through you." I glance down at my pencil skirt which falls just below my knees. *Short skirts and cat walks?* I raise my eyebrows, but she continues, "I can assure you that I—"

"Ms. Sorensen, it's time for you to leave." Owen declares with an authoritative tone I've never heard him use.

"Not until I'm through, it's not," she replies, maintaining her icy glare at me.

"Yes, I need security on the ninth floor," Owen says into his cell. "We're right beside the elevators."

"You called security on *me?*" Mary glowers. "I've never been treated so poorly in my life." She marches to the elevators.

Owen looks back at me for several seconds. I try to think of words that will explain my awkwardness earlier. There is a strange expression on his face that I can't make out. Disappointment? Sadness? He interrupts my thoughts by saying, "I'm going to make sure she finds her way out of this building."

I nod and mouth, "thank you." Owen nods back before turning around to follow the Dorito-colored woman.

* * *

I ignore speed limits as I drive to my parents' house. For Will to send something as large and attention-grabbing as this giant envelope, he must have a good reason. I'm anxious to get it into Eva's hands and find out what it contains. I turn my heater on as high as it will go and finally start to warm up. Even though it's been hours since I've been in the rain, I'm still damp and chilled. My entire body feels like a giant prune.

As I drive, the rain pounds harder. I park my car in the driveway and run to the door. I'm soaked all over again. I open the door and yell, "Eva!"

"Wow, you look like a little ray of sunshine today," Eva says as she comes around the corner smiling. "What's wrong?"

I try to lighten my expression as I say, "Nothing, it's just been a long day." Then I pull the envelope and letter out. "I went to the bank today."

Eva gasps with excitement and grabs me in a hug. "That whole thing is from Will?"

"Yeah, the whole giant envelope that doesn't fit in my purse, it's from Will," I mumble. "I didn't know I was going to need to bring a hobo bag to fit Will's messages." Eva's sitting on the couch poring over the letter. "What's in the envelope, Eva?"

"Hold on," Eva responds, holding up the letter. Frustrated and more impatient, I sit down next to Eva. "Juliet, you probably shouldn't sit there. You're getting the sofa all wet," Eva says without looking up from her letter. I sigh as loud as I can and stand up. Eva continues reading, smiling and laughing as she does so. After several minutes she folds the letter back up and holds it to her heart. I'm disgusted. I can't believe people actually do sentimental stuff like that and now she seems lost in a daydream.

"Eva, what's in the envelope?" I ask, letting my frustration come through in my tone.

"Why are you so impatient?" Eva responds, sounding equally frustrated.

"I want to see what's so important that he sent that big ol' envelope."

"Fine, I'm opening it," Eva grunts. She pulls out a picture of some scenic place, with a frame I'm guessing Will made. It has that home-made look. Eva stares at it for a few seconds. I look closer and see it's a picture of a decorative park bench among a bunch of trees. Will and Eva must have gone there for a date or something. Eva's pulling more stuff out of the envelope. It's a whole bunch of papers.

"What is all of that?" I ask.

"Well this," Eva starts, holding up a paper, "is the menu from the restaurant where you and I were eating when we met Will. And this," she says, holding up another, "is a ticket to Six-Flags that we went to for . . ." Eva continues talking, but I'm not listening anymore.

"So it's a bunch of nostalgic junk?" I immediately regret calling it junk. "I don't mean that, Eva. I know it's not junk. I just mean that I went to the bank expecting the typical letter so all I had was my purse. It wouldn't fit in my purse. And then I saw Owen. He was being so nice to me and then he tried to grab the envelope so I had to pull it away." I know I'm rambling, but it feels good to complain out loud. "Then he was upset with me. I think he thought I was saying 'no' to going to lunch with him, but I wasn't. I just didn't want him to see the stupid envelope since you say we can't trust anybody." I stop myself when I realize I'm yelling. I know the majority of what I said makes no sense to Eva. After I offended Owen this afternoon, I convinced myself that it was okay because whatever was in the envelope was really important. Maybe Will had found a way to prove that P&L was dirty and expose those responsible. Maybe he was coming out of hiding. Maybe me getting the envelope was going to change everything. Instead, it's old menus and tickets he saved.

I look up when I realize Eva's crying. She picks up the papers and walks out of the room. I can hear her go up the stairs and shut her bedroom door. I start to follow her up the stairs when Mom comes out of the kitchen and grabs my hand. "Give her a few minutes." I let Mom pull me into the kitchen. She heats water and gets out boxes of herbal tea. "I'm sorry you had such a lousy day. What happened?"

I look up at Mom. I open my mouth to speak, but there's a big lump in my throat. I'm not going to let myself cry over something so silly. I close my mouth and shake my head. Mom nods. I love that about her. She isn't pushy. She knows I don't feel like talking about today so she drops it. "Do you feel like Bengal Spice or Orange Zest?" Mom asks, opening tea boxes.

"Bengal Spice," I answer quietly. "Thanks, Mom." I quickly wipe away a tear I feel rolling down my check. Mom puts her hand on mine and pats it.

More tears are coming, but I fight them back as I hear the doorbell. While Mom goes to the door, I grab a tissue and wipe my nose. There's a man's voice, but I can't tell what's being said. Mom says something, but she's barely talking above a whisper. I move toward the kitchen door to see if I can make out any of the conversation. "I only want to talk to her," I hear the man say and instantly recognize the voice.

"Right now is not a good time. If you want to talk to her, call her. How did you know where she was or how to get here?" Mom's voice is a mix of irritation and confusion.

"She told me she'd be here. Please, just let me talk to her. It's important."

I head to the front door. I can see Luke trying to push his way into the house. "Luke, what are you doing here?" I ask, my voice giving away my frustration.

"I told you before. I need to talk to you." With that, he shoves my mom aside and walks over to me.

"Yeah . . . and we decided we'd talk tomorrow night. Remember, you're going to come over around seven?"

Luke glances nervously around the room. He leans back and peers into the kitchen. "I know, I know, but I could tell that you were upset about something. Then you said you were coming out here so I thought maybe you were upset about some family thing. I wanted to make sure you were okay. Are you okay? If there's something going on that you want to talk about, you can talk to me."

"I'm fine. Nothing's going on. However, if it were, what's going on between my family and me is between *my family and me*." I walk back to the front door, hinting at Luke to leave. He doesn't follow. He stays in the hallway and glances at the stairs. I continue, "How did you know how to get here?"

"Oh, ah, the Internet."

I shake my head, disgusted by the complete invasion of privacy and he doesn't even seem embarrassed about it. He had to dig pretty deep to find my parents' address. Since they'd moved here in an effort to give Eva somewhere safe, the address wasn't just in the yellow pages. "I'll talk to you tomorrow, Luke." I open the door and motion for him to leave.

"I thought you were hanging out with Eva tonight," he says, slowly walking toward the door.

"Um, no, I said I was going to my parents' house."

"Oh, well I guess I figured since she lives here . . ." he says, trailing off.

"Yeah, but she's busy," I answer briskly, trying to force the door shut while Luke is still in the doorway.

He reaches out and grabs my hand. "Please stop being mad at me. I miss you."

"I'll see you tomorrow, Luke," I say before pushing the door shut. I can't believe he came all the way out here to try to talk to me. As soon as I started avoiding him, he became ten times more interested in me. I look out the windows in the door and shut off the front entry light so Luke won't be able to see me peeking out. I watch him get into his car and drive away.

I walk back into the kitchen and take a sip of my tea. It burns my mouth. I set it down and walk up to Eva's room. Surprised to find the door unlocked, I go in without knocking. Eva's lying on her bed, staring at the framed picture from Will. "Eva, I'm sorry," I start, sitting on the edge of the bed. "I can't even imagine what it must be like to not be able to see Will, to know he's living a life somewhere that you can't know anything about. I know his letters and this stuff is important. I really didn't mean to call it 'junk.' I'm sorry."

"It's okay. It is junk, but the 'nostalgic junk' is all I have right now." She continues to stare at the photo as she talks. "I really don't understand why he sent me all this stuff though. It doesn't make any sense." She turns the photo over and starts prying it out of the frame.

I don't want to push her by questioning further. I watch as she takes the photo out and looks at the back of it. I keep watching her with an inquisitive expression. She glances up and, seeing my face, holds the back of the photo in front of me. It has advertisements for businesses in Eden Falls. Will must have cut the photo out of some Eden Falls magazine. At the bottom of the page, written in Will's chicken scratch, are the words, "You'd love this park." I look at Eva, wondering what the significance of this park is if she's never even been there. Eva stares back. "So," I question, "you've never been to this park? I don't get it. Why did he frame a picture of a place that means nothing to either one of you?"

"I don't know yet," Eva answers. "All of this other stuff is somehow significant, but I don't remember ever even seeing this park. It must be somewhere in Eden Falls, but I don't know why he went to the trouble of framing it."

"For him to write 'you'd love this park' so cryptically on the back of the picture, he must have a good reason for you to go there." Eva nods, deep in thought. "Or maybe," I continue, "he's been in hiding for so long, he's forgotten how to communicate like a normal person." Eva continues staring blankly at the picture, ignoring my comment.

"Okay, let's go find this park," Eva says as she jumps off the bed.

"Right now?"

"Yes. He wants me to find this park bench so I'm going to find it."

"Eva, it's pitch black outside."

"That's even better. I'm harder to follow that way." Eva's already heading for the stairs.

"It's pouring out there. Let's wait 'til tomorrow. Maybe we can figure out why he wants you to go there. Let's look through everything he sent." I can hear Eva running down the stairs and know she's not listening to a word I say. I pick up the mess of papers from the envelope and glance over the menu from the night Eva and I met Will. A wave of sadness rushes over me as I think about how much everything has changed since that night. I pull out another paper; a playbill from Wicked. Will and Eva went to New York together for a few days and that's where Will proposed. My eyes are drawn to the bottom of the playbill where Will wrote, "Day of the week?" I set it aside and start looking through the other papers. There's an ad for Home Depot that has Will's writing on the top, "What time?" I keep looking through to find any other papers that have his writing on them, while running to the stairs.

"Eva, there's more! Come back," I yell.

"Really?" Eva appears at the base of the stairs.

"Really."

As Eva climbs the stairs, I find another piece of paper with Will's writing on it. Eva combs through everything again, assuming she'll catch something I missed, but there aren't any others. She stares at the Home Depot ad for a second and then says, "two o'clock."

"But what does that mean? Why is he asking the time? Why two o'clock?"

"I'm not sure yet, but I know that's what he means. We were supposed to meet at Home Depot at two o'clock to look at tile for the new kitchen, but I was really, really late. There had been this spider that was the size of a quarter on my steering wheel and I didn't want to get anywhere near it. I waited outside my car until the vice-principal, who was parked next to me, came out of the building and took care of it." Eva grimaced. "Anyway, Will always brought it up. Anytime I was supposed to be anywhere, he'd make some joke about a spider."

The other paper I found is apparently something from Will's twenty-sixth birthday and Eva says they went to Wicked on a Friday. I stare at the papers for a minute to try to piece everything together. "So, he wants you at that park on Friday, the twenty-sixth at two o'clock?"

"Is the twenty-sixth a Friday?" Eva asks.

I check the calendar on my phone before nodding. "Why is he being so coded? Why couldn't he just write "I need you to go to this park on Friday, the twenty-sixth, at two" in the letter?

"I'm sure he's trying to be careful. What if the wrong person got a hold of this stuff?" Eva answers, a look of excitement spreading across her face.

"Hold on," I reply, as I answer my ringing phone.

"Jules, where are you?" Everett's voice is desperate. It's barely above a whisper, but I can tell he's angry.

"I'm at Mom and Dad's. What's wrong, Ev?"

"You need to come back here now."

"Where's here? The apartment?"

"Yes. Hurry up," he pleads before hanging up.

Eva picks up where she left off the minute I set my phone down. "Maybe he's going to be there. Maybe all the secrecy is about to be over. I bet he finally found something concrete and he's about to expose P&L." I nod, not feeling nearly as optimistic about the situation as Eva.

"I've got to go. Something's up with Everett. He wants me to hurry and meet him at the apartment."

"He's probably worried you're not making him dinner," Eva says with a smile.

"Yeah, probably," I say, not wanting to alarm Eva, but worried it's much more than that.

I call Everett as I drive, but he's not answering. The heavy rain has cars crawling along the freeway at thirty miles per hour. I tap my foot against the gas pedal, picturing an extra lane opening up and me flooring it. Instead, I move along slowly as tension builds up inside me.

I finally make it home and fumble with my keys until I find the right one to unlock the apartment door. When I open it, a knot takes hold of the pit of my stomach. I stare in disbelief. Our apartment is completely torn apart. The couch is upturned. What was once Everett's beautiful, dark leather sofa, is now only the skeleton with stuffing covering the living room floor. Every cupboard is open with its contents thrown haphazardly around the room. Even one of the lights above the kitchen table is shattered. I carefully move toward the hallway and see that my room looks like the living room. My bed is torn apart. My dresser's empty. I didn't own much, but the few precious possessions I had are destroyed or missing. Everett appears in my doorway.

"I don't believe this," I whisper.

"It has to be about the flash drive, right? Was it here?"

I shake my head and motion toward my purse.

"Good," he says.

"How would anyone know about that? I haven't said a word to anybody besides you and Eva."

"I don't know, but we need to call the police before we erase any evidence that may be here." I follow him to the front room where he calls and reports a break-in. Tears prick the underside of my eyelids, but I try my best to hold them back. Everett's lost a lot more than I have tonight. If he can hold it together, so can I.

We spend all evening and a good part of the night talking to police and then making trips to the dumpster. We get my sofa out of the storage unit and Everett lends me a sleeping bag to use until I can buy a new mattress and bedding.

"If this is about the drive, then do you think they'll come back?" I ask Everett as we're cleaning up the last of the mess in the kitchen.

"Maybe, but they know it's not here. Now they'll go after our cars or us." He looks at me and seeing my horrified look says, "Or not. It may not even be about that. It could be unrelated."

"Uh huh," I say, my mind busy thinking how I'm never going anywhere alone ever again. My peace of mind has been shattered into oblivion.

♡ Chapter 27 ♡

The following evening Everett strolls into the kitchen, gym bag in one hand, an apple in the other. He looks like an ad for vitamin supplements. "All right, I'm ready," he says between bites of his apple. "Let's go."

"I can't go yet," I reply. "I told you seven thirty."

"Why seven thirty? Aren't you ready now?"

"Go for a run outside and when you get back, I'll be ready to go."

"Okay. What's the big secret? Why can't we go now?"

"There's no big secret. Luke is coming over and I told him I wasn't leaving until seven thirty."

"Are you serious?" Everett asks. "You plan on letting Luke come in here? I *do not* want that guy in here."

"I know. I figured it was better here than somewhere else though and I—"

"Why does it have to be anywhere? Just quit seeing him." Everett's nostrils are flaring and the veins in his neck are popping out. "I don't want him around you. C'mon, Jules, you're smarter than this."

"Ev, stop. He's been following me around, begging me to talk to him."

"Is that supposed to be an argument in favor of him coming over tonight? He's been following you around?"

"I told him he could have thirty minutes. That's all."

"Okay. Well I'm going to be here," he states, dropping his gym bag and sitting on the sofa. "After the stuff I've heard about him, there's no way I'm leaving him alone in my apartment with my little sister."

"What do you mean? Have you heard stuff other than what I've told you? Or are you talking about seeing him beat that guy up?"

"I don't know a lot. I just know I don't want him anywhere near you."

"I want to know what you've heard, Everett." I sound whiny, but the fact that Everett knows things about Luke and hasn't told me makes me feel betrayed.

"All I know is the little bit Owen told me. Owen had a really close friend. His name was Kyle or something." Everett swallows his last bite of apple and throws the core at the garbage. When it goes in, he throws his hands up in the air.

"Okay, Owen's friend Kyle," I prompt him to continue.

"No, actually I think his name was Paul."

"Anyway," I nod. I'm on pins and needles waiting to hear this story and Everett is taking his sweet time telling it.

"Anyway, they grew up together and this Paul guy came from a lot of money. I guess Paul kind of went off the deep end as he got older. He spent all of his time with a new group of guys and was always either drunk or high. One of those new guys was Luke. Pretty soon, Paul dropped out of college. He, Luke, and a couple of others had been drinking way too much and decided to try and make some crazy jump with motorcycles. Paul didn't clear the jump and was killed on impact. Luke and the other two guys didn't even call the family. They took his credit cards and spent the next few weeks living off of them until they were caught."

I sit down in the nearest chair. All of this shady stuff about Luke is getting old. This story brings it to a whole new level. He's heartless. However, I have no trouble believing any of it. I trust Owen a whole lot more than I trust Luke. "So, what happened? He must have gone to jail, right? How did he get out? How did the family find out about everything?"

Everett shakes his head. "I don't know. Owen didn't say. He said he hadn't seen Luke since then and wasn't even sure Luke remembered him."

"I'm going to ask him about it. I've been dating someone that he knew was a felon and he didn't feel it was important to tell me?"

"Would you have believed him? You thought Owen was as untrustworthy as they come. Besides, I think he was trying to give Luke the benefit of the doubt, in case he really had changed. He didn't tell me that he knew Luke until the night we saw him beating up on that guy. By that time, you told us that you and Luke weren't together. You acted like you'd already figured out what a jerk he was. I didn't think I would ever have to worry about you telling me he was coming over to this apartment again."

"I was just letting him come up so he could say what he had to say and leave me alone, but now I'm not going to let him in."

"Or, you could have Owen here when he comes over."

I feel a surge of excitement as I think about Owen coming over. "Yeah, that could work, except Luke will be here any second."

"I'm kidding, Jules. Owen's gone. He left yesterday."

My stomach falls. I try to act nonchalant as I ask, "Left where?"

"He had some family thing going on. I'm not really sure," Everett replies, focused on the TV. I nod. I hate the way things ended with us yesterday. All day today I hoped I would run into him at work and everything would be back to normal. When the day passed without any sign of him, I hoped he'd be going to the gym with us tonight.

I'm startled by a quick knock on the door followed by Luke letting himself in. "Hey, ooh . . . you look good."

"Thanks," Everett interjects. "I think these shorts really emphasize my calf muscles."

Luke looks surprised as he turns toward the sofa and sees Everett. He gives Everett a slight nod and then turns to me. "Is there somewhere we can go where we'll be alone?"

"You can go home and be alone," I reply. When Luke stares at me seemingly confused, I add, "No, I'm not going anywhere."

"Okay, this works," he sighs, sitting down at the table. "Did you guys buy a new sofa?

"Uh, yeah." I nod, not wanting to explain that it was my sofa that had been in storage and we needed it because our other one was destroyed by people who had ransacked our apartment.

"How are you doing?"

"Great," I answer half-heartedly. He's the last person I want to be sitting her talking with right now. He fidgets awkwardly. I can't remember ever seeing him act awkward and I'm enjoying it.

He scoots his chair closer to me and leans in. Then in a whisper he says, "Look, I'm really sorry about the other night. I should have stayed right next to you at the club."

"That's what you want to talk about? Luke, I didn't expect you to stay right next to me. It would have been nice if you had—" I stop myself. "No, actually Luke, I don't want to get into that again. It doesn't matter. The more I get to know you, the more reasons I find that you and I will never happen."

"What? What does that even mean?" Luke's eyes are wide. He looks like I just told him I'm moving to Nepal and becoming a Sherpa. Can he really be confused by me not wanting to date him?

"Okay, like why were you beating some guy senseless the other night?"

"HE TOOK MY PARKING SPOT!" Luke bellows, his face reddening. "It says on the asphalt '207,' but he parked there anyway." He lowers his voice again. "You had just gotten mad at me and I was really upset. I started driving around trying to find you and when I got back, that dude looked right at me and pulled into my spot."

I stare at him, waiting for more of an explanation, but he stares right back, obviously feeling like he's provided more than an adequate explanation.

"So you started beating on him?"

Luke opens his eyes wider, giving me an expression that says, "Of course."

I let out a loud sigh and put my head in my hands. "That honestly makes me feel sick, Luke. You and I are such different people. Can you please stop trying to make amends and realize that we're done?"

"Yeah, fine," he grumbles. He pushes his chair back from the table and it falls on its back. He ignores it as he walks to the door and slams it behind him.

"That was easier than I thought," I say, more to myself than to Everett.

"Nice job, Jules." Everett shuts off the TV and grabs his bag again. He walks to me and puts his arm around my shoulders. "I seriously hate that guy."

I hug him. "I'll be ready to go in five minutes," I say, leaving to get my workout clothes.

♡ Chapter 28 ♡

Do you want to get that?" Collin asks, motioning to my phone that's vibrating behind me.

"Nah, that's all right," I respond, opening a desk drawer and dropping it inside. I'm explaining the results of a report I've been working on and I'm ninety-nine percent sure it's Luke calling. Less than a minute later, I hear it vibrating again.

"Juliet, it's fine. I'll finish up some stuff in my office and you answer your phone," Collin says, running his hand through his hair. He's wearing a button-up shirt that's undone a couple buttons too many, allowing some silver chest hair to show. He straightens the collar on his shirt as he waits for my reply.

"No, no really, I don't want to answer it. Let's finish this."

"Okay," he replies skeptically.

"It's just this guy that keeps calling and texting. I don't want to talk to him."

"Oh yeah? Mad at the boyfriend?"

I shake my head. "We broke up weeks ago and I haven't talked to him in days, but he will not stop with the calls, voicemails, and texts."

"Do you want to block him?' He asks. Before I've responded, he grabs my computer and is asking for my login information on my Verizon account. I take the keyboard back and put it on my lap where he can't see it. I smile at him as I type my info. Collin seems nice enough, but I'm not feeling trusting of people lately. I return the keyboard and scoot in next to him so we can both see the computer screen. He's leaning across me to open the drawer I dropped my phone into when Lila opens the door.

She looks at us with a big grin on her face. "Well, don't you two look cozy?"

Collin stands up, "Hey, Miss Bradley." Then he turns to me and points to a tab on the webpage. "Anyway, go there, enter his number, and that's all." As he leaves he says, "I'll see you two later."

"Collin, you can stay," I say as I try to tell him with my eyes that he can't go because I don't want to spend time alone with Lila. Apparently it's too much of a message for my eyes to convey it properly. He waves and continues out the door.

Lila shuts the door behind him. "Trying to dip into the workplace pool again, huh? What would that beautiful boyfriend of yours have to say?"

"It's always a treat to see you, Lila. What do you need?"

"Whoa, I caught somebody on a bad day. I was only coming down here to catch up. It's been a couple of weeks since I got to talk to you." I eye her inquisitively and wonder what kind of game she's up to. "Okay, honestly I miss Owen so much and I need to talk to someone about it." I type Luke's number on the computer and push, "block number." When Lila gets no response from me, she continues, "He's my soul mate, you know? We normally have a hard time making it through the work day without seeing each other, but it's been ten days. Even when we were little, we saw each other nearly every day."

This piques my interest. I've never heard much about Owen's past. "Really?" I don't want to sound overly eager for

Lila to tell me more, but I *am* interested in how they know each other.

"Yeah," Lila says, rolling her eyes. Now I feel dumb for giving her any response at all. "Owen practically lived at our house," she continues condescendingly. "And he's been in love with me for as long as I can remember." She pauses, taking a moment to look me up and down. "So, you haven't heard from him, have you?" she asks, trying to act nonchalant, but not succeeding. "I mean, for work stuff or something or has he called Everett?" I stare directly at her, but say nothing. She starts rambling, "Not that it matters or anything. He's called me several times, but we can't seem to connect. In fact this morning he called me four times while I was at the gym. I was busy on the elliptical and didn't notice my phone. You know how demanding cardio can be." She stops long enough to make a statement by sneering at me and then says, "No, I guess not, but I get so intense that I can't bother with my phone. It's important for me to keep my heart rate up for optimum fat burn . . ." She continues talking while I type information into a spreadsheet. I repeat the lyrics of Simon and Garfunkel's *I am a Rock* in my head to tune her out.

". . . and all of this talking about him is making me miss him so much more. I'm going to go ahead and give him a call."

Now I'm listening. Lila pushes a couple of buttons on her phone and stares at me with a big grin on her face. She sticks her lips out in a pout and whines, "Oh, he must be away from his phone. He always answers when I call. I guess we'll have to leave him a voicem—Owen! Hey, hon, I'm sitting here thinking about you and missing you. This morning I had a frittata and it reminded me of that weekend we had in Italy." Lila laughs into the phone, while glancing at me to get a reaction. "Oh we had some fun, didn't we? Anyway, I'm here with Juliet and we wanted to say 'hi.' She was nice enough to stop throwing herself all over her new man for a few minutes so that we could call you." My face burns and I envision throwing my stapler at her. I take several deep breaths as she continues, "I'm pretty sure we need to talk to Daddy about his policies on PDA in the workplace because Juliet was breaking all of them this morning. Although it is Juliet and you know her, she'll be on to someone new next week so maybe we shouldn't worry." She smiles at me like we're best friends and this teasing is just part of our thing. "Call me when you get this. Oh, and Juliet says to tell you 'hey.'" She gives me a thumbs up. "I love you, Christopher Owen Denny." Lila hangs up the phone and smirks at me. Although I'm frustrated, I'm not going to give her the satisfaction of knowing it. I know she's trying to get under my skin and I hope Owen is smart enough to know that nothing she says has any substance to it. He's the one that told me to never believe anything Lila said.

"Feel better now?" I ask.

"Yes, actually I do," she responds, maintaining her smirk. It really helps to talk to you about him."

"His first name is Christopher?" I ask and instantly regret it. The words are out before I think about who I'm asking.

"Yes, his first name is Christopher." Lila rolls her eyes. "He's named after his dad so he started going by his middle name after his dad turned out to be such a loser. Man, you really don't know him well, do you?"

My cell phone vibrates as Lila talks and I can see that it's Grandma. As much as I don't want to talk to her right now, it's the perfect reason to make Lila leave. "I have to take this," I say.

"I can wait," Lila counters.

"No, it may be a while. You need to go."

"Why? Who is it?"

"It doesn't matter," I reply, pushing Lila toward the door. "Hey," I answer the phone. "Hold on one sec, kay." Then I turn back to Lila, "Bye, Lila."

"Who is it, Juliet?"

I know Lila's thinking it could be Owen and I love how frustrated she looks. I grin at Lila and say, "I'll see you later." Lila spins around angrily and heads toward the door. I put my phone back up to my ear and say, "Hey, sorry about that."

"JULIET EASTON, YOU DON'T EVER TREAT YOUR GRANDMOTHER LIKE THAT AGAIN!" Grandma's voice booms through the phone.

"Sorry," I respond, not wanting to say anything that might prove I'm not talking to Owen. There's a good chance Lila's still waiting outside my door trying to hear every word.

"You don't sound very sorry! It's incredibly rude to answer a phone call by telling me to 'hold on one sec' without giving me a chance to speak. What if I couldn't hold on one sec? And since when is *sec* a word?"

"I'm at work and I was in the middle of talking to someone."

"Was it a boy?" There is no anger in her voice now, only excitement.

"Um, no."

"Well, that's why I'm calling. I've found you a wonderful man and you're going out with him on Saturday. I know you're going to argue, but this one is a keeper. I met him at lunch at the club yesterday. His mother was wearing the most stunning pant suit and she told me that he'd picked it out for her. Can you imagine? Not only does he have fashion sense, he also has a successful career in finance. He worked as a consultant for IWP for almost thirty years and now he's their CFO. He has a cat named Chips and he loves t—"

"For almost thirty years?" I interrupt. "How old is this guy?"

"Fifty-two and as I was saying, he loves something called geo-caching. It's really quite fascinating. You see you find th—"

"Fifty-two?"

"Juliet, stop interrupting me! This is why you're still single. Age isn't important anymore. All sorts of young girls marry older, more sophisticated men. You're going out with him on Saturday. He'll be at your place at six-thirty."

"I already have plans," I lie.

"Then cancel them and please remember to wear pantyhose. I don't want you to run him off by giving him the wrong impression. He's looking for a good, wholesome girl."

"I'm sorry, Grandma, but I really can't do it on Saturday." There's nothing but silence on the other end. I look at my phone and realize Grandma hung up on me. I lean back in the chair and sigh. As often as Grandma bugs me about not being married, I'm unfazed by the phone call. I'm not going to go and that's that. What is eating at me is Lila's call to Owen. I've spent the last week forcing all thoughts of Owen from my mind. He left without telling me so he must be wanting some time to himself. Has he really been calling Lila or did she make that up to upset me? I think of the voicemail Lila left him and hate the thought of him hearing that I'm with some new guy. I wonder if he has any feelings for me at this point. While trying to remember every word of Lila's voicemail to decide if it was *that* bad, I scroll down to Owen's name and push "send."

As it rings, I have an inner battle. What am I doing? *He* is the one who left without telling me where he was going and how long he'd be gone. *He* is the one who's practically engaged to someone else. But, I'm so excited at the thought of talking to him that I let it ring. Besides, it hasn't been all that long ago that he told me how much he cared about me. I replay the words he used the night he told me that I was all he could think about. His voice interrupts my thoughts as he says to leave a voicemail. I freeze. I haven't actually thought about what I'm going to say. "Hey, Owen. It's Juliet." I feel that all too familiar ache in my chest as I say his name. "I really want to talk to you. It feels like you've been gone forever." I stop talking and try to regroup my thoughts before I get too sentimental. "About Lila's call earlier, it was ridiculous. She came into my office while I was talking to Collin and decided there was something going on between us, which of course, there isn't. I don't want you to think any part of what she said is true. There is no new guy every week." I pause again, unsure of where I'm trying to go with this message. "Also, I'm sorry for the way things went that last day I saw you." Bringing that up makes me feel awkward so I switch topics. "I ended things with Luke. I wish you would have told me you knew him. You should have told me what a jerk he was. Okay, this is getting to be a really long message so I'm going to go now. I miss you." Those last three words slip out before I even realize what I'm saying so I hang up quickly, feeling silly.

♡ Chapter 29 ♡

Friday, the 26th

wake to a knock on my door. "Jules," comes Everett's voice. "Your phone has been vibrating all morning. Do you want it?"

It takes me a couple of seconds to process what Everett said. "Oh, yeah, thanks."

He opens my door and sets my phone on the nightstand. "You left it in the kitchen and it's been going off ever since I woke up an hour ago. Someone's really trying to get ahold of you."

"Thanks, Ev," I mumble groggily. "What time is it?" I ask, squinting to make out the numbers on the clock, but they're still blurry.

"Six-thirty-two. I need to get to work early today. Remember to call me as soon as you guys leave the park. See ya." He rushes out the door. I grab my phone and anxiously look at the screen. A surge of excitement passes through me as I check to see if Owen called. It's been three days since I called him and I have yet to hear back. I blink several times so I can see the screen more clearly. It shows one missed call and two texts, all from a number I don't recognize.

"Don't go today" reads the first text. The second text, sent thirty-five minutes after the first, says, "Julie, don't go. It's dangerous." My breath catches in my throat. I jump out of bed and try to decide what I should do next. There's only one person who ever called me Julie, but why would he send Eva coded messages to go to the park and then text me saying not to go to the park? I stare at the number for several seconds before calling it. It's been disconnected. I check the times of the texts and missed call again. I received the last one just twelve minutes ago. Glancing at the clock again as I call Eva, I decide it doesn't matter if I wake her up.

I try to tell Eva about the texts without actually saying anything over the phone about Will or the park. "We have new lunch plans," I explain. She doesn't get what I'm implying.

"I'll be to your place in thirty minutes, Jules. I'll talk to you then.'"

I sit cross-legged on my sleeping bag, nervously clicking a pen until Eva walks in. We spend the better part of an hour arguing about whether or not we should go to the park. "He sent me texts begging me to stop you from going there. He must have a good reason."

"Well he spent a lot of time making clues for me so that I could decode a message telling me I *should* go there," she argues.

"Something must have changed, Eva."

"Either way, if there's a chance he's going to be there, I'm going to be there too. Please don't take this away from me. You don't have to go, Juliet. I'll just go."

"I'm not letting you go by yourself."

This went on and on without either one of us willing to compromise. Eva must have walked at least three miles pacing back and forth in my bedroom. "I've got to leave for work. I'm already going to be late," I groan. Trying to come up with a scenario that will make Eva happy, I settle on, "Okay, we'll go to the park, but not anywhere near that bench. We'll stay in the car and watch from there."

"Yes!" Eva squeals. "That's all I want. Unless I see Will. Then I get to get out." I shake my head, but say nothing. I know this is a terrible idea.

Eva's waiting next to my desk half an hour before we're supposed to leave. She's wearing some white skinny jeans I've never seen before and her hair is in perfect waves. I know she's picturing a sweet reunion with Will and I'm sure she's been planning what she was going to wear for at least two weeks.

She's silent as we drive to the park, but she has an ear to ear smile. The closer we get, the worse I feel. Will specifically asked me to not do this. By the time we get to the north side of the park, the little voice in my head that's been telling me to turn around has turned into a fog horn screaming at me to get Eva away from here. She sets her hand on my arm, "Thanks, Jules." I turn left and head toward the small road that winds around the edge of the park. I tighten my grip on the steering wheel to stop the shaking in my arms. "Stop," Eva yells. "That's the bench. Let's park here so we can watch it."

"I'm not parking right out in the open. We might as well march out there and sit on the bench." I continue on. "Eva, look at those guys by that rock over there. They keep watching us."

"They do not, Juliet. You're trying to find a reason to be scared."

"I'm serious, Eva." A dark-haired female jogs past the bench and two more guys show up from behind the bushes. "We're getting out of here. Something's not right."

"No. Turn around. Juliet, turn around!" Eva's yelling in my ear, but my mind is made up. We shouldn't be anywhere near this place right now. I hold the lock button down just in case Eva's thinking about doing something crazy.

"Juliet, it's not even two o'clock yet. Those people are just hanging out in the park! Turn around."

As soon as we're out of sight, I slam my foot down on the gas pedal and head for the main road. Eva's screams turn into silent tears. I'm pretty sure she's not going to speak to me for years, but I don't care. Something was off. I could feel it.

Instead of going back to TBC, I pull in to Sadie's for some blueberry pancakes. I don't want Eva to have her car yet. I'm afraid she'll speed straight back to the park. "I'm sorry, Eva. I really am. I want you to see Will too, but not like that. I don't even think Will was there. I can't let something happen to you." Eva's wide eyes lock on mine for several seconds. "I haven't eaten all day and I doubt you have either. Let's go get something." I get out, not sure if Eva will follow. As I'm walking through the main door of Sadie's, Eva gets out of the car.

I sit at our favorite corner booth. Eva begrudgingly joins me, though she sits as far from me as possible while still being in the booth.

"There are two of my favorite people," Sadie says as she approaches our table. Her apron is covered in little painted handprints of kids from the preschool down the street. Sadie is a sort of mother to the majority of the community. "Can I get you girls some pie? I whipped up a strawberry rhubarb this morning."

"Hey, Sadie, I'm sure it's delicious, but we're not really in the mood for pie today," I answer. "Can we get some blueberry pancakes instead?"

"I'm not in the mood for blueberry pancakes either," Eva grumbles.

"That's good, because we're all out," Sadie says, putting an arm around Eva's shoulders and squeezing.

"Is there anything that sounds good to you right now, Eva?" I ask.

She sighs as she nods. "Yes, going to the park."

"I mean, foodwise."

She softens a bit. "I don't think so."

"I know," Sadie answers with a grin, her plump, rosy cheeks and white hair reminding me why I used to think she was Mrs. Claus. "One of the girls in the back made some delicious pumpernickel bagels this morning. You'll love them."

I look at Eva.

"I'm going to grab you each one before they're gone," Sadie says. "Don't worry, they're on the house. I can tell my little Miss Eva needs some cheering up. Baked goods always do the trick." She's gone before we can say anything.

I set my hand on Eva's. She watches me with sad eyes before pulling her hand back. "How long will this drag on?" She asks. "I said good-bye over two years ago, and I was upset that he'd be gone a few weeks. Now I wonder if I'll ever see him again."

"Oh my, you girls are going to love these," Sadie swoons, setting down a basket with two bagels inside. She hands me a couple silver packets. "I hope you don't mind fat-free cream cheese. We're all out of the other stuff."

"Not at all. Thank you, Sadie. These smell amazing," I say as I tear open the cream cheese and spread it on. She smiles and walks away.

Eva eyes her silver packet warily. "I can't do it. I hate that stuff."

"Cream cheese? You do not. C'mon, food might help you feel better."

"No, I like cream cheese. It's fat-free that I hate. Fat-free cheese is the biggest scam," she says, nibbling on the edge of her dry bagel. "If all a person knows is fat-free cheese, then it probably tastes good. But, if you've had normal, delicious full-fat cheese and then you try fat-free, it's disgusting."

I laugh. She's letting herself get worked up over cheese, but I'm glad because at least she's talking now.

"It's exactly like love."

"Cheese?"

"Yes, cheese." She sets her bagel down and drops her head into her hand. "Once you've been in love, the real kind. You know, the kind where you're head-over-heels, will do anything to make the other happy kind of love, then all other relationships pale in comparison. They're missing something. They're a little disgusting, just like fat-free cheese."

I look at my bagel smothered in fat-free cheese and smile at her. "That's actually kind of poetic, Eva. I like it."

"Is it okay if we get out of here now? I'm really not in the mood to be around people."

"Sure," I say, wrapping my bagel in the tissue paper from the basket. I can't see Sadie anywhere. She must be in the back. I write a quick thank-you on a napkin and leave a five-dollar tip.

As we drive back to TBC, I can't get Owen's face out of my mind and I vow to never eat fat-free cheese again.

* * *

To make up for lost time, I stay late working. I ignore a call from Elaine, deciding to call her when I leave. I'm overwhelmed by all of the work I should have done today, plus the fact that Eva's not speaking to me. After two more calls from Elaine in five minutes, I answer.

"He lied to me," Elaine blubbers into the phone. "He told me he wasn't feeling well, but when I showed up at his place with soup and a movie, he wasn't there and neither was his car."

I can hardly understand her. She sounds like she's about to hyperventilate. "Josh?" I ask.

"Yes, Jawawawawsh," she bawls. Apparently saying his name makes the crying worse.

"Maybe he had to run to the store to get some medicine or something."

"I d-don't think s-so," she cries. "He w-won't answer his phone."

"I'm so sorry, Elaine, but I don't think you should worry too much yet. He may have a good reason for being gone. Do you want me to come over?"

"N-no, I'm driving around looking for him."

"Why don't you come meet me at my office? We can grab some dinner or ice cream or something."

"Okay, thanks, Juliet. I-I'll be there in a few."

An hour passes and Elaine hasn't shown. I call her phone, but it goes to voicemail. At eight-thirty, I decide to leave while it's still light out. It makes me uneasy when I leave the building after dark, especially when I'm parked in the parking garage. As I get into the car, I get a text from Elaine, "So sorry, found Josh and we've been talking. Call you later." I toss the phone into the passenger seat and take off to find somewhere to eat. I hear my phone ringing and realize it's slid down between the passenger seat and the door. I try to reach over and grab it, but it's way too far out of reach for me to get while I'm driving. A few minutes later, it rings again. A red light forces me to stop so I unbuckle and grab my phone before it stops ringing.

"Hey," I hear Mom's whisper on the other end.

"Hey," I reply inquisitively.

"Luke is here. He called the house several times tonight and I kept telling him you weren't here. Then he showed up!" I push my phone to my ear so I can hear more clearly. Her whisper is difficult to make out. "Dad has him in the front room right now giving him a long talk about respecting your privacy."

"Ugh," I respond. "What's wrong with that guy? I can't believe he drove all the way out to the house again. He's actually starting to scare me." As I finish talking, my phone beeps that someone is calling in. I check it. "Mom, I've got to go. Owen is calling me. I'll call you later."

"Okay, bye, honey."

"Hey," I answer the other line, suddenly nervous. I called Owen several days ago and he's just now calling me back.

"Hey, Jules," his calm tone makes me relax slightly. "Are you busy?"

"Not at all," I answer as I pull into the lot of my apartment building. I wish I hadn't sounded quite so un-busy. It is a Friday night. Maybe I should retract that and say that I am in fact busy so I don't sound too pathetic. "Well, I . . ." I begin, but stop when Owen starts talking.

"I just got your message . . . and Lila's. I was at my mom's house and there is no cell reception there. I'm glad you called, but I hope you know by now that I don't believe anything Lila says.

"Was at your mom's house . . . does that mean you're back now?"

"Yeah, I actually called you a few minutes ago to see if you wanted to grab dinner, but I couldn't get you. Then your brother called so now he and I are getting dinner."

"Oh, my phone had slipped off the seat of my car and I couldn't get to it," I say, feeling disappointed as I unlock the door to my apartment.

"Why don't you come too?" he asks. "I'm about to meet Everett and then we'll come by your place and . . ." I don't hear anything else Owen says. I see a dark outline of a man sitting at my kitchen table and let out a scream. Thoughts flash through my mind of Luke attacking me or men from P&L kidnapping me. The man jumps up and I grab the closest thing I can find; the broom. He seizes me by the arm just as I swing back to hit him with the broom handle.

"Stop. It's me!" I immediately recognize the voice.

"Juliet? Juliet! Are you okay? Jules!" Owen's yelling through the phone.

"Sorry, Owen, I'm fine, but I've got to call you back." I end the call and turn to hug Will.

♡ Chapter 30 ♡

I fire off question after question as to what's going on, why he's here, if it's safe for him to be in Eden Falls, and why he's sitting in the dark.

"Maybe you can set down your deadly weapon and I'll tell you," he smiles. I hadn't realized that I was still holding the broom. I set it down and hug Will again. After a long hug, we sit on the couch and Will explains that he was sitting in the dark because he wasn't sure who'd be coming through that door. He didn't know where the house was that Eva lived in now, but he knew where Everett's apartment was. He said he preferred to be in the dark. Wrinkles crease across his forehead as he talks about how worried he is for Eva and what he's putting her through. As my eyes adjust to the lack of light, I notice he looks at least ten years older than the last time I'd seen him. Dark circles frame the bottoms of his once bright, blue eyes. He explains how the problems with P&L's product that have caused his life to fall apart, Tipro, have been corrected.

"They're in the process of phasing out all of the old product and replacing it with the new one. If they're successful, no one will ever know about the problems the original Tipro caused. Everything would be covered up. The people who knowingly sold a defective, cancer-causing product would never be brought to justice. Besides, I'm quite certain they'd still come after me. They don't want any loose ends and they're unsure what evidence I have against them."

"Yeah, I read about the replacement in the files you sent me."

"Oh good, you got it. Were you able to open everything?"

"Yeah, with some translating help from Eva."

He smiles. "And? Were you able to figure anything out?"

I nod with a smile and walk to my purse. I retrieve the flash drive from its hiding place in an old lipstick tube. "Everything is on here."

Will takes the drive from my hand. "Thank you," he says. "And now, more has happened since I sent you the original drive. The doctor who gave me that information several months ago, the one who noticed the old and new products weren't the same and was helping me, had a heart attack. A thirty-seven-year-old doctor who looked completely healthy suddenly died of a heart attack. I don't think it's a coincidence. I convinced a resident doctor from the same office, who'd worked closely with the doctor who died, to help me. It took a couple of months for her to agree, but she finally gave me some of the old and new product."

"Can't you go to the police now?" I feel naïve as I ask. I know he's doing everything he can, but it seems like it would go a lot quicker if he had some help from the law.

"I did. I took all the evidence I've gathered to the FBI. I told them everything. They told me it was necessary to place Eva in protective custody while they finish their investigation. Because she's watched and followed so often, we agreed it would be best to have a casual meeting place where it wouldn't be obvious that she was going with the FBI. Hence, the meeting at the park was arranged. They said they could get Eva, and she and I would be protected until everything with P&L was taken care of." Will rubs his eyes and takes a deep breath.

"Okay, so why was it dangerous? Now the FBI's not involved?" I urge him to continue.

"Yesterday, an agent called me and told me something strange was going on. He said he wouldn't trust someone he loved in the hands of a couple of those FBI agents; that they would do anything for the right amount of money. P&L has so much power in this town. Of course they have connections on the inside," he said, shaking his head. "So I didn't want her in the hands of a group of men I don't know if I can trust. I was terrified she'd go to that park and something terrible would happen to her. I'm sorry that I caused so much drama this morning trying to get you the message. I have to be so careful." He looks pathetic, slumped over on the couch trying to explain everything. I put my hand on his, trying to comfort him. He looks up at me, trying to force a small grin and continues, "I needed to make sure she was okay."

"It's great seeing you and finding out what's going on, but what if someone sees you? I mean, you're so close to getting this all taken care of, right?"

"I need to get the flash drive back from you with anything you've figured out so far." He pauses with a pained expression. "And I need to see Eva." He rubs his hands through is hair. "If people from the FBI are helping P&L, P&L knows I'm in contact with her. They'll go after her to get to me."

I reach towards him and he wraps his arms around me. The front door opens and light pours into the apartment. In an instant Will disappears into the back. I look up at Everett standing in the doorway staring at me, his eyes filled with questions. Next to him is Owen with a similar expression. Everett glances toward the back and then to me.

"Please tell me that wasn't Luke," Everett says, shaking his head.

"That wasn't Luke!" I respond, hurt that he thinks it's possible for me to be so stupid.

"Then who was it?" he asks, his tone sounding more curious than angry now. I say nothing, but motion for him to go to the back as well. He walks down the hallway where Will disappeared.

Owen looks at me and then to the floor. "You sounded so scared on the phone," he mutters, shaking his head. "I was worried something was wrong." He turns to go back out the door and says, "I'm glad you're okay."

The disappointment on his face makes me want to tell him every detail about Will and why I was sitting on the couch in the dark, hugging him. I fight the words back and instead say, "I'm sorry. I didn't mean to scare you."

He watches me, waiting for more of an explanation, but when he gets none, walks away. I watch him go, feeling a sharp ache in my stomach. This is like the envelope incident all over again and for what? Do I really think Owen is going to tell someone about Will? No, but a few months ago I would never have thought he was involved in some enigmatic relationship with Lila either. I run out the door and grab him. I know I can't tell him about Will, but I can't let him walk away thinking so little of me. "Owen, that wasn't what it looked like."

He stops and looks at me for several seconds. "What was it then?" he asks, a hint of desperation in his voice. I search for what to say. He looks down, disappointed.

"You just have to trust me on this one," I plead. "I'll explain it to you as soon as I can." I know how pathetic it sounds, but I don't know what else to tell him.

He nods. Everett comes out of the apartment and down the stairs and stands next to us, seemingly oblivious he's interrupting anything. He explains to Owen that he better go get food without us; that we have some family stuff to take care of. Owen tells us to let him know if we need anything and walks away as Everett goes back inside. Before getting into his car, Owen stops and turns back to look at me. I smile and he tries to smile back, but he just looks tired.

♡ Chapter 31 ♡

Everett peeks out the peephole in the door to see who is knocking. Nearly ten minutes ago, he called Eva and told her it was important that she come over. She must have sensed the seriousness in his voice because she immediately agreed. She said she was still in Eden Falls and would be right over. Everett and I are certain she has no idea Will is here. Everett nods to Will to let him know that it *is* Eva, and Will grins. He's been pacing back and forth in anticipation since Everett called her. Everett opens the door and there stands Eva wearing a worried look. "What's going on, Ev?" she asks, stepping inside. "Something's wrong, isn't it?" She stares at him, eagerly awaiting his response. "Did Juliet put you up to this?" She grows increasingly anxious with each word. Everett looks next to the sofa, where Will is standing. Eva's eyes follow Everett's. She gasps and covers her mouth and tears start pouring down her cheeks. Will runs to her and picks her up. She wraps her arms around him and cries harder.

Tears roll down Will's cheeks as well. All his worries seem to have disappeared for the moment. I read his lips as he whispers, "I love you, Eva," and buries his face in next to her neck. Tears push at the corners of my eyes. Nothing can show how much you love someone like being forced apart. Feeling like I'm interrupting a private moment, I motion for Everett to leave with me.

We walk silently to my car. Seeing Will and Eva so emotional makes me want to hug everyone I see and tell them what they mean to me. As I back out of my parking space, Everett quietly says, "Nearly two years apart, the only communication the occasional vague letter, and they still love each other that much. It's pretty incredible." He spoke in awe as if somewhat envious of what Eva and Will have. I only nod. After several minutes of silence, Everett asks, "As long as we're driving around, can we pick up my car? It's still at Owen's place." I nod again. "And, Jules?" he says, sounding hesitant.

I face him.

"What's with all the awkwardness between you and Owen? It always seems so tense between you two."

I flash a disheartened grin. "I really don't know, Ev. Every time I think we're right for each other, there's some ridiculous misunderstanding and everything falls apart. All this secrecy about Will hasn't helped."

"It's not the Lila thing bugging you?" Hearing Lila's name makes me cringe. Before I respond, he continues, "Because he really can't stand her."

"What makes you say that?" I ask, wondering when Owen started talking to Everett about Lila.

"I asked him about his trip and he told me he went home because his dad died."

"Oh," I respond, my heart sinking.

"Then he told me an entire soap opera between his family and the Bradleys."

"Really?" I perk up at the prospect of finally getting some answers.

"His dad used to work with Mr. Bradley. The two of them started TBC together and they each owned half of the company."

I'm surprised I've never heard anything about this. "His dad helped start the company?"

"Yeah. Mr. Bradley came from a famous entrepreneurial family and Mr. Denny had spent something like fifteen years working surveillance technology in the military. A few years after they started TBC and the company was becoming successful, the two men had a major falling out. Mr. Bradley accused Owen's dad of embezzling from the company."

Just hearing Mr. Bradley's name gives me a bad taste in my mouth.

"Mr. Denny, who insisted it was a set-up, owed thousands upon thousands of dollars in gambling debts, which didn't help his plea of innocence. They were able to settle it without Mr. Denny having to serve time, but he lost his place at The Bradley Corporation. Losing everything he'd worked so hard to build, he fell apart. The gambling got worse and he drank excessively. Owen says he remembers his dad disappearing for weeks at a time. When he would finally show up, his alcohol-induced temper made the whole family wish he was still gone.

"I've heard Owen mention before that he learned to fight from his dad. I didn't realize it was because he was fighting *against* his dad. Anyway, he told me that his dad would come back and beat up on his mom. Sometimes, he'd even go after the kids."

I grow more furious as I listen. I can picture a young Owen trying to protect his family from his dad and it breaks my heart. What kind of a man would do that to his wife and his own children?

"Owen's mom took the five kids and moved into a much smaller home, working two jobs to make ends meet. Owen was the oldest so it sounds like a lot of the responsibility fell on his shoulders, but all he talks about is how the Bradley family helped out a lot." Everett says the name "Bradley" in a mocking tone, showing his dislike for them. "He seems to feel any comforts his family had are entirely a result of charity from the Bradleys. They often helped Owen with the other kids while his mom worked late and Owen spent a lot of time at their house. He also said Mr. Bradley helped pay some of his dad's debt so people would stop going after Mr. Denny and his family."

I think back to the way Owen spoke of the Bradley family back when I hardly knew him and we were driving back from Penn. He'd spoken about their generosity and how they were a second family for him. I try to feel some appreciation for the Bradleys and how they've helped Owen, but I can't. The way they try to manipulate him is disgusting and I can feel nothing but dislike for them. Everett's still talking, "and by then Owen and their son, Paul, were best friends. You know that whole story I told you about the motorcycle accident and Luke?"

I nod.

"They guy who died was Paul Bradley. He was supposed to become vice president at TBC once he graduated from college, but after he died, Mr. Bradley wanted Owen to do it. He accepted the offer, partly because he felt so indebted to the Bradleys and partly because his family needed the money. He really liked the job and was able to start paying off the debt his dad ran up in his mom's name. Then Mr. Bradley asked Owen if he could help look after Lila. She was in college and starting to scare her dad with all her partying. She was acting too much like Paul. Owen agreed to help out in any way he could. He said it was no big deal at first. He'd invite her to do stuff with him and his friends and try to keep her from doing anything crazy. Everything at TBC was still going great, especially the pay. His mom had been able to quit one of her jobs and two of his younger siblings were able to start college.

"Lila began showing a lot of interest in Owen and when that girl wants something, she generally gets it. Owen said he truly believed she'd changed and was likeable."

I raise my eyebrows. "Likeable? Lila?"

Everett rolls his eyes at me. "He still didn't have any actual feelings for her, but they spent quite a bit of time together. Anyway, one afternoon Mr. Bradley came into Owen's office and made it clear the family believed Owen and Lila were dating. When Owen told him that wasn't the case, he flat out told Owen they better be dating—and dating exclusively—or he would be out of a job. Although he didn't like the idea of being bribed into dating someone, he didn't mind Lila and he needed the money to help support his family so he went along with it. That's when Mr. Bradley started surprising them with trips to foreign countries or romantic weekend getaways. Finally Owen felt things were going too far. He tried to end things. Again, Mr. Bradley told him his career would be over, not only with TBC, but with any reputable company." Everett stops talking and points to his car as we pull into the parking lot at Owen's apartment. I park my car next to his.

I'm glad when, instead of going to his car, he continues talking. "About that time, Owen's mom started getting threatening phone calls. Mr. Denny's gambling was still haunting them nearly two decades later. Owen's youngest brother, still in high school, came home to find three men sitting in the living room. They asked him where his dad was and when he told them he didn't know, they beat him up pretty badly. Threatening calls laced with death threats continued. Owen and his mom tried to find Mr. Denny, but found a bunch of dead ends. They decided the best thing to do for now would be to leave Eden Falls. Mrs. Denny and her two youngest children moved to a very remote town about two hundred miles away, which meant Mrs. Denny had to quit her job. This put even more pressure on Owen to keep his job with TBC. He was now fully supporting his family. He said he knows it sounds like an excuse and that's why he never tried to justify it, but he feels like his family's relying on him. For whatever reason, the Bradleys want him and Lila together and by doing what they want, his mom is able to stay safe and not work, his siblings can all go to college, and they don't have a massive amount of debt looming over their heads."

I don't think it sounds like an excuse. I feel terrible for Owen, having to go through everything Everett just told me. I see Everett watching me intently, apparently waiting for a reaction. I shake my head and say, "That's definitely not the explanation I expected. Why didn't he tell you sooner?"

"I don't know. He rarely says anything about his past."

"Why do the Bradleys care about Owen and Lila being together? I don't get it and how did his dad die? Did Owen care that he'd died?"

Everett smiles at my long list of questions and answers, "By the time Owen told me all about the Bradleys, we were at the apartment and he was worried about you after hearing you scream on the phone. We ran inside as quickly as possible so I don't know anything more about his dad or what happened with Owen while he was at his mom's house."

"Oh," I sigh, a fresh wave of guilt spreading over me as I think of Owen's face when he entered the apartment to find Will and I alone in the dark. Thinking of Will reminds me of our current situation. "We should probably get back to the apartment and help them figure out what they're going to do before someone realizes he's here."

Everett nods before getting out of my car and into his own.

I speed through a yellow light and watch in my rearview mirror as Everett has to sit and wait while it's red. I hurry back to the apartment. As I'm parking, I see Ev's car come into the parking lot. "Way to run that light, Jules," he yells, grinning as he pulls in next to me.

"I didn't run it. It was yellow," I argue, running up the stairs. I immediately go silent when I'm close enough to see our apartment door. It's open several inches, the lights are on inside, and I can hear voices. Panic rising in me, I'm torn between wanting to see who's in there and knowing it could be dangerous. I turn and run back down the stairs. Everett follows my cue. I hear my name yelled and see Luke waiting at the bottom of the stairs.

"I thought I heard you two yelling out here." Then sensing our rush, he asks, "Are you guys all right?"

"Fine, thanks," I say as we continue to the parking lot.

"Seriously, I know you don't like me much right now, but let me help."

"We're on our way out and we're late," interjects Everett.

Luke wedges himself in between me and my car. "Call me if you need anything. You can always hang out at my place if those people won't leave," he says, motioning towards our apartment.

"You saw them?" I ask, noticing Everett's already in his car and waving for me to hurry up.

"Yeah, three guys were trying to bang your door down. Several of us came out to see what was going on. Within a few minutes, two more guys showed up. You two must be into something pretty serious, huh?" Luke nudges me and smiles, like all of this is no big deal.

"You watched all this and didn't do anything?" I asked, my insides feeling like I just ate three pans of brownies.

"I figured it was none of my business."

"Did you think to call the police?"

"Somebody had already called them. They showed up, talked to a couple of the men, told them to quiet down, and left," Luke answers nonchalantly.

Everett backs his car out and pulls up next to me so I can get in the passenger side. We pull away and Luke yells, "My apartment will be open!"

Without any idea of where we're going, we drive in complete silence for several minutes, the air thick with worry. It's Everett who finally breaks the silence, "They have to be fine, right? Those men wouldn't have still been in the apartment if they'd already found them." Hoping he's right, I nod enthusiastically. Similar thoughts have already been running through my mind. Still, I feel sick with anxiety. Maybe Will and Eva are still in the apartment being interrogated. Doubtful since I'm fairly certain the only way they want Will is dead. Maybe some of the guys had already left with Will and Eva, and a couple of others stayed in the apartment to try and find Will's research. Maybe they already killed Will *and* Eva and they were inside the apartment celebrating. I have to force myself to stop thinking of possible scenarios, since they're only getting worse and worse. "Why wouldn't the police have done more?" Everett asks. "I can't believe they didn't arrest them for breaking and entering."

I'd thought about that too, but Will had mentioned someone in the FBI working for P&L. That probably meant there were more dirty cops. I decide not to share my theory. It will make things seem too dismal. "Should we try to call Eva?" I ask.

"She's not going to risk them being able to track her through her phone. I hope she was smart enough to shut it off."

"Yeah, you're right," I agree, but on the off chance that she did have it on, I dial the number. It goes straight to voicemail. I try to comfort myself thinking that her phone being off is a good sign. If someone had gotten to her, she wouldn't have ever shut her phone off. It would still be sitting in her purse, inside the apartment, ringing.

"They're following us," Everett says casually, like it doesn't matter.

My heart races as I look in my side mirror. "Where should we go? Are we going to keep driving around?"

"Until we can come up with another idea, yeah, I guess the best thing to do is to drive around." Everett turns on some music and, clearly realizing it's only making things tenser, immediately shuts it off again. Then he says, "You know, we're not going to be able to help them at all, even if we figure out what's going on and where they are. As long as we're being followed, there's not a lot we can do. Plus, our phones are probably no good at this point. I'm sure they've figured out a way to monitor them." He takes his phone out of his pocket and shuts the power off.

I get my phone out of my purse and do the same. Several months ago, I read an article online about how people can listen to you through your phone even when you're not using it. Apparently there's a program you can install, and once you do, you can tap into a phone's mic as a listening device. It's advertised as a way to "catch your spouse cheating" or "bug meeting rooms."

"We're going to need help. We should stop and pick up a phone. If we do figure out where they are, we're going to have to call someone else."

"Who? Mom and Dad's house would be one of the first places people would think about looking for Will and Eva. Someone's probably out there watching by now and I don't know who else to trust." As soon as I finish my sentence, I think of Owen. Everett looks slightly skeptical when I suggest his name.

"That's who I was thinking too," he says, looking uncomfortable. "The only thing is he was the only other person who saw Will in our apartment so what if he was the one . . ." He trails off and then says, "No, it couldn't have been him.

I know we can trust him. I bet this all has something to do with Luke. Somehow, he saw Will and knew who he was or something."

"I thought about that, but Luke was getting a lecture from Dad when Will showed up at the apartment. Mom had just called me and told me he was out at the house. I don't know how he could be involved."

Everett shakes his head. "I don't know, but I bet he is. We know he'll do anything for the right amount of money." He checks the rearview mirror and suddenly takes a hard left, causing me to smack my head against the window. "Sorry," he says as I wince. "Those guys were right on my bumper. They're way more aggressive than usual. They're not even trying to blend in. It feels like they're actually after *us* this time, not just to see where we're going or if we'll lead them to Will." Then he adds, "Hang on" before he takes another quick turn and gasses it. I'm grateful Everett has a love of fast cars. I've never appreciated this Mustang's speed until now. I brace myself as he takes several more turns. He nods toward Wal-Mart and says, "I'll pull up next to the door and you run in and grab a phone. Do you know where they are?" I nod. "Okay, meet me in the back next to the garden center when you're done." He slams on the brakes and I'm running through the automatic doors before I have time to question his plan.

I pick up the cheapest, most basic prepaid phone I see. "Nah, you don't want that one," a kid wearing a blue Wal-Mart shirt says, pulling it out of my hands.

"I do want that one," I reply, reaching for the phone as he holds it above his head.

"No, let me tell you about some of these others," he says, fanning his hand out toward the assortment of phones, "like this one. It has a three-point-five-inch touch screen, a built in—"

"I want *that* one."

He looks surprised. "It doesn't do anything remotely cool."

I glance around, expecting to see someone who looks like Tommy Lee Jones in *Men in Black*. That's how I picture the men involved with P&L. My eyes dart from side to side, taking in my surroundings. I keep telling myself no one is following me; that they didn't see me go into Wal-Mart, but I can't shake the feeling that someone is going to reach out and grab me at any second. "Will it make phone calls? Because that's all I care about," I respond, sounding ruder than I intended.

"Oh?" he responds, inquisitively, followed by another "oh," but this time it's long and drawn out, as if something finally makes sense to him.

Unsure what to say to speed this process along, I stare at him. "I'm in a bit of a hurry and I'd really like that phone." He carefully walks behind the glass counter and gets the phone ready.

With my new phone safely tucked inside my pocket, I walk toward where I'm supposed to meet Everett. I want to sprint as fast as I can but instead remain calm and walk at a regular pace as to not attract any unwanted attention. A man in an oversized John Deere sweatshirt stares at me as I pass. He reaches into his pocket so I quickly dart behind a display of movies. He gives me a confused look and answers the cell phone he pulls out of his pocket. I take a deep breath, tell myself to quit being so jumpy, and continue walking. Wal-Mart has never seemed so big. I make it outside and creep slowly around the side of the store until I see the garden center. I can't see Everett's car anywhere. Should I walk back toward the parking lot and see if he's there or stay put? My skin turns clammy as I imagine what could have happened to Everett. Maybe I should use the phone I bought and call him. His phone would still be off, but I could leave a message. Would P&L be able to get the number of the new phone, even if it was just from a voicemail on Ev's phone? I don't think so, but I don't want to risk it. I finally have a phone that I know isn't being listened in on and I don't want it to somehow lead them to me. Ev will come. I sit down against the building, in the darkest spot I can find.

I have no way of telling time since my only clock is on my phone and I haven't turned it on. My legs are cramping from holding so still. The cool, autumn air now feels bitterly cold as the wind pierces through my clothes. I wonder if that's what's causing me to shiver so hard or if the chill I feel is brought on by fear. Either way, my body is shaking and I want it to stop before the movement gives away my hiding spot.

When I'm sure I've been sitting here for at least an hour, I know something's gone wrong. Pulling out my new phone, I decide to call Owen. As I start to push the buttons, I realize I don't know his number. Panic starts to set in. Whose number do I know? I think through contacts in my phone, whose numbers I actually know; Eva, Ev, and my parents. None of those numbers will help right now. P&L will be listening to all of their lines. I try to think through my options. I can go back inside the store, but what if there are people from P&L in there? If they spotted Everett, they would know that I'm somewhere near here and they would be looking for me. I could try to run across the street, where there's a movie theater. I know I can blend in well there, but I'm not sure how dangerous it will be to run into a well-lit street. Besides, I'm not even sure if the theater is still open. It may be the middle of the night by now. I decide to turn on my personal cell to see if Everett left a message and get Owen's phone number. I know I can be tracked on it, but P&L probably already knows I'm somewhere around here anyway. The notes my phone plays as it powers on are so loud I'm sure it can be heard from across the parking lot. I shove it under my coat to mute it.

Beep Beep. I have a new text. As I'm opening it, another one shows up. Butterflies course through my stomach when I see it's from Everett. I try to hold my shaky hands steady and push the button to open it. It says, "Stay there." Although it doesn't give me any information, I'm relieved to know I'm in the right spot. Everett will be back to help me. The other text is from a number I don't recognize. I open it, "14th bday place, 212." It's definitely Eva. When I turned fourteen, Eva and Mom planned a big party for me at The Applebay Resort. It had an indoor water park and suites that, to a fourteen-year-old, seemed like the epitome of luxury. I'm sure the 212 is a room number. Either Will or Eva is hiding out there or they left some sort of a message in that room. Now I just need to find a way to get there.

I scroll to Owen's number and memorize it. I find myself making up a song in my head to help me remember it before I power down my cell. Afraid I've given away my hiding spot by using my phone, I creep alongside the wall slowly. When I'm a few feet away from some parked cars, I run until I'm next to a black Yukon. I crouch behind it. It isn't the best hiding spot, but it's better than sitting in the exact spot where I'd been. Unsure how accurate the GPS trackers on phones are or what resources P&L has, I hope they're not too exact. I don't want to leave until Everett comes back. Once I get into a position that doesn't hurt my legs too much, I lean against the wheel well. While watching the garden center, I take out the phone I bought inside Wal-Mart and dial Owen's number.

Owen's voice cuts off the fourth ring. "Hello," he says, half asleep. I realize I forgot to look at the time on the phone. It could be two or three in the morning by now.

"Hey, Owen," I whisper. It's silent. I try again, a little louder. "Owen?" I say in a quiet voice, slightly above a whisper.

"Yeah?" He sounds more alert now.

"It's Juliet, I'm—"

"Jules? What's going on? Are you okay?" Comfort floods over me as I hear the concern in his voice. All the stress of the night comes rushing forward and I fight to hold back tears. I have to hold it together or I won't be any help to Eva. He continues, "Where are you?"

"I'm okay, I'm . . ." I look around, wondering how I should finish that sentence. "I'm at Wal-Mart, but I could use some help."

"Of course. Can I come get you?"

I'm excited at the thought of leaving this cold, scary parking lot and going with Owen. I let my mind wander as I consider having him come get me. I can explain everything to him and let him make it all right. I'm thinking of his warm arms wrapped around me when I force myself to snap out of it and focus on reality. "No, I actually need you to help Eva. This is all going to seem crazy and I know I'm asking a lot of you when you don't even know what's going on, but she's in trouble and I don't trust anyone else to help her."

"Okay, what do you want me to do?" He sounds calm, but different than usual. It's like he's trying to mask other feelings like worry and fear.

"She's with a man named Will, actually, he's the guy you saw at my apartment earlier. They're stuck. Some people are hunting all over for them. They need to get far away from Eden Falls. Is there any way you could h—"

"Where are they? I'm headed to my car right now," he agrees before I can finish asking. I tell him where I think they are and say they'll explain everything to him when he gets there. He asks again if I'm okay and if he can come get me first.

"There's not enough time to come here first. They've got to get away from here as quickly as possible and I need to stay here and wait for Ev." I pause and then add, "Thank you, Owen."

It's quiet for a couple of seconds and I hear Owen start his car. Finally he responds, "You'd tell me if you weren't okay, right? Are you really at Wal-Mart?"

I take a breath, hoping I'll sound calmer than I feel. "I'm really at Wal-Mart and I'm really okay, or at least I will be after Eva's safe."

"Okay, I'll make sure she's safe and then I'll call you back. Do I call this number?"

"Yeah." My throat tries to close off as tears start flowing so I quickly finish with, "I'll talk to you then. Thank you." It's strange how the comfort of his voice and his willingness to help make me so emotional. The tears on my cheeks are making me even colder so I wipe them off and pull my face down inside my coat. To help pass time, I replay our conversation in my head. I like that he was trying to cover up the worry in his voice to keep me calm. The whole idea of him being worried about me makes me feel significantly warmer.

♡ Chapter 32 ♡

'm lost in thought when a dark, shadowy figure seems to come out of nowhere and squats beside me. There's a hand over my mouth before I can react. If I can bite the hand hard enough, maybe the person will be forced to let go and I can scream for help. I grab the arm that's up by my face and bite down as hard as I can on my attacker's hand.

"Jules! Stop!" comes a familiar whisper.

I stop and turn to see Everett, rubbing his hand where I bit him. "Ev?" I throw my arms around him. "Why did you cover my mouth? You should have known I'd be scared."

"I didn't want you to scream when you saw someone beside you, and you didn't give me time to say anything before you went into full-on attack mode." He grabs me again, but this time in a big hug. "Are you okay?"

I nod, but realize it's probably too dark for him to see me so I say, "I'm fine. What about you? What happened?"

"I'm fine too," Everett huffs as he lets go of me, "but we need to get out of here. I'll tell you about it later." He stands up and peeks over the top of the Yukon, then looks side to side, "C'mon, we can go this way." He squats back down and looks at me to make sure I'm ready, then slowly moves toward the next car. We work our way from car to car, until we're on the front side of the store. Now that the lights from the parking lot make us more visible, Everett moves quicker. I try to keep up, but all that sitting still has my legs feeling like Jello. Everett notices the space between us is growing so he stops next to a big truck and waits for me. I catch up and sit next to him, my breath heavy.

He points across the street to the movie theater. "Let's head over there. You go first. Don't stop running 'til you've made it across the street and inside the movie theater."

"Okay," I agree. I take a minute to let my legs get their feeling back and take off in a sprint across the street.

A couple minutes later I run through the front doors of the Newport 16 Cinema. A dark theater full of people is the perfect place to hide if we can figure a way out of here before all of the movies are over. I glance at the list of movie times. There are several that list midnight showings. They'll all be at least half over by now. I choose the longest movie and am buying two tickets when Everett comes through the doors. He hurries me down the long hallway and through the double doors of theater number eight. The theater isn't even a third full so we grab two seats near the back. I'm not used to seeing Everett on edge like this. His uneasiness scares me.

As soon as we're seated, I lean in to Ev, "Okay, now what happened?"

I have to strain to hear Everett over the movie as he speaks in a low whisper. "I'm so sorry you had to sit out there by yourself for so long. When I dropped you off, I really thought everything would be fine. I figured you could buy the phone and be out before any of them spotted my car." He rubs his temples and sighs. "After I dropped you off, I pulled around the backside of Wal-Mart. Right away that car was following me again. I sped back onto the main road and took off. I thought I could lose it and get back to pick you up, but I couldn't get rid of it. Every time I'd get ahead, it would be right back within a minute. I decided that once I could lose them for a few seconds, I'd ditch the car so I could run back and get you." Everett shakes as he talks. My heart races faster. He continues, "I found an area without streetlights, jumped out of my car, and hid in a backyard about fifty yards away. Not thirty seconds later, the car that was following me parked behind my Mustang. Two men got out and both had guns. I hunched down as low as I could and stayed still while they searched the area. They ransacked the Mustang and made several phone calls, but I was too far away to hear what was being said. I was afraid they were calling in more help to search for me, but no else showed up. Nearly an hour later, they gave up. They got back in their car and sped away. I made my way back toward Wal-Mart, but stayed off the main roads, which meant a lot of fences to climb and angry dogs to avoid." His breathing gets heavier just recounting the story. "I was terrified they'd gotten you," he said, squeezing my arm "We won't split up anymore."

"I can't believe they had guns," I said, the reality of the situation growing graver. "They've never tried to hurt *us* before."

"It surprised me too. Maybe they thought Will was in our car or something. I don't get it."

I tell Everett about the text from Eva and how I'd called Owen. I explain he's on his way to Applebay to see if Eva and Will are there. This seems to help Everett relax slightly.

"One thing I can't figure out," starts Everett, "is how P&L knew Will was in our apartment. The obvious answer is Owen since he was the only other person who saw Will, but there's no way he would betray us like that. The more I think about it, the more I think Luke is to blame. You said he wasn't there, but somehow he's to blame. Why don't you call him and tell him Eva's in trouble? Tell him she's hiding somewhere like Falls View Park and she needs him to come get her. Actually, say Wal-Mart so we can see what happens. I bet a bunch of guys from P&L show up."

There's a knot in the pit of my stomach picturing Luke behind all of this. "If he really is involved, then calling him right now will only hurt us. It will just give them another way of tracking us," I whisper back.

"Yeah, you're right," he says with a sigh. "But I know it's him." He unclenches his fists and asks, "Where's the phone you bought?"

I eye him skeptically.

"I'm not going to do anything about Luke. I just want to see the phone," he assures. I hand it to him. "This number here is Owen's, right?" he asks, pointing to the only number in the phone's call history. I nod and he pushes "send."

"You don't think talking on the phone in the middle of a movie is going to draw unwanted attention?" I ask, surprised.

"It's better than walking out there, where I can easily be spotted," he replies, pointing to the exit. "This movie's loud anyway. No one will even notice me."

"He said he'd call as soon as they were safe."

"He's not answering anyway," Everett says, handing the phone back to me.

That can't be a good sign. Why won't he answer his phone? I try to mask my worry as I say, "He'll call us back any minute." I'm saying it more for my benefit than for Everett's. It doesn't seem to faze him that Owen didn't answer. If he's not worried, then there's no reason for me to be worried. Everett settles back into his seat and looks as if he's turned his attention to the movie. I follow suit.

Vibrations from the Wal-Mart phone make me jump. I realize that although my eyes have been on the movie screen for several minutes, I have no idea what's happening in the movie. My mind is in a hundred different places, but not one of those places is here in this theater. I dig the phone out and see a text. It's not Eva's or Owen's number.

It says, "Thanks J, Please tell me you guys are safe! Thanks for the help you sent. Love you." I hold the phone out so Everett can read it. Eva must have a phone of Will's and have gotten this number from Owen. A wave of relief rushes over me. As I feel a release of pressure in my chest, I realize how worked up I've let myself get. Where breathing has taken some effort for the last couple of hours, it feels easy now. Knowing Eva and Will are safe makes everything feel better. I quickly type Eva a response telling her we're safe and force myself to focus on how happy I am that everyone's okay, instead of thinking about how long it might be until I see Eva again.

Everett and I sit in silence, watching, or at least appearing to watch, the movie. When the end credits roll and the majority of the audience leaves, we decide it's a good time to walk out. "Why don't you go into the bathroom while I make sure no one's here looking for us and I'll come back and get you?" Everett suggests.

"You just finished telling me we wouldn't split up anymore. I'm coming too."

"Okay," he says, surprised by my outburst. "Why don't we go check the back lot first? They probably don't even know we're here." As we wind around the hallway toward a backdoor, he continues talking quietly. It sounds like he's trying to comfort himself. "In fact, they're probably still at Wal-Mart looking for us . . . or back by my car . . . or maybe they've given up by now and they're all home sleeping."

Buzzzzz buzz buzzzzzzzzzz. The phone in my pocket buzzes and both Everett and I jump. I grab it, but my shaky hands fumble it to the ground. Everett snatches it up. Suddenly feeling vulnerable at the end of the long hall, I motion back to the crowded lobby. We move that direction as Everett answers the phone. "Hey," he says, his voice barely above a whisper. I want to hear what's being said on the other end as Everett listens for several seconds. "Oh man," he responds to whatever is said and lets out a relieved sigh. "Your timing couldn't be more perfect. We've been hiding out in the Newport Theater, but it's about to close." More silence as I strain to hear what I assume is Owen's voice. I can't make out anything, but Everett replies, "Yeah, they chased me for a while so I know they're trying. Can you pull around by the back door on the East side and let us know if it's clear? We'll be waiting inside 'til we hear from you."

"He's about ten minutes away," Everett says as he hands me the phone. He points back at theater number eight and says, "Let's go back in there for a little while."

The credits are still rolling when we walk back in, but no one is watching. The only other person in the room is a short, plump woman who's straining to bend over and pick up trash. She looks at the two of us and raises an eyebrow. "Movie's over," she huffs, out of breath. Then, exerting a great amount of effort, she bends back over to grab more trash.

"Yeah, we know. We were on our way out when we realized she lost her bracelet. We thought we'd check and make sure it wasn't in here somewhere," he lies.

"Mm," the woman responds, not looking up.

I scan the walkways for my fictitious bracelet and then move toward some chairs and squat down next to them. Everett's doing the same. "Wow, you really have a big job picking up all this junk. People throw stuff all over, don't they?" Everett says. He picks up a couple of soda cups and throws them in her garbage bag. The woman watches him, shocked. He continues, "They just have no respect. What's your name?"

After looking at him for several seconds like she's trying to figure out his angle, she responds, "Madge."

"Madge, nice to meet you. I'm Everett. They have no respect, do they, Madge?" She lets out another grunt in reply. Everett continues picking up garbage and putting it in her bag. Within a couple of minutes, he has Madge telling him all about her job.

The phone buzzes again. "It's not in here, Ev. Maybe it's in the bathroom," I say, motioning to the door and trying to sound bummed about not finding a bracelet.

"Okay," he says. "Good luck in here, Madge."

"Thanks," she replies, a small grin playing at the corners of her mouth.

As soon as we're in the hallway, I answer the phone and hear Owen's voice, "Hey, I'm here, by the back East door and it's totally clear."

"Okay, see you in a sec." We make our way to the side door, push it open, and jump in Owen's car. We pull out of the parking lot and onto the main road before Owen asks where he's taking us.

"Definitely nowhere near our apartment," Everett says. "And I'm sure they're watching Mom and Dad's by now."

"They've always been watching Mom and Dad's. So what if they see us drive out there? That's something we'd normally do and I'm sure Mom and Dad are kind of freaking out right now since Eva never came home and they can't reach of any of us."

"So what if they see us drive out there?" Everett echoes, his voice an octave higher than usual. "They were looking around a nice little neighborhood for me with guns loaded and ready to fire. I'm not ready to drive right past them waving yet!"

"You want to leave Mom and Dad out there, clueless, surrounded by the people with guns?" I ask.

"We can go to my place," Owen suggests, "and try to get them a message to meet us there."

"Thanks, Owen." I barely get the words out before Everett's talking again.

"We should go to the cabin. I'm sure Mom and Dad know something is up and they probably left the house hours ago. I bet they're at the cabin waiting for us by now."

"You're right," I agree. I tell myself that Mom and Dad are probably at the cabin waiting to hear good news.

"Okay, where's this cabin?" Owen asks. Everett tells him what road to take and Owen laughs quietly.

"What?" Everett asks.

Owen shakes his head and then, still smiling, says, "This is crazy. You think that people following your every move for years is normal. Then you have a bunch of men chasing you with guns and now I'm taking you to your family's safe house."

For the first time in hours, I grin. I turn away, but see Owen look at me in the rearview mirror.

Everett smiles too and says, "It was only two men with guns."

"Did Eva have time to explain everything to you?" I ask.

Owen's smile fades as he nods. After several seconds of silence, he adds, "Yeah, they told me the whole story." Then the lines by his eyes crinkle hinting at a smile. "We had plenty of time for it."

"What happened? They must have been in the room I told you about, right?" I ask and wait anxiously for the answer.

"You haven't talked to her?" Owen seems surprised.

"No, she texted me and said she was safe, but that was all."

"Will had a phone he'd picked up for her. I figured she'd probably call and explain everything to you."

"Knowing Eva, she'll be overly cautious for a while until everything settles down," Everett says.

"Yeah, they were in that room," Owen begins, "but they were pretty nervous to let me help. They told me how they'd been in your apartment and apparently Will kept telling Eva they needed to go somewhere else. He was worried that someone would know he was there. She thought he was so used to running that he was paranoid. When Will saw several cars pull into the parking lot, he convinced her they needed to go down the fire escape. He had parked two blocks away so they needed to run to his car. Eva said it wasn't even thirty seconds after they made it down the fire escape when men came around the backside of the building and started climbing up. One man saw Will and Eva and ran after them. They made it to Will's car and took off, but they were pretty sure that the guy had gotten a decent view of Will's car. After a few miles, they ditched the car and checked into a room at Applebay and that's where—"

"How did they get a room? Isn't it too risky to use a credit card when it can be traced?" I ask.

"I didn't ask how they got the room, but I know Will had fake IDs for both of them. That probably means he had credit cards to match those identities."

"For Eva too?" I say, more to myself than for the others to hear. "That means he's been planning on her leaving with him for a while."

"He said it was too risky for her to be here and now that he didn't trust the FBI to put her into protective custody, he wanted her to come with him," Owen explains.

I feel like a balloon is being inflated inside my stomach as anger pours through me. I can't believe Will would be so selfish. He can't possibly believe that a life on the run will be safer for Eva. He just wants her with him. "More dangerous here than with *him*?" I ask, unable to hide my frustration.

"He's probably right, Jules," Everett says in a comforting tone. "I'm sure Will knows exactly what's going on and if he thinks it's safer for Eva to go with him, then that must be the case. Will would never purposely jeopardize Eva's safety."

Even though I know Everett's right, I refuse to admit it. I like having someone to feel angry with right now. I'm not going to see my sister for a long time and it feels good to blame that on Will. Not wanting to respond to Everett, I turn to Owen and say, "Sorry, I interrupted you. So they checked into the Applebay and then what?"

"After a lot of persuasion, they let me in. Eva was willing to let me help, but Will was far less enthusiastic. He finally relented."

"Oh, go right here," I say almost too late for Owen to make the turn. He jerks the wheel all the way to the right. We slide off the pavement and onto some gravel before he's able to straighten the car out. "Sorry, I forgot you didn't know where to go. Anyway, they let you in," I prompt.

"Yeah, they let me in. Will's contact at the FBI had given him fake IDs, but since he was short on time, those IDs didn't include passports. He'd originally wanted to leave the country, but now that's going to have to wait. They just needed help getting as far from Eden Falls as they could. Will was worried that P&L might have people waiting at the airport and it's so small that it would be nearly impossible to stay hidden so that wasn't an option." Owen stops talking when his phone rings. He looks at the screen and sets it back down.

"Where did you take them?" Everett asks.

Owen looks distracted and glances at his phone again before replying, "They asked me not to say exactly where they are because that could put you in danger." He said it quietly. I can't tell whether he's feeling bad that he can't say where he'd taken them or if he's simply distracted by the call he ignored.

"C'mon man, you have to tell us something," Everett complains. "You weren't gone long enough to get them very far from here. Are you sure they're safe?"

"They're safe," he says confidently. His phone rings again. "Sorry," he says before silencing the ringer. I hope he'll offer more of an explanation, but he adds nothing.

"You can answer your phone, Owen. Tell us about all of this when you're done," I say, my interest growing.

"No, that's okay. It's not you guys. I just really don't want to deal with *this*," he says, pointing to his phone, "right now." I nod, but have a hard time hiding my curiosity. He must realize how curious I am because he quickly adds, "It was Mr. Bradley."

"Oh," I respond, wishing he'd elaborate. "He calls you in the middle of the night?"

Owen nods. "If it's important enough to him."

"So can you give us the general direction you took them?" Everett asks, not at all distracted by Owen's phone calls. I wish I could reach Everett so I could punch him discreetly. Owen was about to tell us why Mr. Bradley was calling in the middle of the night and Everett took the conversation in a complete one-eighty.

"Okay, sure. I took them north . . . ish. His phone lights up again. He'd already silenced the ringer, but in the dark car, the light is just as distracting. Still calm, he grabs the phone and drops it into the middle console and shuts the lid. I look at him inquisitively. He notices my expression and smiles. He opens his mouth to say something, but stops. Seeming to weigh the options, he starts talking again. "I may have used the company plane to get Eva and Will out of here." He says it like it's an everyday thing, as if it's no big deal at all.

Now Everett is interested in the ignored phone calls. "You took Mr. Bradley's plane?"

"No, I didn't take it. That would have been impossible," he says, as if Everett's crazy for jumping to that conclusion. "I didn't know where he kept the key to the hanger. I asked him for it."

"So why is he call—," Everett starts before Owen answers.

"I *sort of* implied I was using it to surprise Lila with a little trip."

"Sort of?" Everett repeats.

"Well, I didn't straight out lie, but I knew what conclusion he'd come to if I gave a few little hints . . . and I'm guessing he just figured out that Lila didn't come with me. Although I really didn't expect him to figure it out that quickly . . ."

I try to hide my grin, but can't. Owen took Mr. Bradley's plane to help Will and Eva, all because I asked him for a favor. When he agrees to help, he goes all out. "You know how to fly a plane?" I ask, still trying to keep a straight face.

"Not well," he answers. "Mr. Bradley gave me flying lessons when I was a kid, but I never put in the hours I needed to get a pilot's license."

"And he was still willing to let you take the plane tonight?"

"It took a little coaxing, but he has more faith in my flying abilities than he probably should. I think he was excited I was taking the initiative and planning something for Lila."

"How far did you take them?" Everett asks.

"Quite a ways. You're awfully curious for someone who's not supposed to know where they are," Owen says. "It won't matter a whole lot though, because Will figured they'd fly out of there tonight and get farther from here, but Eva was so worried about you guys finding them and the danger that might bring to you."

Everett laughs. "I can't believe you had access to a plane and actually flew them out of here. You're a good person to know."

I laugh too, but add, "You completely saved us tonight."

"It was actually kind of fun. At first I felt terrible for them, but they seemed so wrapped up in each other that having to run didn't bother them. They were so happy to be together. How long had it been since they'd seen each other?"

"Two years," I answer.

"In two years, you'd think Eva would have moved on, but I've never seen her even close to being as happy as she was tonight. She was a completely different person." Owen stops talking and looks uncomfortable. "I mean, I'm sure she was happy spending time with you guys, but she was so . . ."

"No, we know." I offer with a smile. "We're not offended that Will makes her happier than we do."

"I'm a little offended," Everett chimes in.

I wish I could take back all the mean thoughts I had about Will a few minutes ago. It was selfish of me to feel that way. Of course Eva is happier with Will and she's probably safer with him than staying near Eden Falls. "Eva had a theory about her time away from Will," I start. "It's all about cheese."

"This ought to be good," Everett says.

"Actually it is good. She says that if fat-free cheese is all a person knows, then it probably tastes pretty good. But, if you've had normal cheese and then you try fat-free, it's gross. She compares it to love. Once you've been in love, the kind of love she has with Will, then other relationships pale in comparison. They're gross, like fat-free cheese," I finish.

Everett laughs and Owen grins. As I watch Owen's expression in the mirror, he stares back at me. Still smiling, he says, "Sounds about right." I hold his gaze for several seconds before he looks away to watch the road.

"Well Eva has always hated fat-free cheese," Everett says.

Silence falls over the car. The longer we drive in the dark, the more the adrenaline wears off. Everett's head starts bobbing.

"Are you okay driving?" I ask Owen as I fight off a yawn.

"I'm all right. I don't think my night was quite as exhausting as yours."

I smile, but say nothing as I think how to respond. There's so much I want to say to him. Now that he knows all about Will and why I've been so secretive, I want to know how he feels toward me. I'm tired of hiding how I feel, but what should I say? I'm not even one-hundred percent sure Everett's asleep and I don't want to share my feelings for Owen with my brother listening in. Instead, I say, "Everett told me about your dad. I'm sorry."

"Oh thanks, but it's not a big deal. I haven't seen him since I was ten. I made peace with losing him a long time ago."

"Yeah, he actually told me about that too," I say sheepishly, feeling like I've somehow invaded his privacy.

"Wow, he doesn't mess around with news, does he? I just told him about that tonight. I'm surprised with all of the drama you guys had on your hands that he even had time to tell you."

"Sorry, it was my fault. I kind of pulled it out of him," I say, hoping I haven't made him distrust Everett.

"It's fine. I've wanted to tell you all about the Bradleys for a while, but the timing was never quite right." He pauses, "So what all did he tell you?"

"Basically that you and Lila will be getting married any day and you work for the Bradleys because you're obsessed with becoming rich."

His serious expression makes me want to take it back. I was trying to lighten the mood, but apparently went too far. A big grin spreads across his face. "Man, I really lost something in that translation."

I laugh and let out a sigh of relief. "He told me about the Bradleys taking care of you when you were young and how Mr. Bradley has helped your family a lot."

"Yeah, he's done more for me and my family than I can ever repay him for. When my dad first left, there were a lot of people angry with him; people who he owed a lot of money. I can remember one night when a man broke into our house looking for my dad. When my mom told him he'd been gone for weeks, he didn't believe her. He threatened her. I was too young to really understand what was being said, but I remember the terror in my mom's eyes, along with the evil look of that man.

"Mom claimed she was putting us kids to bed, but sneaked us out the back door. I was the oldest so she handed me my one-year-old brother, instructed my three sisters to listen to everything I said, and she told me to get to the Bradley's house. I tried to argue and say I was going to help her, but she begged me to go. It was one of the hardest things I've ever had to do to leave my mom that night. She was trying so hard to fight back tears as she sent us away. It was weird for me to see her like that. She'd always seemed strong, you know, like nothing could faze her. I watched her walk back into the house and toward that horrible man. I was afraid I'd never see her again."

I want to reach out to comfort Owen, but sitting behind him makes that awkward and difficult so I sit still with my hands in my lap.

"The Bradley's house was the closest house to ours. It was about half a mile away, which doesn't sound like far, but it seemed to take hours. My baby brother was screaming 'Mama' over and over, which made my youngest sister cry and say she wanted Mom." He stops talking and stares out the front, eyes wide, lost in thought. Finally, he shakes his head and continues, "Anyway, we made it and the Bradleys took care of everything. Mrs. Bradley took my younger siblings and helped calm them down. She made us food and rocked my brother to sleep. Mr. Bradley went to our house. Mom said when he got there, he took the man aside and talked to him. We figure he must have paid off the debt. After that,

Mr. Bradley continued watching out for us. So, years later when he started asking me to watch out for Lila, it was the least I could do. When it turned into something more and I tried to end it, he told me he was going to stop protecting us. Within days, a couple of men showed up at my mom's house demanding money that my dad owed them and my little brother got beat up. It was easier to keep seeing Lila than be responsible for pain being inflicted on my family." He looks at me in the mirror and keeps his eyes locked on mine. "It's really important to me that *you* understand I do not have any feelings for Lila."

I nod as an electric pulse runs through my body.

"I'm sorry I've made it awkward for you. I should have explained all of this a long time ago," he says.

"It's okay, Owen. I'm sorry I jumped to conclus—"

"You didn't jump to anything. What else were you supposed to believe?"

"I should have let you explain when you tried," I respond. "Why does it matter so much to Mr. Bradley that you date Lila?"

"I honestly don't know. I think maybe after Paul died— Oh, did Everett tell you about Paul Bradley?"

"Yeah," I smile.

"He really covered everything, didn't he?" Owen smiles back. "Anyway, I think after Paul died, they were so worried that Lila might get herself into trouble, they became overprotective. I don't know. It still doesn't make sense. I've wondered about that a lot too. Mr. Bradley became a different person when Paul died. It made him bitter and I don't understand why he does most of the things he does anymore."

Owen gets off on the exit Everett described earlier. I wish we weren't so close to the cabin already. I'm anxious to see if my parents are here and let them know everything is okay, but I don't want this conversation to end. "So, what is Mr.

Bradley going to do now that he knows you took his plane and didn't take Lila?"

He smiles as he shrugs. "He gave me permission to take the plane."

"Somehow I don't think he'll see it that way," I reply. "What if something happens to your mom or siblings as a result of this? I'll feel horrible if my family is safe only because you put yours in jeopardy."

"I can't live my whole life doing exactly what Mr. Bradley wants. I have to get out from under his thumb some time, but I'll make sure my family doesn't suffer when I do."

I nod, but the pit in my stomach grows.

"Is this the road?" he asks, stopping next to the gravel trail that leads to the cabin.

"Yes."

"There's a car here. Is it your parents'?" Owen asks.

I shake my head, my heart pounding. How would anyone know about the cabin? It isn't even in my parents' names. When everything with P&L started happening, Dad was overly cautious about everything. He transferred the title to the name of a close family friend, Duncan Hefner. Had people dug so deep as to figure that out? I push myself forward so I can look out the front window. Sure enough, there's a dark-colored car sitting out front and my parents' car is nowhere to be seen.

"Ev!" I whisper, shaking Everett. "Ev, wake up." He sits straight up, eyes wide.

Before I can say anything more, he says, "Huh, I wonder why they brought Grandma's car. I look back to the dark-colored car. I laugh as I sit back in my seat. It's Grandma's maroon Cadillac.

"Where should I park?" Owen asks. Everett motions to a spot right of the Cadillac and Owen pulls in. As I reach for my handle, Owen grabs my door and pulls it open. I step out and look up to thank him, but find my face only inches from his. I can smell the spearmint from his gum on his breath.

"Thanks," I barely manage to whisper as every hair on my body prickles.

He leans in closer so he can shut the door. Now I feel his breath on my neck when he answers, "No problem." It sends shivers down my spine.

"Oh, thank heaven!" Mom yells as she swings open the front door. She's holding a lantern. Dad, a flashlight in hand, comes out as well. The cabin doesn't have electricity. This is another reason I consider it a shanty instead of a cabin. Everett hugs Mom and kisses her on the cheek. As I get closer, I can see that her eyes are red and puffy from crying. She looks at me and back at Everett and then, searching for an answer, asks, "Eva?"

"She's fine, Mom," Everett assures. "She's with Will." Mom's eyes stay wide and her mouth agape.

"Why doesn't everyone come inside and we can talk?" Dad suggests.

"I'm going to go ahead and head back," Owen says.

"Owen, don't feel like you need to run off," Mom says. "Why don't you come inside?"

"Stay," I agree, grabbing his arm. He nods and follows us inside.

"Why'd you drive Grandma's Caddy?" Everett asks as soon as we all sit down.

"A car parked itself out by the front gate earlier this evening," Dad says, shaking his head. "Then every time we called any of your phones, we got your voicemail. After a couple of hours, your mother was a wreck and couldn't take it any longer—"

"And you were calm?" Mom interrupts.

"We were both worried," he corrects. "So we grabbed the emergency phone and sneaked out back through the trees.

We called Grandpa and Grandma and they met us with Grandma's car."

"I'm surprised they weren't following Grandma and Grandpa, as hard as they're trying tonight," Everett says.

"Why? What happened? And how is Eva with Will?" Mom quizzes anxiously.

Everett looks at me so I tell about Will showing up at the apartment. He takes over at the part where he dropped me off at Wal-Mart. As he relates the events of the night, I lean back on the sofa and quit fighting the heaviness of my eyelids.

♡ Chapter 33 ♡

I realize Everett's quit talking. It's quiet all around me. Opening my eyes to see what's caused the lull in conversation, I find I'm all alone. I'm lying across the sofa, my head on a pillow from one of the beds and a fluffy green comforter tucked around me. The phone in my pocket says it's 5:53 a.m. It's been almost two hours since Everett and I started telling Mom and Dad the story. The door to the only bedroom in the cabin is shut. I sit up. Everett's in a sleeping bag a few feet from me and Owen's in a recliner.

There's a flicker of orange flame through the window. I wrap the comforter around me and walk outside. Dad is adding wood to a fire so I walk over next to him. When he sees me, he wraps an arm around me and kisses the top of my head. When I look at his face, there's a difference in him. His eyes seem far off and his wrinkles deeper. "I'm going to Lakeside," he says, referring to a small gas station and store about ten miles away. "There isn't any food here and I figure we could all use a good breakfast. Do you need anything, sweets?" he asks, using the nickname he'd given me when I was little and I haven't heard him use in years.

"Thanks, Dad. Breakfast sounds great. I don't need anything else though."

"Okay. Will you make sure your mom knows where I am when she wakes up?"

"Sure."

He pauses for a second, watching me. "I love you, Juliet. I'm really proud of you, of all of my kids."

I lean in and hug him again. "Thanks, Dad. I love you too." He looks down and walks away, leaving me melancholy. My eyes wander out toward the lake. The sun is coming up. The sky is a mixture of dark purple and a brilliant shade of orange. Bright reflections from the sky swirl through the water. I readjust my blanket, wrapping it tighter against my body, and walk down to the lake. I sit on a log that Dad cut into a makeshift bench several years ago. This is my favorite time of day, when everything smells crisp and looks bright. A boat moves slowly across the water, probably fishermen. Generally, not many other people are out in boats at six a.m. I take in a big breath, feeling the chill of the fresh morning air as it hits my lungs. The sound of footsteps behind me causes me to jerk my head around.

"Hey," Owen says. He walks toward me, rubbing his hands together to get them warm. "Sorry, I wasn't trying to scare you."

I smile. "It's fine. I guess I'm still a little jumpy."

He sits down beside me on the bench. "Couldn't sleep?" he asks.

"I probably could if I really tried, but I like it better out here."

Owen looks out across the water. "Yeah, it's beautiful here. I haven't been up to this lake since I was a kid, and I'd forgotten how serene it is."

I turn to Owen and watch his face as he stares at the reflection of the sunrise on the water. "Owen," I pause and he turns to look at me. "Thank you . . . for everything you did last night; going to that hotel without even knowing what was going on, taking a plane and flying them out of there, picking up me and Everett and bringing us here. It means a lot."

He nods and continues looking at me. I stare back and feel light-headed as he leans toward me. I close my eyes and his lips brush mine. I'm glad I'm sitting because suddenly the phrase "weak at the knees" has new meaning. My stomach feels as if it's filled with firecrackers. As we kiss, I move the green comforter out of the way and scoot closer. He puts one hand on my back and pulls me in and places his other hand below my ear and traces my jawline. The warmth of his hand sends heat all through my body. Yet, somehow I also have shivers.

He draws back. I move closer to try to prolong the kiss. He smiles and nods toward the cabin. The door is shutting as Everett tries to sneak back inside. I laugh. Owen puts his hand on my leg and his touch sends another wave of electricity through me. He kisses my forehead before wrapping his hand around mine.

"This is the last thing I want to say right now, but I need to get back to Eden Falls," he says quietly, "and clear some things up with the Bradleys."

"Like why you stole their plane?" I ask with a grin.

"Yeah, that might be part of it." His expression changes to a serious one. "What are you going to do? Are you going to be able to go back to your apartment?"

"I really don't know. I bet this will all blow over and they'll leave us alone before too long, just like when Will disappeared the first time, but we'll probably have to hang out here for a bit to make sure. Do you need to leave right now? My dad went to get us breakfast."

"I'm sure Mr. Bradley is waiting to hear from me, and your parents would probably like to have some family time." He puts his hand on the side of my face and kisses me again.

♡ Chapter 34 ♡

think it's best if we hang out here for a few days," Dad says. We finished eating breakfast and are sitting in the living room.

"Dad, we need to get back home and act like nothing big is going on," Everett argues. "They know Eva's with Will and far away from here by now. As long as they understand we don't know where they are, we'll be fine."

"I'm not comfortable with that," Dad says. He rubs his hands over his face. "I want us here where I know nothing can happen to any of you."

"Dad, Jules and I have jobs. We can't just disappear for several days."

All of us are overly tired and no one's agreeing on the next step. "So, you think it's perfectly safe for us to go back to our apartment?" I ask.

"Since they know Will was there, maybe the apartment's not safe yet." Everett says.

"No, the apartment's not safe. Somehow P&L knew Will was in your apartment. I would say that's the least safe place for you to go." Dad says, getting louder with each word.

"Okay, let's all at least agree to stay here for now," Mom says. "We'll get some much needed sleep and talk this over later."

"Like this afternoon? What do you mean by stay here for now? How long is now?" Everett's pacing back and forth between the kitchen and living room.

I'm exhausted and this conversation's going nowhere. "Mom, can I lie down on your bed until we decide what we're doing?" Mom nods. Dark circles frame the underside of her eyes. I give her a quick hug and walk to the bedroom. I snuggle under the covers and drift in and out of sleep. I wake up enough to know the conversation hasn't changed much and let myself fall back asleep.

I wake with a start as someone grabs my arm. I roll over and see Everett standing above me. "What time is it?" I ask, my mind in a fog.

"A little after two," he replies. Apparently the drifting in and out had stopped and a heavy sleep had taken over. "I need to talk to you, Jules."

"Okay, talk," I yawn.

"I wanted to find out what happened when the cops showed up at our apartment last night," he says, sitting down on the bed next to me. "Luke said they came, told people to quiet down, and left. I was curious to know if there was more to the story. I figured they must have done more than just tell people to quiet down. It didn't make any sense. I asked Owen if he would call the police station when he got back and see if they would tell him any of the details about last night."

"Uh huh," I sit up.

"Well, Owen called me a few minutes ago. Jules, no one called the police last night. They said they were never called to our place."

"What?"

"Luke never saw the police come. He lied to you and the only reason he'd lie to you . . ."

"Is because he's helping P&L," I finish.

"Yeah," he nods. "I have no idea how he knew Will was there, especially if he was out at Mom and Dad's when Will got to our apartment, but why else would he tell us the police had been called if they hadn't?"

I lie back down. I feel like Everett kicked me in the stomach. I'm the reason for all of this craziness. P&L knew Will had been in our apartment because of me. Eva was on the run now because I'd been caught up with blue eyes and muscular arms.

Everett places his hand on my arm. "Anyway, I've convinced Dad that it's best if we head back today, probably in an hour or two. We're going to take Grandma's car back and then stay the night at Mom and Dad's."

I nod. Everett watches me closely before patting my back and walking away. "Oh, and sorry," he says as he stops in the doorway, "for interrupting you and Owen earlier. I didn't mean to ruin your moment."

"You couldn't have ruined it if you'd tried," I say. I can't help the smile spreading across my face. Everett smirks and shakes his head before he leaves.

The euphoria I experience when I think of Owen is highlighted by the nausea I get over Luke so I reflect on nothing but kissing Owen all the way back to my grandma and grandpa's house.

All four of us sit still in the car without anyone trying to open a door and get out. Dad sighs and says, "I really wish we could return the car without explaining anything. Your *mother* is the last person I want to—"

"I know," Mom says, cutting him off. "We'll keep this as short as we can, but I think we need to tell them what's going on. I'm sure they're worried and they deserve to be assured that Eva's all right. Let's go."

Everett's the first one to open his door. Slowly, everyone gets out.

247

Grandpa answers the door and breaths a loud sigh of relief. "Ruth, they're here," he yells. We step inside as Grandma walks out of the kitchen.

"I'm glad you are all okay," she says seriously. Then scanning us once more, she says, "What about Eva?"

"We need to come in, Grandma," Everett says.

"What's going on? What's wrong? Where is Eva?"

We push our way inside the door. Once we're safely in the house and the door's shut, Mom begins explaining the situation. Grandma and Grandpa are both silent, even after Mom's finished talking. Finally, Grandma says, "Good." Then she grabs my hand. "I'm especially glad to see you. I thought you might try and stand up your date." I shoot her a confused look. "Six-thirty, your apartment, tonight?"

I groan. "Grandma, I told you, I'm not going on a date." The stare she gives me could freeze lightning. "Especially now," I add.

"Oh horse feathers," Grandma snorts. "You *are* going on a date. He's going out of his way to do me a favor and you're going. I'll ask if he can pick you up here instead." She walks toward the phone. "That's better, actually," she says to herself. "Now I can help you get ready and make sure you're presentable."

"Grandma, tonight will not work." I look at my family, giving them a silent plea for help. They all look confused, still trying to figure out why Grandma hasn't given them the second degree about Eva.

"Yeah, Grandma," Everett steps in to help. "Tonight's really not a good night. She shouldn't be going out. Besides, Juliet's dating someone else." I try to stop him as he says the last part, but it's too late.

Grandma sets the phone down. "Oh no, did you meet him on the Internet?" she asks, eyes bulging. Everett laughs.

"What? No," I answer.

"Juliet, I've heard atrocious stories. Girls don't want to get all dressed up and go out to meet men so they stay home at those computers and try their luck. It's no good. Half the time, they end up with some crazy person or a fake person altogether."

"I don't think it's because they don't want to dress up, Grandma," I say. Then I quickly add, "But no, I didn't meet him online."

"Okay," says Grandma, skeptically. Then turning to everyone else, she says, "I was just finishing making supper. Why don't you all come sit down and we can eat?"

"No thanks," Mom answers. "We're all tired and ready to be home."

"Nonsense, Janie. I know you didn't make anything for supper yet and I made plenty so let's all sit down as a family and eat. We can't take you home right now or our food will get cold. Now come eat. I want to hear more about this man Juliet is dating."

Everett mouths, "sorry," and Grandma goes to the cupboard to get plates. I turn my phone on.

"Does this boy wear his pants beneath his bum?" I look up, only half hearing what Grandma's saying. "You know, trying to seduce women with his underwear. Lots of boys do it now. I say boys because men wouldn't ever wear pants like that."

"No, Grandma. He keeps his pants up over his bum," Everett says, smiling at me. My phone beeps, showing several voicemails and texts.

I walk into the hall as I dial my voicemail. "Hey there, uh, Juliet. This uh is Marcus Reed. You probably don't remember me, but I need to talk to you. Please call me back." As he rattles off his number, Grandma snatches my phone.

"We have a rule here, Juliet. There are no phones at the dinner table." I want to argue that I'm not at the dinner table yet, but my mind is too busy thinking about Marcus to get any words out of my mouth. Marcus Reed? Is that the Marcus I met at the club I went to with Luke? If so, I definitely remember him. Like I remember slicing my hand open with a box cutter when I was eleven. Traumatizing experiences like that park themselves clearly in my memory. The thought of Marcus trying to reach me sends chills from head to toe.

We sit down and the questions about Owen keep coming. Finally, Everett says, "Grandma, don't you need to call the guy you tried to set Juliet up with? You don't want him driving all the way to our apartment."

"Oh yes, darn it. This is so tacky giving him late notice like this. He's such a catch too." She stares at me as she speaks. A phone rings. It takes me several seconds to realize it's the phone from Wal-Mart. Maybe Eva's calling to tell us where they are. I dig through my jacket and find the phone, but not in time to get the call. It was Owen. I start to call him back when my other phone rings. Owen must be checking to see if I have my cell back on. I run over to where Grandma set my phone on the counter and quickly answer it.

"Hey." I walk to the other room so Grandma can't confiscate my phone again.

"Juliet? I've called you at least twenty times. Didn't you get my voicemails? Where are you?" Luke's voice conjures a giant knot in my stomach. I'm pretty sure my intestines are wrapping themselves around all my other organs.

"I'm having dinner with my family," I answer curtly, wishing I hadn't answered my phone. He must have figured out I blocked his number and be using someone else's. I want to scream at him, tell him I know he's been stabbing me in the back, but maybe acting like I don't know can work to my advantage.

"Where are you having dinner with your family?"

I don't answer.

"Where did you go last night?" he asks.

"I was with my family."

"Where? And when are you coming back to your apartment?"

I take a deep breath. "I don't know."

He's quiet.

After several quiet seconds, he says, "I was really worried about you. You seemed so upset when you left and then you never came back and I couldn't get ahold of you."

Knowing Luke is a liar is frustrating enough, but trying to maintain composure as he lies to me has my head spinning. I feel like my off-balance washing machine is in my chest, trying to beat its way out. It's hard to believe that my heart can be causing such chaos inside me.

"I appreciate you worrying, but I'm fine. I was a little freaked out by a bunch of random people in my apartment so I stayed with my family."

"When are you coming back? We can meet and talk about it."

"Thanks, but there's nothing to talk about," I say with fake optimism through gritted teeth. I have to end this conversation or I'm going to explode. I suddenly have a better understanding of internal combustion. "I need to go."

"Wait, Juliet. What are you not telling me?"

"Oh, actually there is something. Did you give my number to Marcus?"

"Marcus?"

"Yeah, Marcus. Your friend I met at the Orchid Lounge."

"What? No. Why would I give your number to Marcus? I barely even know the guy."

I want to point out that after I left the club and was mad that he'd let Marcus lead me away, he'd tried to assure me that Marcus was harmless. Now he's telling me he doesn't even know him.

"I haven't seen him since that night," he continues. "Why?"

I ignore the question. "Is his name Marcus Reed?" I ask.

"Uh, yeah, that sounds right."

"Hmmm," I say. "Okay, well I really need to go."

"Juli—"

I hang up the phone and fall onto the sofa, taking a deep breath. I'm afraid I'll throw one of Grandma's porcelain *Precious Moments* figurines if I don't calm down. I lay my head back and try to forget about Luke. Thinking about him will only frustrate me more and it won't accomplish anything,

I decide to get some fresh air, but when I open the door Grandma yells, "We're still eating dinner in here. All of us. Together." I ignore her and walk outside, fighting the urge to slam the large, cherrywood door. I dial Owen's number.

I forget how angry I am when I hear his voice. "Hey, Jules."

As we talk, calmness envelops me. Even though I just saw him this morning, hearing his voice makes me realize how much I miss him. He tells me how purple Mr. Bradley's face got when Owen acted innocent and said he'd never planned on taking Lila on the plane. He tells me how pouty Lila's been, complaining he's been so busy lately. I tell him about my conversation with Luke and how gullible I feel.

"Hey, Grandpa says he'll take us home now," Everett says, peeking his head out the door, "but Grandma is insisting that you at least taste her rhubarb pie before you leave. She's quite distraught that you missed the end of dinner."

I nod and repeat to Owen what's going on.

"Are you coming back to Eden Falls tomorrow?" Owen asks.

"Mom and Dad want us to stay together right now so Ev and I will both stay here at least one more day." I pause, wishing I could say I was coming back and I'd love to spend the entire day with him. "Why don't you come out here tomorrow? I mean, we're probably not doing anything very exciting, but I'd love—"

"Yeah, I'll come out there."

"Really?"

"Juliet." It's Everett again. "Grandma's holding us hostage 'til you eat some pie. Get in here." I tell Owen good-bye and follow Everett inside.

"You must be feeling better," Mom whispers when she sees me. "You sounded ready to kill someone before you went outside and now you can't stop smiling."

"Juliet Easton! I hope you have a good reason for breaking all of my dinner rules and . . ." Grandma keeps ranting, but I tune her out and think of Owen.

♡ Chapter 35 ♡

The next morning the sky through the window is ugly. The air is damp. Even the smell in the house is musty. My head is filled with gray. I know something isn't right long before the knock at the door.

"Is this the home of Randy and Jane Easton?" the police officer with a severe overbite asks. The second police officer stares at the ground.

"Yes," I answer. "I'll get them." It's like I'm a small girl again running for Mom and Dad to make everything feel better. I'll get them and this looming dread will go away.

I watch from a distance as the police officer talks. I can't get any closer or the ominous feeling intensifies. The gray on Mom's face matches the gray that fills my head. She leans on Dad, but he looks too weak to be much support. She's shaking.

"What is it?" Everett appears at my side.

I can't take my eyes off of the chilling scene.

He grabs my arm. "Jules, what's going on?"

I shake my head and swallow to get the cotton out of my mouth. "Eva," I whisper.

"What happened?" Everett has both of my arms now.

I shake my head again. He rushes to the doorway and

pulls Mom into his arms. Dad looks so small standing next to them with his shoulders slumped. My six foot, two-inch dad has never appeared small to me before.

The policemen leave. My feet seem to be trapped in mounds of concrete. It takes every last bit of strength in me to walk to the door.

"Eva and Will," Mom says as I stumble toward her.

"What about Eva and Will?" I have a pretty good idea what she's going to say before she ever answers.

"They're gone."

"Gone, like missing? Like left the country?" I ask.

Mom shakes her head. "Juliet, they're dead."

Every ounce of strength leaves my legs and I lean against the wall before sliding down to the floor. Dead? I can't move other than the shivers that have taken over my body.

"No they're not," I say to no one in particular before my throat closes off. I wipe the tears off of my cheeks, but fresh ones continue streaming down my face.

Everett wraps his arms around me. His body is shaking as much as mine. When I finally find my voice again, I say, "I don't understand. Where? How?"

"The US consul said their bodies were found last night. They washed up on the shore of Haiti," Mom answers, her face resembling a gray stone.

As the pain pulsates through my head, I check to see if I'm hitting it on something. How else could it hurt so badly? Time is nonexistent. The only sound is my erratic breathing as I try to get a breath and keep my tears under control.

When it feels like the tears should stop; like there shouldn't be anything left to cry, I walk to Mom. Hugging her only makes it hurt more. Unsure how to handle all the emotion, Everett asks, "So what do we need to do now?"

Mom holds out a paper the officer gave her. "We need to contact the consulate staff and decide what we'd like done with her body. Will's family will be doing the same for his."

Everett takes the paper and he and Dad begin discussing options. I can't listen to this. How can they possibly be making plans for her body already? There doesn't seem to be enough air in this house. I can't get a decent breath. I numbly make my way outside and breathe in the slightly less stagnant air.

"Jules, it's going to rain," Everett calls after me. "Why don't you come inside?"

"I won't be long. I need . . . walk . . . fresh air," I trail off with a mumble.

I run until I can't see the house and then keep going up the hill. My feet hurt from little rocks poking my feet through my sandals and my lungs burn. Somehow the pain is welcome. It makes me have something besides Eva to think about. I keep going. When every part of my body is protesting, I slow to a walk. Still, there is no rain.

"Juliet. Hey, Juliet." My name is called in the distance. I've run farther than I thought so I'm hoping Everett is coming to offer a ride back. "Juliet."

The crunch of the gravel under the tires gets closer. The nearer he gets, the more certain I am that I don't recognize the voice calling my name. A glance over my shoulder reveals a dirty red truck and a face that sends chills down my spine.

♡ Chapter 36 ♡

His face conjures strength from somewhere inside me and I run, but I'm at least three miles from the house. The fields around me aren't going to provide any concealment.

He pulls up next to me and lowers his window. "Please stop running, Juliet."

I feel like I'm back in the club and he's forcing me to the door. I run faster and move sideways into the field.

"I'm sorry I scared you. I need to talk to you," Marcus yells.

I will not be taken with his apologetic performance. I move further into the field and slow to a walk. My lungs feel like they've been dipped in liquid nitrogen and my legs won't run another inch.

"It's about your sister," he yells. "Look, I won't even get out of my truck. Just come over here so I can talk to you."

"Jules, what are you doing out there?" Everett's voice echoes off the mountains.

Marcus and his filthy truck ramble on down the road. A wave of relief floods over me. I move toward the road, where Everett sits in Dad's truck.

"Um, I, I was just thinking."

"Who was that guy?"

I take a second to decide whether to explain it to Everett or not. If Marcus is coming all the way out here, it might be good to clue my family in about what happened, but I don't want them to have one more worry right now when it might be nothing at all.

"I met him at a club a few weeks ago."

"Okay, and why was he all the way out here?"

"Honestly, I have no idea. He said he wanted to talk." I decide a half-truth is the way to go right now. "That's not important right now, Ev," I say, getting in the truck.

He glances at my sandals. "You ran all the way out here in those?"

"Yeah." I take them off and empty out the rocks that had worked their way in between my feet and the soles of my shoes.

"I know you want some time out here alone to think, but maybe you could come back to the yard. There's going to be a storm and Mom's really worried about you," he says as he glances at my face. "I think we should all stick together right now."

I nod and he puts the truck in gear.

Now that Marcus's face isn't paralyzing my thoughts with fear, I try to make sense out of him showing up. Besides the obvious questions I have about how he got my phone number or found out where my parents live, I'm dying to know how he knows anything about Eva. How much did Luke tell him about me? Maybe he's working with P&L too. Anyway, none of that matters now. Eva's gone. It doesn't matter if I can figure out what P&L is up to. It won't bring her back.

"What are you thinking about?" Everett breaks the silence.

"You know what I'm thinking about."

"I guess so. There's one part of it I don't understand though."

"Only one?" I ask. "None of it makes any sense." I realize I'm yelling and sit back in the seat with a deep breath.

"Well, one that's really bothering me."

"And it is?" I urge him to continue.

"How were Eva and Will identified? They had fake IDs on them. How was the US consul able to notify us less than twenty-four hours after they found them?"

"Maybe they still had their old IDs too, in case they needed them for something."

"That doesn't make sense to me. And, why would they have Owen take them somewhere near an airport just so they could stow away on a boat?"

"I, I don't know, Ev. We don't know it was a boat. Maybe they were in a plane that crashed, but I'm not sure I have the energy to question any of it right now." I'm afraid to let myself hope that these odd circumstances might mean there's a mistake.

"Yeah, I get it."

"I'll meet you inside. I'm going to stay out here for a sec," I say.

"Sure," Everett says, leaving me alone in the truck.

I need to call Luke. I keep putting it off and telling myself it will somehow help for him to think that I don't know anything, but I'm burning up inside. I need answers. His betrayal has resulted in the deaths of two people I love. My fingers shake as I scroll down to his name and push send.

"Hey babe," Luke answers.

"Please don't."

"Huh?"

"Luke, I need you to be honest. No calling me 'babe,' no telling me you miss me, and no saying how much I mean to you."

"Okaaay. Uh, when are you coming back to your place?"

"Do you know that Eva died?"

I count the seconds of silence. Three-four-five. "What?"

I wonder whether the silence means he already knows or if he really is surprised. "Eva, my sister. She's dead. They found her body in the ocean."

"Oh, Juliet, I'm so sorry. I had no idea. When? How?"

"You really hadn't heard?"

"No, I, I didn't even know she had left. Why was she in the ocean?" he asks. He sounds genuinely concerned, but I don't trust myself when it comes to reading him. I wouldn't be in this situation if I were good at figuring him out.

"Look, Luke, I know you played a part in this."

Silence again. "Juliet, I never did anything to Eva."

"How long have you been working for P&L?"

"Who?"

"Luke, you owe me some answers," I say desperately.

"I wish I knew what you were talking about."

"Fine!" I fume. "I thought just maybe you cared about me a little tiny bit and might actually tell me the truth, but obviously I was wrong. I hoped some of the horrible things I'd heard about you were blown out of proportion. I hoped there was some sort of a soul left in the lying, traitorous p—"

"Stop, Juliet," he raises his voice. I quit talking. Quietly he continues, "That's not fair. I do care about you."

"So you help people kill my sister."

"You have to believe me that I had no idea your sister was dead. I didn't think any harm would come out of it."

"Would come out of what, exactly?"

He takes a deep breath. "Yeah, I was asked to watch you, to see who went in and out of your apartment, but I don't get the big deal. I liked what I saw. I enjoyed being around you. Besides, when they asked me to put a video bug into your apartment, I declined. I thought that was too invasive so I only did one with sound. I helped you out."

"You bugged my place?" I try not to scream, but I'm so angry I'm shaking.

"Calm down, Juliet. It wasn't a big deal. I think I'm falling in love with you."

"Are you serious? Because of you, my sister's dead!"

"I did not harm your sister."

"Yes, you did. Maybe you didn't directly do it, but you helped the people who wanted her dead."

"How was I supposed to know you guys had such a big secret?"

"Why else would you be asked to watch us?"

"I'm sorry. I am. I had no idea you could lose your sister over this. Let's talk about this when you get home. Why don't we get lunch tomorrow?"

"Instead, you can meet Everett and me at our place and show us where that bug is." I yell, shaking. "Or are there more than that?"

"No, there's only one."

"Wonderful," I say, hoping somehow my glare can be heard in my voice.

"Juliet, I'm not the only one, you know. I know there's another source that talks to someone in your family in person. I don't know anything else about it, but they kept threatening to fire me if I couldn't get information because they had someone else who could."

"Good to know. I can't trust anyone. Thanks." I hang up. How had I been so stupid? My naïvete is the reason Will and Eva are dead. It was probably also the reason our apartment was ransacked. If Luke bugged our place, P&L had heard me talking to Eva and Everett about the flash drive.

I take a few minutes to calm down and then walk inside. Dad, Mom, and Everett are sitting at the kitchen table. Mom's head is in her hands and Dad's explaining something. "They said they couldn't match the medical records we sent."

"What is it?" I ask.

"We don't know," Dad says. "They initially used passports to identify the bodies, but now they need more conclusive results. They keep talking about the medical records we sent, but we never sent any medical records. Now they want dental records so they can be sure."

Everett shoots me a glance that says "see?"

Maybe he's right that something is off. I think about what Marcus yelled to me, "It's about your sister." I rush into the other room to get my phone and listen to my old voice-mails, several from Luke and one from Marcus. As he gives his phone number, I type it into my Walmart phone.

Before I can think about how crazy this is, I push send.

"Hello?"

"Uh, y-yeah, th-this is Juliet. I want to hear what you have to say."

He lets out a sigh. "Oh good, okay, I need to see you in person. I'm turning around now."

"My brother's coming too," I say. "Meet us in our driveway."

"All right. Give me ten minutes."

♡ Chapter 37 ♡

I wave Marcus into the garage after he gets out of his truck. I already gave Everett an abbreviated version of everything while we waited for Marcus to get there. He's upset with me for not telling him earlier, but we can deal with that after we find out more.

"Look, before your brother tries to beat me up," Marcus says with his hands in the air, stepping inside the garage, "let me explain some things."

"No one's going to be beating anyone up," I say, watching Everett glower at Marcus.

"That night at the club, it wasn't what you thought," Marcus says, taking a seat in a folding chair next to me. "Yes, I was trying to get you outside, but not for the reasons you thought."

"Then what was the reason?" Everett's voice is gruff.

"Will wanted to talk to you."

"Will?" Everett and I say in unison.

"Yes, Will. He'd given you that flash drive and he wanted to explain a few things and make sure you understood what he was asking of you."

"What is your connection to Will?"

"I've known him my entire life. How do you think the letters he wrote to Eva got into that safety deposit box and vice versa?"

I'm trying to make sense of this, but my head is spinning. "If you were trying to help him that night, why didn't you tell me you were friends with Will?"

Marcus holds his hands wide. "Are you kidding? I told you over and over, but you were too busy trying to fight me."

"Yeah, because you were acting like a sexual predator!"

"I didn't realize you thought that until later. You were acting weird, like you were drugged or something. I couldn't make you understand anything."

I think back to that night, the flashing lights, the spinning, and the nausea. *Was is possible that I'd been drugged?* I mentally add one more reason to the list of reasons to hate Luke.

Anyway, I'm sorry. I wasn't trying to scare you, but that's not why I'm here. I'm here because Will wanted me to give you a message."

"What message? When did he give it to you?" Everett asks.

"He called me Friday night. Actually, I guess it was Saturday morning since it was like four a.m. He wanted me to be sure and find you. They had concocted some plan with help from his contact at the FBI. I don't know all of the details, but he said I had to tell you guys that they were staying in the country for a couple of days." He runs his fingers through his gelled hair. "He was adamant that I find you yesterday and tell you that their old passports were being used in some scheme on a boat, but that they had new identities."

I sigh and Everett grabs me in a hug.

"Did he say anything else?" I ask.

"No, nothing important. He was in a hurry." Marcus stands up. "I tried as hard as I could to find you yesterday, but you are hard to track down. And even once I found you . . ."

"Sorry," I say. "Thanks for making sure I got the message."

Everett shakes Marcus's hand and Marcus leaves.

We walk inside and sit down next to Dad and Mom. Everett relays the message Marcus gave us. Mom looks skeptical.

Dad laughs. "Of course. Think of how much easier things will be for them if people at P&L think they're already dead."

"How do we know this Marcus guy can be trusted? How do we know he doesn't work for P&L?" Mom asks.

"He knew about the safety deposit box, the flash drive, and details that only someone close to Will would know," I answer.

"Plus," Everett adds. "This explains why the US consul has medical records that we never sent. Whoever is setting this up sent those. They're probably doctored to make that dead body look like Eva."

"We're still going to have to act like we're really upset," Dad says. "Until Will comes forward with all the evidence, everyone close to us has to believe Eva died."

"That should be easy since I'm still not sure I believe she's alive." Mom says, but she relaxes as she says it and wipes tears off of her cheeks. "We have a funeral to plan."

♡ Chapter 38 ♡

I lie awake early Wednesday morning, watching my room get lighter and lighter as the sun comes up. My alarm hasn't gone off yet, but I've been awake for over an hour. Everett and I both took the week off from work. I've spent most of the last two days at my parents' house and can't stop thinking about how perfect those days have been. Owen took work off on Monday and spent all day with my family. On Tuesday evening, he came out to the house. He seems completely comfortable around the family. I love the way he treats me, like when he kissed my hand during the movie, smiled at me from across the room while talking to Everett, and cornered me in the hallway to kiss me. When he isn't making me laugh, I can't stop myself from smiling. Even now as I lie in bed thinking about him, I smile.

A shiver runs through my body as I get out from under the covers. I grab the clothes I'm going to wear and take them into the bathroom. I'm still nervous that parts of the apartment could be bugged. It creeps me out to think of some P&L exec watching me change clothes. Luke did come over and show us the bug he'd installed and promised again that it was the only one he'd ever put in there. However, our apartment was filled with strangers on Friday night; the kind of strangers that wouldn't feel bad putting bugs all over. Plus, after I told Everett that Luke told me there were other people we talked to working for P&L, we spent half of the night scanning every corner of the apartment, making sure it was clear of any listening device, but I still don't feel safe. Luckily, Everett has already found three apartments for us to look at as possibilities to move into.

I sit down at the kitchen table next to Everett and we eat breakfast in silence. Even though the funeral this afternoon won't be real, it still masks the day in a feeling of melancholy. As we drive to the church, the silence is broken only once when Ev asks me if I'm ready for this and I nod. By now it's practically second nature to put on an act for all of our close friends. We've been acting like we knew nothing about Will for the last two years.

I walk into the chapel and immediately spot Owen. Excitement swells within my chest as I watch him talk to Dad. Suddenly this day doesn't seem so dreadful. The funeral goes as normal as can be expected. I even manage to produce some tears. They aren't entirely fake, since I am thinking about how far away Eva is and that I don't know when I'll see her again. Everett gives a eulogy that, according to an old neighbor, is "emotional and compelling." Our family gives and receives more hugs than I care to count. I'm struggling to feel positive feelings for any of our friends. I stare at each one and wonder if that man or woman is willing to betray us for money.

Following the service, a few close friends and family are invited out to my parents' house for a more intimate gathering and luncheon. I sit at a table on the patio, along with Everett, Owen, Elaine, and Josh. Apparently everything's working out between Elaine and Josh because they can't seem to keep their hands off each other.

As Josh tells interesting facts about giraffes—interesting by his description only—I excuse myself. Acting distraught over Eva's supposed death makes getting out of boring situations much easier. "They whistle, but they can also moo. They're fascinating creatures . . ."

Owen looks at me with concern. "I better make sure she's okay," he says, following me to the food table. He puts his arm around me and whispers "Did you know giraffes have four stomachs and eat seventy-five pounds of leaves each day?"

My first instinct is to laugh and push him away, but that doesn't seem appropriate with the circumstances so I kiss him on the cheek. I love being able to be with Owen in public without worrying about who will see or if they will tell one of the Bradleys. "Juliet, honey, come here," says Mom, motioning for me to join her. "This is Eva's good friend, Meg. She was one of Eva's fellow teachers." I spend the next few minutes making small talk with Meg and thanking her for coming. "Juliet, sorry to interrupt." It's Mom again. "Would you please grab some more ice inside? We seem to have run out." I'm thankful for a reason to get away from all the watchful eyes. It's exhausting acting as if your sister has died.

I walk into the kitchen and let out a sigh. My stomach leaps into my throat when I hear floorboards creak upstairs. My pulse quickens. I tip-toe toward the stairs, listening intently. All I can hear is the loud beating of my own heart. I lean against the wall in an effort to calm down. I can't believe how jumpy I feel. I've been so tense the past few days. Before my heart jumps into my throat, I remember I haven't seen Everett in a while. He's probably up there getting something. I check outside and can't see him anywhere. Letting out a sigh of relief, I grab a glass of lemonade and head up the stairs to take it to him. While walking toward the den, I notice Eva's door is open. Eva's door is never open. My heart is going triple-time again. I take a step inside Eva's room, but quickly change my mind. I don't want to know who is in here, at least not when I'm by myself. I take a step backward in an attempt to get back outside quickly when someone grabs me and a hand goes over my mouth. I kick and flail, sending the glass of lemonade crashing to the floor. I try to scream over the sound of shattering glass, but get slammed into the wall. I'm dazed and there's a throbbing pain pulsating through my head. I twist my head around to see who has me, but whoever it is jerks my head back straight and slams me into the wall a second time. When my vision comes back into focus, I see blood on the wall. It takes me a few seconds to realize the blood is mine. There is a tan hand in front of my face and an arm with a white shirt covering it. I try to focus on details. My view is extremely limited, but I can feel a ring on his right hand. It's being pushed against my chin, which means it's probably on his ring finger. The man tries to force something over my head, but I'm able to keep free of whatever it is. He shakes me and throws me to the floor. There's a pop in my ankle and pain shoots up my calf and down to my toes. He whispers, "Put this purse over your head and wait in the closet for ten minutes. If you try to look at me or get away, I will shoot." His sharp whiskers poke into my cheek and his warm breath covers my face. He grabs my chin one last time. I'm afraid he's going to throw me into the wall again so I quickly try to do as I've been told. Adrenaline is pumping through me fast and I'm trembling, making it difficult for me to put the purse over my head. I'm forced into the closet, where I sit with the purse over my head for several minutes. Should I really wait for ten minutes? I'm sitting here doing nothing while he gets away. If I could just get a good look at him, I could help answer some of the questions we have. On the other hand, I really don't need some guy pulling out a gun on my friends and family. After a couple more minutes of an internal debate, I crawl out. I hobble to the window and look down at the patio, but nothing seems out of the ordinary.

I limp down the stairs and around the corner into the kitchen, practically running over Mom. Owen's standing next to Mom, deep wrinkles in his forehead. "Jules, what happened?" He asks, staring at my forehead. "Where have you been?" He wipes at a drop of blood that's landed on my arm.

Mom dabs my forehead with a wet cloth. "Owen and I have been looking all over for you," Mom gushes. "Where were you? What happened to your face?"

"Someone was in Eva's room," I say quickly, trying to get back outside. "I didn't see who it was, but they . . ." My voice trails off as I look out the window, my eyes scanning all of the visitors who are sitting on the patio. Practically every man here has on a white shirt or a suit coat over a white shirt. It could be anyone and he easily could have left by now. "Did anyone leave in the last few minutes?"

"I didn't see anyone," Owen says.

Mom shakes her head. "No, I don't think anyone did, but Owen and I were walking all around the house and yard looking for you so we could have missed it. We need to call the police. What happened to your forehead? Honey, I think you need to sit down. You're getting awfully pale." Mom continues talking, but I don't hear a word of it. My eyes are narrowed in on the table where I sat earlier. There sits a beaming Elaine listening intently to something Josh is saying. Josh, who's waving his hands wildly telling a story, has a shiny ring on his right hand. It glistens as he moves, but his hands won't slow down enough for me to see which finger it's on. I glance at his face, his *whiskery*, innocent-looking face, and try to picture him capable of being so forceful with me. The room starts spinning so I move toward a chair. Owen grabs me and helps me sit down.

"Mom, why don't you call the police now?" I suggest, still reeling at the idea that Josh could have a mean bone in his body.

The door opens and Everett walks in. His eyes grow wide. "Are you okay?" he asks. I must look terrible.

"Somebody attacked her in Eva's room," Mom says.

"Who?" he asks. I want to tell them I think it may have been Josh, but know it sounds crazy. I need to be sure. I don't think a ring and whiskers are enough to incriminate him. Besides that, I'm afraid Everett and Owen might try to be heroes and get Josh. The man who attacked me mentioned having a gun and I can't risk Everett and Owen up against that.

Mom calls the police while I give a recount of exactly what happened. I glance back outside and Elaine and Josh are gone. "Where did Josh go?" I gasp.

"He mentioned having some family thing he was going to have to get back to," Everett says. "They must have had to leave. I'm surprised they didn't tell you good-bye."

"They can't leave yet!" I shout as I stand up, but sit back down quickly when everything starts spinning.

Owen's eyebrows are furrowed. Everett looks at me like I'm crazy. "Jules, I think you should probably go lie down. We'll figure everything out. I'm sure Josh and Elaine will be fine."

"I—I think it might have been Josh," I stammer.

"What might have been Josh?" Owen asks.

I take a deep breath. "He may have been in Eva's room."

"Josh?" Owen asks, his voice an octave higher than usual.

"Are you sure, Jules?" Everett asks skeptically.

I sigh. "No, I'm not sure. There's a good chance I'm wrong, but he was wearing a ring on his right hand and had whiskers."

"There are probably plenty of people here with whiskers and a ring . . ." Moms says, trailing off. Everett and Owen are already running out the door. I let out a huge sigh of relief as sirens blare in the distance. The sirens might scare Josh off, but at least Owen and Everett won't get hurt.

By the time I make it out to the driveway, Owen and Everett have blocked Josh's car and the police are pulling in. As soon as the two policemen get out of their car, Everett's pointing at Josh and yelling. Elaine, completely oblivious of what's going on, is wide-eyed and pale.

"I didn't do anything. What is this about? Is it the extra sandwich I took?" Josh asks. "I thought it was for anyone." He looks as pale as the night at the club when he saved me from Marcus. One policeman handcuffs him while the other slowly takes statements from everyone. Tears stream down Josh's face, telling me I've made a huge mistake. He's probably going to be scarred for life from the trauma of this experience.

I lean against the car Josh is sitting in. "I'm sorry, Josh. We'll figure all this out and make it right."

"Figure what out? What is going on?" Josh's red eyes and sweaty forehead sweep a fresh wave of guilt over me. "When are they going to explain everything to me? Should I get a lawyer? I've watched a lot of *Castle*. This is usually the time where the innocent person gets a lawyer and gets out of this mess."

"It's a simple mistake, Josh. Everything will be fine. You don't need a lawyer."

I jog to Owen and grab his arm. "It wasn't Josh. We have to get them to release him."

He wraps his arm around me. "What? Why do you say that?"

"Just look at him. That guy couldn't be malicious if he tried. I was scared and blamed the first person I saw with a ring and whiskers." I put my face in my hands. "I feel so stupid right now."

Owen shakes his head. "You shouldn't. He's putting on an amazing show for you, but he's guilty."

"Why do you think he's guilty?"

"Hey, Everett, come here man," Owen yells. "Tell Jules what you and Elaine were talking about.

"We were just saying Josh left for several minutes to use the restroom, but it was right before you disappeared."

"That doesn't mean he's guilty." I wave my hand dismissing the so-called evidence. "But it does remind me I haven't talked to Elaine. She must want to kill me right now. Where is she?" I peer around the driveway and spot her talking to an officer. I head her direction when Everett runs after me.

"What about these? Do these convince you he's guilty?" he asks, waving a handful of papers in my face.

I grab them from his hands. "What are they?" I ask, but as I skim the first few papers, I answer my own question. They're letters from Will to Eva.

"They were in the console of Josh's car. He had to have gone into Eva's room to get these."

I stare at them in disbelief. "But why? How would these help him?"

"Maybe he was checking if any evidence against P&L was in them."

"Yeah, maybe." I sit down in the gravel. I still can't picture Josh behind this. He must have had a great reason for doing it. He's always seemed so nice. Odd, but nice. I can't imagine him being two-faced. I close my eyes and think of the way he slammed me into the wall and don't feel bad for him anymore.

I look back at the police car and meet Josh's wide eyes. I need to talk to him now. When will I have a chance to speak with him face-to-face again? I walk toward him, intensifying my glare as I get closer. "How could you?"

"I, uh, I don't get it. Why are you mad at me?"

I question myself again. Could I be wrong? I hold his stare. "We found the letters in your car, Josh."

I expect him to play dumb, but instead his demeanor completely shifts. His eyes get darker, meaner. Innocent, baby-faced Josh is gone. "I will get out of this and you will pay," he spits.

I step backwards, shaking my head.

How could this possibly be the same guy who raved to me about scallions and French food? The guy who saved me when he thought Marcus was trying to hurt me. Was it all just an act? Or maybe he didn't think Marcus was trying to hurt me. "Why did you help me that night at The Orchid Lounge?" I blurt out.

He gives a cocky smirk. "It wasn't about you. I'd given you a little extra treat in your drink to get you talking and th—" He stops midsentence. "I, I just want to go home. Will they at least tell me what they think I've done?" I'm confused by the sudden change of tone, but one of the police officers walks by. He continues his act while the police officer is in earshot and grins and winks at me before I walk away.

Owen grabs me in a hug as I walk by him and I try to force that creepy wink out of my mind. "Why don't we get out of here and get some dinner? You need a break from all of this," he says in my ear.

"Yes, I do."

♡ Chapter 39 ♡

On Thursday morning, I'm ready to return to work. I've had enough drama to last a lifetime. Josh was arrested, but wouldn't admit to anything so we'll have to rely on the evidence.

I'm excited to return to the day-to-day dealings of TBC; to see what it's like to be with Owen when we're not being chased or attacked. I spend a little extra time on my make-up and change my shirt twice. After eating breakfast and yelling "good-bye" to Everett, I head to TBC. When I walk into the marketing department, people watch me with apprehension. Did I wear too much make-up? Why is everyone staring at me? I self-consciously smooth down my hair. Kat shakes her head and Collin mouths "sorry." I open the door to my office to find Lila sitting behind my desk in my chair.

"Shut the door," Lila commands.

I laugh at the expression on her face. "I'm not sure I want to shut the door. You look like you might crawl across that desk and strangle me," I reply, nudging the door shut.

"Is this funny to you? Is Owen losing everything funny to you?"

I say nothing and set my bag down.

"Juliet, he needs this job. His family needs him to have this job. The only reason they're not out on the street is because of the money Owen gets from TBC."

"What do you want me to say, that I'm glad he has this job?"

"You need to back off!" she growls.

"If you're worried about him losing his job, you should probably be talking to your dad."

"My *dad* is the only reason Owen has anything. Owen should be showing him a little more respect. He's never had a hard time with that before, before *you*. What are you thinking? That now his dad is dead, the family will be safe so Owen can do whatever he wants? It doesn't work like that."

"I have work to do," I say.

"You won't for long if you keep this up," glowers Lila. "I don't know what all you've heard so I'm going to do you a favor and let you know what's going on. Owen's dad was scum. Owen will agree. Unfortunately, Owen has to make up for a lot of mistakes his dad made. Without the generous amount of money he gets from this job, not to mention my dad keeping him safe, there will be a lot of bad people coming after him and his family."

"Owen can make his own decisions," I say, trying to act unbothered. The problem is Lila is hitting on a few things that have been gnawing at me. Owen told me that Mr. Bradley had helped his family, that he was dating Lila so he could keep helping his family financially. His dad dying wouldn't change that. Owen needs this job to help his family and dating me could jeopardize that. I push my way past Lila to answer my ringing phone. She doesn't leave. She stares at my face. "This is Juliet," I answer.

"Ms. Easton, you're needed in Mr. Bradley's office immediately."

"Okay, thanks," I reply, trying not to let the confusion or frustration I feel show on my face. I don't want to give Lila the satisfaction.

"See," Lila grins. "There are always consequences for your actions, Juliet."

I respond with silence. I pick up my bag and head out the door. Lila's right on my heels, still talking about how selfish I'm being by *making* Owen lose his job. Would Mr. Bradley really fire Owen because he's dating me? I can't let Owen's family suffer just so I can be with him. I know Lila's trying to get to me, to make me question things with Owen, so I can't analyze this too much until I talk to Mr. Bradley. I walk all of the way to his office without speaking a word to Lila.

I sit down in the waiting area, but the secretary immediately says, "Oh he's ready for you right now, Ms. Easton." Lila gives me a little wave and an arrogant smile. I'm shaking from nervousness. I have to focus on putting one foot in front of the other to make it through the door to Mr. Bradley's office.

"Sit down," he says immediately. It is an order, not a request. I do as I'm told. Mr. Bradley stares at me. I'm not sure if it's a scare tactic or not, but I hold his stare just in case. "Ms. Easton, Owen tells me what a fantastic person you are." Unsure how to respond, I give a faint smile. "He says you're extremely intelligent, funny, an outstanding athlete, and his list goes on. He makes you sound quite impressive."

"Thank you? . . . Sir," I respond quietly, still confused. Hearing the compliments Owen gave me helps me calm down.

"Oh, I'm not saying I agree. In fact, I have another source that tells me quite the opposite and unfortunately, since you're not seducing the other source, I consider it more valid."

The heat rises in my face. My ears are on fire. Seducing? I can't believe what I'm hearing. "I'm not trying to *seduce* anyone," I reply.

"Well, this isn't a discussion about whether or not you're trying to. That's not why I brought you here. You're here so we can talk about the things my other source said. I've received a formal complaint about you. Actually I should say *complaints* since it goes on for nearly three pages. The way you treated this poor Ms. Sorensen was extremely unprofessional and that's not how we operate here at The Bradley Corporation. I'm afraid you're not the kind of employee we want here so we're going to have to let you go."

I was expecting to be reprimanded for being a bad influence on Owen, but not to be fired. I sit still for several seconds, thinking through the words I just heard. Is there any way I misunderstood? When I decide that I did, in fact, hear him correctly, my anxiety is replaced with fury. "What's even worse," Mr. Bradley continues, "is that Owen treated her poorly as well. I really will miss having *him* here. He's been a great employee. More than that, he's been like a son to me." I shake my head. "Don't just shake your head, Ms. Easton," he says. "Say what you're thinking."

"I'm thinking that I don't agree with Owen's opinion of *you* either. He thinks you stepped in and helped his family because you're such a great guy, that you actually care for him. He doesn't see that everything you do has a selfish motive behind it. And I don't think men showing up at his mom's and beating up his brother just happened because you stopped protecting them. I think you sent those men." I snap before turning to leave.

Pretending I've said nothing, he tries to reason, "Maybe there is a way you can both keep your jobs." Something inside me tells me to walk away, but I feel guilty that Owen might lose his job because of me. I don't respond, but wait motionless by the door. "You know, Owen's paycheck supports his entire family. Things could get ugly if those stop coming. Plus, if he's fired from TBC, I'm afraid I couldn't let another reputable company be tarnished by his name. I'd be forced to let others know not to hire him. However, this can all be fixed if you straighten Owen out. Help him see that *my* way is best for him."

"I've been thinking it's about time for a new job anyway," I say curtly, opening the door to his office. As I do so, I run into Owen, who is in the process of barging in. He looks angrier than I've ever seen him. His cheeks are red and his eyes are big.

He grabs my hand and growls, "Leave her out of this."

"Out of what?" Mr. Bradley says calmly, rolling his eyes. "Be serious, Owen. We've received complaints about her and, as one of our employees, I expect better. She and I just needed to have a chat."

"You received that complaint weeks ago. What makes it relevant today?" Owen asks.

Mr. Bradley pulls out a pack of gum and opens a piece. He looks entirely bored with the conversation.

"You can't fire her," Owen says and Mr. Bradley smiles. I tug on Owen's hand and he follows me into the waiting room, where Lila's waiting for us with an ear-to-ear grin. "Come here," Owen murmurs in my ear before leading me to his office. Once inside, he pulls me close and kisses me. "I'm so sorry," he whispers. "I'll get him to give you your job back."

I want to stand here and kiss him, to forget everything, but I know I can't. I can't let him lose everything, let his family lose everything. I kiss him again, but pull away when I feel tears coming. I try to stop them.

Owen sees I'm crying and pulls me close again. "Jules, we'll make this right. You still have a job here."

I shake my head. "I don't care about the job, Owen." He looks at me, confused. "How does your family support themselves?" I ask. Owen's quiet. "It won't just be me losing my job. He basically said if we don't break up, you will lose your job and your family will have nothing. I can't be the reason that you have to quit helping your family."

"This is exactly what he wants you to do. He'll do whatever it takes to get his way."

I kiss him. "I can't do it, Owen. I'm not going to mess everything up for you," I say through tears as I walk away.

"Don't do this, Juliet, please," he pleads.

I walk out the door and find the nearest restroom. Regretting my decision to spend extra time on my makeup this morning, I clean up the mascara under my eyes. When I'm finished, I walk to my office, intent on cleaning out my desk. When I get there, I find Owen and Lila inside, Lila grabbing at Owen.

"Oh, Juliet, what sad news," Lila says, sticking her bottom lip out in her signature pout. She slides her hands inside Owen's jacket and I've never wanted to punch someone so badly in my life.

Owen shoves her away. "Look, I'm quitting either way. You and I being apart is not going to change that," he says, grabbing my hand.

Lila's jaw looks like it's going to hit the floor. "Think about what you're saying, O, what you're doing to your family," she argues.

Owen glares at Lila. "Don't call me that." He looks at me and continues, "I can work somewhere else. Mr. Bradley doesn't have as much control as he thinks he does. I'm tired of doing what he tells me. Anyway, my siblings are older now. They can get jobs to help my mom. We'll make it work." He grabs me and pulls me toward him again. "Please, Jules."

I see the desperation blazing in his eyes and want so badly to give in. Maybe the Bradleys are dramatizing things to get what they want. I reach up and put my arms around his neck. A smile is tugging on the corners of his mouth as he nods to Lila and adds, "I can't *stand* fat-free cheese."

I laugh and he kisses me again.

♡ Chapter 40 ♡

Six Weeks Later

I rub my eyes. I've been staring at the computer screen all morning, browsing through job openings. My eyes burn, my back aches, and my stomach keeps growling. I've applied for at least thirty positions and had two interviews, but so far nothing has turned into a job offer. It may be time to go back to a diet of Malt-O-Meal. I glance out the window. Bright red and orange are everywhere. It's such a beautiful fall day I find it hard to stay inside sitting at a computer when it looks so enticing outside. However, I've wasted far too much time playing the last six weeks. With Owen and me both out of jobs, we've spent our days together, accomplishing absolutely nothing. I squint at the computer to check the time; 11:13. Owen's been at his mom's the last two days. Boxes containing everything his dad owned were delivered to her this week, and Owen is helping her sort through everything. He thought he would be back sometime this afternoon and *afternoon* cannot come quickly enough.

Standing up to stretch my back, Monday's newspaper catches my eye from its spot on my desk. I pick it up, lie down on my bed, and begin to read the article I've read at least fifty times. Just as it has every other time I've read this article, relief fills my entire body. The title reads *P&L Execs Found with Hands Dirty*. It goes on to explain that evidence has recently come to light that a certain P&L product is linked to endometrial cancer and that several employees in the company knew about it. An enormous amount of effort has gone into covering it up, possibly including the murder of Matt Kirkpatrick. The author of the article specifically names two executives who have been arrested and states there are many others who could be facing charges.

I know there are a lot more than two guilty people, but it's a start. It proves that Will is getting somewhere. Someone, maybe his contact at the FBI, is listening and using Will's evidence against P&L. It also helps that Josh hasn't dealt with jail well. He quickly made a deal to tell what he knew in exchange for a reduced sentence. His dad was a major P&L investor and had a lot riding on the success of Tipro. Josh knew he'd hired "some young guy" to spy on me and my family to find anything that could lead them to Will. Offended that his dad hadn't trusted him to do it instead of hiring a random guy, he was determined to prove to his dad that he was capable of doing it. After Eva and Will supposedly died, he took it upon himself to figure out if they were really dead or not.

Elaine, though crushed initially, hasn't visited Josh. Grandma set her up with her Pinochle partner's grandson and Josh seems to be a distant memory.

I set down the article, which I've practically memorized now, and I walk back to the computer. As I sit down, my phone rings.

"Let's go to lunch. I'll be there in fifteen minutes," Owen says as soon as I answer.

"Wow, you're feeling extravagant today. We're actually going to spend money?" I reply. Both of us have been saving every penny since getting fired.

"*I'm* going to spend money because I'm taking you to lunch," he gushes.

"Okay," I agree enthusiastically. I miss going out to eat. "How did it go?"

"Really well, actually. It was a little weird going through his stuff. I haven't seen him in almost twenty years so it felt like I was in some strange dream from when I was a kid. Anyway, we finished. I'll tell you all about it at lunch. I have to make a couple of calls first."

Twenty minutes later, we're seated across from each other ordering Mexican food. He's told me some of the details of his trip and I'm talking about my job search. Owen's surprised when I tell him that Collin, from TBC, called and asked me to come back. He said they needed me and that he'd okayed it with Mr. Bradley. Owen's even more surprised when I tell him I'm considering it.

"After weeks of searching, it's tempting to just go back, but I really don't ever want to give Mr. Bradley control over me again. I hope I find something soon or I'm afraid I'll give in and take the offer," I say, my mouth watering as the food for the table next to ours is brought out.

"I think you should work with me," Owen responds. I give him a smile, but am more focused on the smell of the enchiladas and flautas. My stomach growls in anticipation. I drink some more ice water trying to stave off the hunger a few minutes longer.

I turn back to face him and notice he's staring at me intently so I smile again and try to recall what he just said. I tilt my head sideways and ask, "And how exactly will I work with you?"

"Well, you'll still be working at TBC, but it will be with me instead of Mr. Bradley." I'm confused by his joke and look at him inquisitively. "My dad owned fifty percent of TBC."

I nod, wondering if he doesn't realize I already know that.

"When he got caught embezzling and had a huge amount of debt, we were told he'd lost his half. It turns out that's not entirely true. The board made him leave TBC and said he could no longer be an owner, but my dad had already given up his half of the company." There's a glint in Owen's eyes as he watches for my reaction. I'm still too confused by what he's saying to give a reaction. He continues, "When his gambling got out of control, he'd put his half of the company in my name so he couldn't touch it, and he didn't have any say in TBC's decisions. My dad asked that Mr. Bradley make all decisions for the fifty percent that was in my name, until my dad died. Then I was to be notified and take ownership of them."

I stare at him in shock and try to let it sink it. "Why didn't debt collectors take his asset? How was he able to transfer it to you if he owed so much?"

Owen smiles. "His debt wasn't the legal kind. They couldn't come after his share of TBC. That's probably why they kept harassing us. They figured there was money there."

"Why would he wait until he died for you to find out?"

"He was so addicted to gambling. My mom thinks maybe he knew he'd come after me for money if I had access to it while he was alive or maybe he thought he'd figure out a way to get it back before I ever found out about it. I'd like to think the former since it paints a prettier picture of him. When we were going through his stuff, there was a letter to my mom. It said that I owned half of TBC and it gave the name of a man who used to be a financial advisor for the company. My dad said he could help us." Owen takes a drink and gives a sad grin. "That's my dad for you. Even as he's dying, he can't write a decent letter for her saying he's sorry for any part of what he put her through, but that he did something nice for our financial future. Instead, he gives her two very cold sentences."

"Maybe he felt like he'd put her through more than he could ever apologize for. This was his small gesture of making things right," I suggest.

"Yeah, maybe. Anyway, we tracked down that financial advisor and my dad was telling the truth. Mr. Bradley has been making decisions for my fifty percent. He's done everything he could to cover up that it's not actually his, but there are legal documents stating otherwise."

I smile as everything finally makes sense. "That's why he needs you to marry Lila. You're taking half of his company."

"Yes," Owen smiles back, "but it gets even better. He sold off part of his half. Now I own more of the company than he does."

"Why would he . . ."

"I don't know. I guess he was pretty confident that I would marry Lila before I found out or maybe he thought I'd never find out. He was always asking if Dad ever tried to make contact with us. I thought it was odd that every couple of months he'd either ask me or call Mom to see if we'd heard from him," he answers. Then he continues, "And it explains why he always tried so hard to help my dad out. When my dad first left, Mr. Bradley talked about the people he'd paid off so they wouldn't hurt my dad. I thought it was because he wanted to help. No. He just knew that as soon as my dad died, he'd lose control over my fifty percent of the company." Owen stops talking as the food comes.

I laugh. "You own half of TBC." I have to repeat it a couple of times as I try to believe it. Owen laughs as I continue saying it. We finish eating and walk outside. I walk toward the car, but Owen pulls me the other way.

"Come with me," he says, nodding at the sidewalk. We walk past a café, where several people are dining on a patio under colorful umbrellas. Right around the corner, Owen stops walking and pulls an envelope out of his pocket. "This was in my mail this morning." An ear to ear smile spreads across his face as he hands it to me. I feel him watching me intently as I look at the envelope and gasp. The round, swooping letters are so familiar they cause an ache in my chest. It's handwriting I've seen hundreds of times growing up, handwriting that's unique to Eva. I can't get the envelope open fast enough. It has already been opened by Owen once, but my shaky hands add a degree of difficulty to the seemingly simple task. I pull a single picture from the envelope. It's a picture of colorful buildings sitting on a rocky hillside overlooking the ocean.

I look up at Owen. "Greece?" I ask.

He nods and motions for me to turn it over. At the bottom, in small round letters, it says, "Thanks so much. See you soon. Love, Mr. and Mrs. Stavros." They're finally married. I smile and wipe away the tears that are beginning to spill out of my eyes. Seeing the phrase see you soon and knowing Eva is safe gives me an optimism I haven't allowed myself to feel in months.

I lean into Owen as he pulls me closer. A song by the Beatles is playing softly through the café's speakers;

Little darling, the smiles returning to the faces
Little darling, It seems like years since it's been here
Here comes the sun
Here comes the sun, and I say
It's all right

With the picture from Eva in my hands and Owen's arms wrapped around me, I feel overwhelmed with excitement for what is to come; today and every day to follow.

♡ Acknowledgments ♡

This book could not exist without the following:

The wonderful team at Cedar Fort, especially Emma Parker, who gave me a chance.

Talented writers who assisted me even while they were busy with books of their own. Thanks to Lauren Farnsworth and Jessica Day George for their help, and a huge thanks to Kirsten Hobbs for her feedback, encouragement, and friendship.

My amazing family—

My mom and sisters, Shari Edwards, Lisa Puente, Yvonne Kinghorn, and Lyndsi Wischmeier, for countless hours of encouragement, reading each draft of the manuscript, and listening to me talk about the characters in my head. Their help truly made this book a reality.

My dad, Denny Edwards, and my brother, Travis Edwards, for reading my manuscript, even though it wasn't in their typical genre, and offering invaluable insights.

My best friend and husband, Brian, and our children, Addie, Taylor, and Preston, who smiled through less than stellar meals and a messy house and who dealt with a distracted wife and mother while I immersed myself in writing. They bring me more support and joy than they know.

The people at Godiva, who make delicious chocolate-covered almonds, which I consumed by the handful during writer's block.

Lastly, this wouldn't be complete without thanking my Heavenly Father, whose blessings and gifts make it possible for me to write.

Discussion Questions

1. What do you think of the relationship between Owen and Lila? Did Owen do the right thing all along, or do you think he could have or should have behaved differently?

2. Are appearances always reality in the book? Think of Josh or Luke.

3. What are your first impressions of Juliet, Lila, Owen, Elaine, and so on? Do the characters turn out like you expected them to? Who surprised you the most?

4. Who do you think of as Juliet's allies? Who are her enemies? Is it always clear in your life who plays these roles?

5. Do you think Juliet is secure with who she is? What makes her feel insecure? What makes her feel confident? Do you see a pattern of vacillating between confidence and insecurity in women you know? How important is it to choose people who will support and strengthen us rather than tear us down?

6. When Owen asks Juliet to trust him even though she doesn't know what's going on with Lila, she doesn't. When she asks him to trust her about Will, he does. What does this tell you about the characters? Are you able to trust easily without knowing all the details or are you more cautious? How do you know when to trust someone?

7. This book compares love to cheese—genuine love to genuine cheese and artificial love to fat-free cheese. How would you characterize each of the relationships in the book (Juliet and Owen, Lila and Owen, Will and Eva, Elaine and Josh)?

8. The saying goes, "Absence makes the heart grow fonder." We see this is the case with Will and Eva. Is it always the case? Is the result always indicative of how genuine the love was?

9. Not a lot of information is given about Will. What suspicions about him did you have as the story progressed and were they dispelled?

♡ About the Author ♡

Crissy Sharp is an author, runner, and sports enthusiast. She has a special knack for avoiding cooking and cleaning so she can focus on her true love: writing. She is in awe of people who can do a One-Legged King Pigeon without pulling something and detests everything about fat-free cheese. Though she'll always be a Montana girl at heart, she also loves Tennessee, where she currently lives with her husband and three children.

SCAN TO VISIT

www.crissydsharp.com